"What do you reme[...] father disappeared?"

"I went to fetch Mr. Ma[...] out to the car. Mrs. Maguire was yelling and crying. He told her she was imagining things again. Then he kissed her on the forehead like nothing was wrong, got in his car, and drove away. That's the last we ever saw of him."

"Did you know he was carrying a lot of money with him?" I asked.

"No." Figgy licked her lips nervously. "Why would I know something like that?"

Giselle leaned toward the old lady and spoke softly. "Tell me honestly, Figgy. What do you know about his gambling?"

"Not much." She sighed. "He had a problem that your grandfather had to fix a few times. Their arguments were pretty loud. But for several months before he disappeared, things quieted down, and I assumed he'd stopped gambling."

"So, what do you think happened to him?" I asked.

"I'm sure someone killed him. Maybe someone he owed money to. Maybe someone who was jealous. It wasn't Mrs. Maguire, because right after he left, she locked herself in her room and refused to eat for two days. And it wasn't Mrs. Eagan, because she took care of both Mrs. Maguire and Miss Giselle during that time."

"What about Jerome Eagan? Do you think he could've killed his son-in-law or hired someone to do it?"

Figgy looked at Giselle as if to ask for permission to speak.

G gave a slight nod of her head. "It's okay. We just want the truth."

The old woman blinked rapidly and pushed her shoulders back. "I always thought it could've happened that way . . ."

Books by Mary Marks

FORGET ME KNOT

KNOT IN MY BACKYARD

GONE BUT KNOT FORGOTTEN

SOMETHING'S KNOT KOSHER

KNOT WHAT YOU THINK

KNOT MY SISTER'S KEEPER

Published by Kensington Publishing Corporation

KNOT MY SISTER'S KEEPER

MARY MARKS

KENSINGTON PUBLISHING CORP.

www.kensingtonbooks.com

ISBN-13: 978-1-4967-0184-8
ISBN-10: 1-4967-0184-4

First printing: August 2018

10 9 8 7 6 5 4 3 2 1

Printed in the United States of America

First electronic edition: August 2018

ISBN-13: 978-1-4967-0185-5
ISBN-10: 1-4967-0185-2

*For my own sissie, Ruthie Marks,
of blessed memory.*

ACKNOWLEDGMENTS

My deepest thanks to the brilliant Nancy Jane Isenhart Holmes, who not only inspired this story, but provided valuable feedback and support. To my critique group Jerrilyn Farmer, Cyndra Gernet, and Lori Dillman, I also submit my gratitude for your honesty and great ideas. I couldn't write a decent story without you. Sincere affection and appreciation for the greatest editor John Scognamiglio and all the helpful people at Kensington. Last but certainly not least, I want to thank my hardworking agent, Dawn Dowdle at Blue Ridge Literary Agency.

CHAPTER 1

Jazz Fletcher put down his needle and raised his hand to block his eyes. "That rock is blinding me! Who did you have to sleep with to get *that*?" He pointed to my left hand and grinned, tan cheeks spreading wide at his own joke.

I glanced at the rainbow-colored sparkles coming from the enormous engagement ring on my finger. My fiancé, Yossi Levy, aka Crusher, insisted I wear it to ward off any unwanted advances. Not that there were a hundred men waiting in line for me. After all, I was in my late fifties with a head full of unruly gray curls and wore size-sixteen jeans. No, Crusher was more concerned about sending a clear message to his rival, my ex-boyfriend LAPD Detective Arlo Beavers.

"Yossi officially gave up his apartment and moved in yesterday, and I thought it was the right thing to do." Tiny motes of dust danced in the beams of strong LA sunlight streaming through my living room windows. I straightened my arm and wiggled my finger. "It is beautiful. But I still think fabric stores, and not diamonds, are a girl's best friend."

My name is Martha Rose, and it was Quilty Tuesday, the day my friends and I got together to sew, no matter what. My best friend, Lucy Mondello, sat on one end of my cream-colored sofa, while Jazz Fletcher, the newest member of our little group, sat at the other end. Our weekly gathering felt strangely incomplete without our friend Birdie Watson. She and her new husband were off on a one-month road trip in their Winnebago.

Jazz reached toward the glass coffee table and removed yet another slice of banana-walnut bread from my favorite china plate with the pink roses. He waved it briefly before shoving it in his mouth. "I'm going to have to put some extra time in at the gym."

Like me, he was in his fifties, but that was where the resemblance ended. He colored over his gray hair with a warm brown and worked out four times a week. A formfitting blue silk shirt showed off his firm abs and biceps. I hated that men aged better than women. It so wasn't fair.

"Is it time to start planning another wedding?" My orange-haired friend Lucy stopped sewing the pink Sunbonnet Sue quilt block for her newest granddaughter. She stood and headed for the kitchen with her empty cup. Even though she was in her sixties, the five-foot-eleven-inch-tall Lucy Mondello still had the bearing of a runway model.

I rolled my eyes. "Give me a break. Yossi only moved in twenty-four hours ago. I need time to decide whether this arrangement is going to work out before even thinking about the next step."

"When you do decide, I've got dibs on making your wedding gown." Jazz, a former costumer for female impersonators, now designed high-end menswear and clothing for dogs.

I smiled at the suggestion. I'd seen photos of some of the elaborate gowns he'd made thirty years ago. "No offense, Jazz, but when I get married again—and I'm not saying I will—it won't be in a green satin gown with a bustle and a ten-foot train."

He sniffed down his nose at my outfit. "Well, friends don't let friends get married in jeans and a T-shirt. I hate to say this, Martha, but my Zsa Zsa dresses better than you." He reached down and stroked the petite white Maltese sleeping on the sofa next to him. Today she wore a matching blue silk pinafore. She did look more stylish than me.

Lucy returned from the kitchen. "I'm sure there's a middle ground somewhere in there." She held out her still-empty cup. "There's no more coffee in the pot."

Grateful for the distraction, I jumped up. "I'll make some more."

As I finished pouring everyone a refill from a steaming pot of fresh Italian roast, someone knocked on my front door. Through the peephole, I spotted the back of a brown uniform walking away toward a brown delivery truck. I retrieved a small package sitting on the front porch; a little white cardboard box with a green double helix logo and the name *Deep Roots.* I thought UPS had made a mistake until I saw my name clearly printed on the mailing label.

What was Deep Roots, and who sent the package?

"Who was that?" Lucy asked as I returned to the living room.

I handed her the box. "This is addressed to me, but I have no idea what it is."

Her eyes lit up. "A mysterious package? Open it!"

Sewing scissors should never be used to cut anything but fabric and thread, otherwise the blades lose their edge. I retrieved a pair of utility scissors from a drawer in the kitchen, returned to the living room, and raked the open blade through the tape that sealed the package. A smaller box with a return label sat inside, along with an empty glass vial, a questionnaire, and instructions printed on a card.

"Read it." Jazz had moved next to my chair and looked over my shoulder.

Congratulations. You are about to embark on a fascinating journey into your own unique personal history. Fill the vial with saliva and screw on the top securely. Complete the enclosed form and return both in the container provided. Because you chose the expedited service, your results will be available within a week.

Jazz moved back to his place on the sofa. "Spitting in a bottle? Sounds like one of those DNA testing services. I didn't know you were into genealogy."

I slowly moved my head from side to side, bewildered. "I'm not. It's true I know nothing about my father's side of the family, but I certainly didn't order this test."

Jazz sank back into the soft cushion and spoke gently. "If you don't mind my asking, why the big mystery about your father?"

"There's not much to tell. I never knew him. I grew up thinking he'd died in a train wreck before I was born. But a couple of years ago I learned the truth."

Jazz leaned forward. "I'm all ears. Dish."

Lucy, who had heard the story before, sat quietly sipping her coffee.

"It was the mid-fifties. My mother, Shirley, was only eighteen. She lived with her mother and her brother—my bubbie and my uncle Isaac—in Iowa. She was always a little, well, *different*, and spent most of her time alone."

"What do you mean by 'different'?" Jazz bit another man-sized chunk out of the banana bread.

I shook my head sadly, remembering how I grew up believing her detachment was my fault. "I don't know what you'd call it. She just failed to connect with the world. She lived in a reality that existed only inside her head."

"And your father?" asked Jazz. "How did they meet?"

I shrugged. "All she would say was he'd come one summer to paint the bluffs along the Missouri River that separated Council Bluffs from Omaha."

"So he was an artist?"

"I guess so. As soon as he learned my mother was pregnant, he left town. That's the last anybody saw of him."

"Didn't anyone try to find him?"

"Uncle Isaac discovered my mother had been a frequent visitor to the man's hotel room. My uncle went to the hotel and found he'd registered with just one name, Quinn. We didn't know if that was his first or last name."

"Wait." Jazz held up his hand. "Surely your mother knew?"

"She only ever called him Quinn. Anyway, he had vanished."

Jazz covered his mouth with his hand. "How awful for your poor mother."

I nodded. "Having an illegitimate child in the nineteen fifties would've made her an outcast and ruined the family. So, Uncle Isaac and Bubbie whisked my mother away to Los Angeles, where nobody knew them, and reinvented her life. I was born in June of the following year."

"How did your family explain away the absence of a father?"

"Uncle Isaac and Bubbie convinced my mother to pose as a tragic young widow. The story they told everyone—including me—was that my father died in a train accident. Uncle Isaac opened a tailoring business on Pico Boulevard and supported the four of us. He's the only father I ever had."

"Don't you know *anything* more?"

"Unfortunately, no. I grew up believing the story about Quinn's tragic death. So, when my daughter was born, I named her Quincy to honor the father I never knew. It's traditional for an Ashkenazi Jewish child to be named after a close relative who is deceased."

"Ashke-who?" he asked.

"Ashkenazi Jews are from northern and eastern Europe. Sephardi Jews are from the Mediterranean and the Middle East. The two groups often have different customs. Anyway, according to the European tradition, naming a child after a living relative might confuse the *malach hamoved*, the angel of death, into snatching the child instead of the adult."

"What happened when you learned the real story? I find it hard to believe you didn't try to find him."

"When I learned the truth two years ago, I tried the Internet. I thought I might be able to trace him through his paintings but came up empty."

I studied the faces of my two friends and held up the glass vial. "Do you know who's responsible for this?"

Lucy shrugged and Jazz turned up the palms of his hands. "How could I? This is the first time I've heard your story. But obviously, someone is encouraging you to find out. Maybe your daughter, Quincy?

After all, it's her family, too. Besides, aren't you a teensy bit curious?"

I didn't respond at first. Hadn't I always felt a huge gap in my life? Quinn didn't seem like a Jewish name. So, who was my father? "To be honest, I have wondered. More so since I learned the real story."

Lucy stirred in her seat and joined the conversation. "Well then, go for it, girlfriend. You could be related to English aristocracy for all you know."

"In which case," Jazz added, "you'd be obligated to let me redo your wardrobe. A touch of *Downton Abbey* wouldn't hurt you, even if you are a bit ample in the chest area." He ignored the stink eye I threw his way. "I'm just saying . . ."

"I'll decide whether to go through with the test when I discover who sent it to me and why."

"Oh, go ahead," Lucy said. "It's time you knew."

At six that evening, I was chopping veggies for a salad when I heard Crusher's key in the lock.

His voice boomed from the open doorway. "I'm home, babe." He dropped his keys into the brass dish on the hall table and tossed his leather jacket over the back of a chair.

If this living together thing was going to work, either he would have to learn to hang up his own clothes, or I'd have to learn to let his sloppy habits slide. I was more likely to fit into size-four jeans before that happened. I looked pointedly at the chair and raised my eyebrows.

He got the message and barked out a laugh. "Aye, aye, Captain." After hanging the jacket in the closet, he clomped into the kitchen with his size-fourteen brown boots. I stood at five feet two, forcing him to bend way down to kiss the crook of my neck. His mostly gray beard tickled my skin, sending an electrical charge through my body. "How was your day, Mrs. Levy?" He lifted me with a bear hug and planted another kiss on my mouth.

"I'm not Mrs. Levy yet," I reminded him, as he lowered me to the ground.

Crusher raised my left hand and looked at the sparkly diamond he'd placed there yesterday. His blue eyes softened and he smiled. "As good as."

He was right. The ring finally defined our relationship as exclusive and serious. For the first time since my divorce from Aaron Rose twenty years ago, I felt safe enough to take another chance on marriage. Almost.

I picked up the knife again and began slicing a Persian cucumber. "I received a package today. From Deep Roots. Did you buy me a DNA test kit?"

He popped three slices into his mouth, crunching. "DNA? Why would I do that?"

"Well, maybe your Orthodox family back in New York wants you to make sure I'm really Jewish before you marry me."

He coughed vigorously, choking momentarily on the cucumber. "You serious? *I* know you're Jewish. That's enough for them. Besides, if they were to object, it'd be because we won't be having children." He lifted his hand to the bandana he always wore as a religious head covering. "*Pru u'revu.* Be fruitful and multiply. It's the first commandment in Torah."

"Well, how *do* they feel about your marrying a woman who's too old to have any more children? After all, you're only fifty. Maybe they still hope you'll find a young wife and start a family." I stopped slicing and turned to face him. I wanted to gauge the sincerity of his response. I would never marry a man whose family wouldn't accept me or my daughter.

"Tay-Sachs." He looked at the floor as he spoke about the genetic Jewish disease. "There's too much of it in our family. I'm a carrier. Everyone knows I chose years ago never to have children because of that."

I stepped toward him, encircled the big man with my arms, and laid my cheek on his chest. "I'm so sorry, Yossi. You would've made the best dad."

We stood like that in silence for several seconds, each lost in our own thoughts. Then he kissed the top of my head. "I bet it was Quincy. Ask her if she sent you the kit."

After dinner, I called my daughter, who lived three thousand miles away in Boston.

"Hi, Mom. I'm glad you phoned. I wondered when it would arrive. I paid extra for expedited service, so the sooner you send them your sample, the sooner we'll know."

"Wait, honey. Slow down. What is it you're looking for?"

"Okay. After you told me the real story about my

mysterious grandfather, I couldn't stop thinking about him. I mean, who was he? Where did he come from? I figured you had to be curious, too. Right? Consider this an early Hanukkah present."

"That's very generous, Quincy. Thanks. But why can't you just send in your own DNA? Won't you get the same answers?"

"I have sent in a sample. But you've inherited fifty percent of your father's DNA. I've only got a twenty-five percent share. Your sample will get a more complete picture of who he was and where he came from. Besides, don't you deserve to know who you really are after all those years of deception? Be brave, Mom. Do it for yourself. Do it for me. And when you fill out the form, be sure to check the option to share information with other subscribers so I can see the results, too."

I sighed. "Well, if it means that much to you, I'll send off the sample tomorrow."

"Awesome. Who knows? We could be related to English aristocracy."

Oh my God. Didn't Lucy say the same thing? "But what if we're related to a Sardinian pig farmer, instead?"

She giggled. "In that case, those little piggies would have nothing to fear from you. Besides, what's the worst that could happen?"

CHAPTER 2

Eight days after I dropped my DNA sample in the mail, a message from Deep Roots arrived in my in-box. My heart sped up a little and I stared at my computer screen. After such a long time, was I finally ready to learn the truth about my father?

Crusher wasn't around to give me moral support, so I called my best friend. "Lucy, I just got a message saying my DNA results are ready. You may think I'm crazy, but I'm all by myself and I'm kind of scared to look."

Fifteen minutes later, she strode through my door, wearing an Ann Taylor gray pantsuit and a rope of twisted yellow gold around her neck.

"You look great," I said. "Why are you all dressed up?"

"Ray and I have a meeting with our lawyer in a half hour. I've only got a few minutes."

We sat at my kitchen table, where I had parked my laptop. The cursor blinked beside the link on the e-mail.

"Okay, hon." She leaned in so closely I could smell her Jungle Gardenia perfume. "Take a deep breath and click on the link."

"Here goes nothing." One tap on the keyboard and a green double helix logo filled the home page of Deep Roots. I followed the instructions to log in and got a welcome message, along with a menu of options. *Ancestry* sat at the top of the list. I glanced at Lucy.

"Go on," she urged.

I tapped again and a pie chart filled the screen. Half was colored blue and the other half was divided into different-colored slices. "Look. Only half of my DNA is Ashkenazi Jewish. I now know for sure my father was Gentile." The other pieces of the pie revealed I had Northwestern European ancestry, with a heavy dose of British and Irish genes, and just a smattering of German.

"Are you surprised?" Lucy asked.

"Not really. There weren't many Jews in the small town in Iowa where my family lived, so I kind of expected as much. Besides, Quinn isn't a Jewish name—it's Irish. I looked it up once. It can be either a first or a last name."

Lucy pursed her lips. "Irish. Is that where Quincy gets her red hair?"

My daughter had a head full of spectacular copper-colored curls, milky skin, and hazel eyes.

"I think so. When Quincy was a baby, my mother used to look at her funny. 'She looks just like your father,' she'd say. Then Uncle Isaac would rush in and change the subject. Now I know why. He was keeping me from asking too many questions."

"Your uncle was only trying to protect you."

"Still, I should have pressed my mother for more details. It's too late now. Whatever else she knew about my father, she took to her grave."

Lucy tapped the computer screen. "Let's see what else you can find out."

I returned to the home page and looked at the other options. "This one says *DNA Relatives.* Quincy has already signed up, so she should be listed." I clicked on the link and gasped.

Of the hundreds of thousands of people who had registered with Deep Roots, I had fifteen hundred relatives, mostly distant cousins with names I'd never heard of. The list was sorted in descending order of shared DNA, with the closest relatives at the top.

"Dang!" Lucy turned to look at me. "Did you know?"

I covered my mouth with my hands, trying to overcome the shock. As expected, Quincy's name topped the list with her relationship listed as daughter and shared DNA as 50 percent. It was the next name that emptied my head and filled my stomach with butterflies.

Giselle Cole. Half sister. 25% shared DNA.

"I, I guess I shouldn't be surprised." I stammered. "A man like Quinn probably left a dozen offspring spread across the country."

"Do you think your daughter knew about her?"

I stared at my friend. "You're right! Quincy submitted her own DNA to Deep Roots. She must've known. Giselle Cole would've shown up on her list as an aunt. Why didn't she just come right out and tell me?"

Lucy cocked her head to the side and raised her well-drawn eyebrows. "Maybe she didn't know how. Or maybe she wanted more information before saying anything. After all, she is a news reporter. She probably wanted to get her facts straight. The real question is, what are you going to do now that you know you have a sister somewhere?"

"I should contact her." I followed the link that led me to Giselle's page, with a space to type in a message. I swallowed the panic rising in my throat. "What should I say?"

"I don't think there's a rule book for this."

The keyboard clacked as I typed, *Hi. My name is Martha, and, as you can see, we're sisters. I'd really like to talk. Please contact me or let me know how I can contact you.* I entered my e-mail and phone number.

"Looks good to me." Lucy pushed her chair away from the table and stood to leave.

"Right." I sent off the message. "Now we just wait."

After Lucy left, I tried searching for Giselle on Facebook but ran into a dead end. I called Quincy. With the three-hour time difference, I figured she'd be back from lunch. But I only got her voice mail. "Hi, honey. I got my DNA results today. Obviously,

I don't have to tell you what I found out. Call me back ASAP."

I thought about calling Uncle Isaac with the news but decided to wait until I had a chance to get some answers about my half sister, Giselle. My head felt like a pinball machine, with questions bouncing around in random patterns. How old was she? Where did she live? How much could she tell me about our father? Did she even know him, or did he abandon her mother the way he did mine?

Finally, I turned to the one thing that always helped me order my thoughts. I retrieved my newest quilt from the sewing room. This was an election year, and I was sick to death of all the political ads on television. Besides, daytime TV never appealed to me. I tuned my radio to the classical music station. I settled on my sofa and let Beethoven and Telemann calm me down. I soon became lost in the rhythm of laying down small, even stitches through the three layers of my Prairie Braid quilt. The rectangular pieces of cloth were joined at an angle to form a herringbone pattern. As I sewed up and down the middle of each piece, a secondary design emerged in the stitching: chevrons marching across the top.

The insistent shrill of the phone jolted me out of my reverie.

"Hi, Mom. I'm so glad you found out about your sister, because we can finally talk about it. I knew once you saw the DNA evidence, you'd probably want to know more. Are you mad at me for not telling you sooner?"

"No. Discovering I have a sister was shocking. I'm still reeling. But what else can you expect from a man who seduces a naïve eighteen-year-old and then abandons her when she becomes pregnant?"

"So, what are you going to do?"

"I've already sent Giselle Cole a message on the Deep Roots website. I'm hoping she'll respond." A new thought hit me. "Did you try to contact her?"

"No. I decided that was your decision to make. And I'm glad you did. Um, there's another reason I called. I've booked a flight from Boston to LA on Sunday to see Noah again."

Crap! Crap! Crap! Three months ago, Quincy began dating LAPD Detective Noah Kaplan. I could see why young women would be attracted to his dark eyes, olive skin, and thick head of black curls. Kaplan was tall, fit, and presented the perfect package, at least on the outside.

But I couldn't stand the guy. He'd arrested me once and I had to spend the night in jail. After that, our paths crossed during a couple of murder investigations. Each time they did, he was arrogant and rude and totally disrespectful. To make the situation much worse, his senior partner was Arlo Beavers, my ex-boyfriend.

When Kaplan met my beautiful daughter, Quincy, his attitude toward me abruptly changed. He became overly polite. Almost smarmy. And Quincy seemed blind to his posturing.

I missed my daughter and didn't want to spoil my chances and alienate her by challenging her judgment in men. I swallowed my objections. "Fabulous. We always look forward to your visits. Especially Uncle Isaac. You know how much he adores you."

"Yeah. He's really pushing me to find a nice Jewish boy and settle down." She chuckled. "I think he wants it to be Noah."

I gritted my teeth when I remembered how my uncle had invited Kaplan to Passover earlier this year. Ever since then, Kaplan and Quincy had plunged into a bicoastal romance. I kept hoping the long separations might dump ice on the fire, but so far, it seemed to have the opposite effect.

"And you know what, Mom? I think Uncle Isaac is right. I think Noah is the one."

Just shoot me.

"There's another thing," she continued. "Don't bother to get my old room ready. I'll be staying with him."

"Who? Uncle Isaac?"

"No, silly. With Noah."

My stomach felt like I was in an elevator plunging ten stories down. Could I think of some way to stop this love affair before it was too late? I shuddered at the possibility of Kaplan calling me Mom one day.

"Quincy, honey, do you think that's such a good idea? After all, you don't really know much about him." *Like what an arrogant little weasel he is.*

"That's the whole point. How can I find out if we don't spend more time together?"

Dear God, please let Kaplan screw up this visit. Amen. "Well, you can always stay here if—you know—things don't work out."

"Come on, Mom. I'm thirty-two, not some dumb little teenager. I'm a pretty good judge of character."

Except in this situation. I realized there was nothing I could do but bite my tongue and hope she discovered the real Kaplan on her own.

"I've gotta run. Call me the moment you hear from your sister."

I stared at the silent phone. Uncle Isaac had encouraged me to settle down with Crusher, and he'd been right. Now he was encouraging Quincy to settle down with Kaplan. I wished I could trust his wisdom on this one, but I couldn't ignore my past experiences. Hopefully, the attraction between the two lovers would run its course and fizzle out before it was too late.

Crusher returned home at six, just as I took the chicken out of the oven.

He greeted me with a kiss and plopped in a chair at the kitchen table. "How was your day, babe?"

I transferred the succulent bird to a serving platter, being careful not to break the crispy skin I had carefully basted. "Like no other." I turned to look at him. "I've got good news and I've got bad news."

He frowned. "Let's get the bad news out of the way first."

"I spoke to Quincy and she told me she's coming for a visit on Sunday."

"What's so bad about that?"

"She'll be staying with Noah Kaplan."

"Oh." I could tell he wanted to say more, but he didn't comment. "So, what's the good news?"

"My DNA results came back and I now know my father was definitely Gentile. Mostly Irish, which explains my daughter's red hair."

"How do you feel? Are you okay with that?"

"Yeah. But that's not the only news." I took a deep breath. "I have a half sister somewhere."

He slowly combed his fingertips through his beard. "A sister? Wow! What's her name? How old is she? Where does she live? Are you going to contact her?"

"Her name is Giselle Cole. I tried looking for her on Facebook. I even tried G. Cole. But there were forty-two of them. I gave up after scrolling through the list. Since I didn't have more information to go on, they all could've been her. I did, however, send her an e-mail on the Deep Roots website. Hopefully she'll get in touch."

We enjoyed a dinner of baked chicken, roasted asparagus, rosemary potatoes, and my favorite Ruffino Classico Chianti. Since I cooked, Crusher cleared the dishes and loaded the dishwasher. I headed for the living room to turn on *Jeopardy!*

Just then my phone rang. The number on caller ID was local, but I didn't recognize it.

A woman's voice said, "Is this Martha Rose?"

I rolled my eyes. I detested phone solicitors,

especially when they called after five. "Do you always bother people at dinnertime? Whatever you're selling, I'm not interested. Take me off your list!" I ended the call abruptly.

Almost immediately, the phone rang again, showing the same number on caller ID.

"Are you some kind of *idiot*? Did you not just hear me? I'm not interested!"

"Don't be so tiresome."

"What?"

"This is Giselle Cole, and you're the idiot."

CHAPTER 3

Nine hours ago I didn't even know I had a half sister and now I'd just insulted her. "Sorry about that. I thought you were just another phone jockey making a cold call."

"Obviously." Her tone was unmistakably frosty.

"I hope we didn't get off on the wrong foot, Giselle. I mean, I just found out about you this morning and I'm still in shock."

"How do you think *I* feel? When I opened my e-mail this evening, I found a notice from Deep Roots saying a relative had contacted me. I almost didn't bother going to the website because finding a third or fourth cousin is common. Everyone has *hundreds* of them. I've even been contacted by a few in the past, but the connections were too distant to be helpful. But discovering a half sister? That's exactly the kind of thing I was hoping for when I sent in my DNA."

"What are you looking for?"

"I want to know what happened to Daddy."

Daddy? So, she knew him! Quinn had stuck around for Giselle, at least long enough for her to call him Daddy.

"We need to talk," I said. "I see by your area code you're calling from West LA. I live in Encino, not that far away. Let's get together tomorrow. Maybe for coffee at my house?"

"Encino? Not likely. I avoid going to the Valley if I can. We'll be more comfortable here. I live south of Sunset on Napoli Drive. It's across from the greens of the Riviera Country Club in the Palisades. Do you know it?"

Sunset Boulevard ran through a string of wealthy communities, with thousands of multimillion-dollar homes beginning at the ocean in Malibu and cutting east through the foothills of the Santa Monica Mountains into Hollywood. A house next to the greens of one of the country's premier golf courses must've been worth millions. When I was married to Aaron Rose, MD, we owned a modest home in the expensive zip code just east of the Palisades. "Yes. I know the area. I used to live in Brentwood."

"Really? And you ended up in the *Valley?*" She clicked her tongue. "What happened?"

I couldn't decide if she was being condescending or just insensitive. Either way, I tried not to growl. "Fine. Why don't you give me your address and we'll talk more tomorrow."

Crusher finished in the kitchen, sat next to me on the sofa, and handed me a cup of mint tea. "You seem upset, babe. Who was that?"

I told him I'd just spoken to my half sister. "I'm not looking forward to meeting her in the morning." I frowned and stared at the steam rising from the white mug. "She's a bit of a snob."

"Do you want me to go with you?"

I looked over at the six-foot-six-inch bearded biker and shook my head. His looks could intimidate anyone into silence. "Thanks, Yossi, but I've got to do this alone. She might speak more freely if it's just the two of us."

The following morning, I agonized over what to wear. My usual stretch denim jeans, T-shirt, and Crocs would send the wrong message to a member of the country club set. I finally settled on a white linen pantsuit Jazz had forced me to buy "In case you actually go somewhere" and white espadrilles. For color I wore a turquoise silk tank top under the tailored jacket. And, of course, my three-carat diamond engagement ring. I'd show Giselle she wasn't the only one with nice things.

I drove south on the 405 Freeway and exited at Sunset in Brentwood. I continued west for miles past a parade of luxurious homes flanking the boulevard on both sides. How did Giselle Cole end up living in such affluence? Did she marry into it? Did she earn it on her own? Did she inherit money?

My gut began to burn with a dawning anger that caught me off guard. If Giselle's money came from my father—the one who abandoned me before I was even born, the one who dumped my mother to raise me on her own—I was prepared to be really pissed off.

I turned left on Napoli Drive at precisely eleven and pulled into the driveway of a massive two-story French chateau–style home with gray stucco and a copper mansard roof. Dozens of lavender bushes filled her front yard, sending up blue clusters on long, delicate stems. I loved lavender and tried many times to grow it in the Valley, but it couldn't survive the hot summers. In *her* yard, however, it flourished.

I checked my lipstick in the mirror, swiped my curls out of my face one last time, and got out of the car. My heart pounded faster the nearer I got to the front door. What was I getting myself into? I rang the doorbell and held my breath as the door swung slowly open.

A dark-haired Latina in a white work uniform led me to a massive living room with brown exposed beams and hand-plastered walls. A bank of mullioned windows looked onto a covered patio, with a pool beyond, and a wide vista of golfing greens in the distance. "Mrs. Giselle will be right with you."

Warm, primary colors filled the room, with a riot of printed fabrics and red Persian carpets. The art on the walls looked original, including a pencil drawing by Picasso. I didn't have long to wait.

Giselle Cole was much taller than me, at least ten years younger, and elegantly dressed in a sleeveless green silk dress that clung to her slender, athletic body. Her straight auburn hair, parted on the side, hung in an expert cut to her shoulders. Her face was suspiciously absent of wrinkles. The only thing even remotely hinting at a familial connection were her hazel eyes, the same color and shape as mine and Quincy's.

"Martha?" She smiled and stretched out her smooth hand with shiny pink fingernails. "Good of you to come."

Her grip was strong and brief. "You're not at all what I expected. Please sit down." She sat on the green and white striped sofa.

"Oh?" I sank into a plump chair upholstered in a flowery blue chintz directly across from her. "What, exactly, were you expecting?"

She shrugged her shoulders and glanced at my engagement ring. "I don't know, really. Maybe some sad little divorcée who was forced to move to the Valley and live in one of those dinky little tract homes."

I couldn't hold back any longer and narrowed my eyes. "Are you always this insulting, or is that an acquired skill?"

She waved her hand. "Honestly, I'm not being judgmental. I just say what I think. You'll get used to me. Would you like a mimosa?"

"No. And just so you know"—I leaned forward—"I also say what I think. And right now, I'm thinking I was right last night to call you an idiot."

Her laughter surprised me. "It's really great to

have a sister. I can see we're going to become best friends."

That's not going to happen.

I stared at the simple gold band on her left hand. "You're married. Children? Brothers and sisters?"

"I'm a widow. I have one son, Nicholas. He's away at Harvard right now. *Harvard Law*," she said for emphasis. "I never had any siblings. What about you? I've been admiring that ring on your finger."

"As you guessed, I am divorced, but definitely not sad. I have a fiancé and one grown child."

The corner of her mouth turned up slightly. "When I saw your name on the Deep Roots website last night, I also learned about your daughter, Quincy. Did you name her after Daddy? Where did *she* go to school?"

"As for the name, it's a long story." I wasn't going to let her get away with dropping the H-bomb on me. Her son might be attending Harvard, but my daughter was no slouch. "Quincy was courted by Stanford. But she chose to attend Brown because they had a better department." I sat back and watched a flicker of annoyance quickly pass through my half sister's eyes.

"How nice for her," she drawled.

I continued, satisfied I'd made my point. "Like your son, my Quincy also lives in Boston. She has red hair like yours, but it's curly like mine."

"We both get that color from Daddy. I remember he had thick, auburn hair." She paused and blew out her breath. "I didn't know he'd been married before."

"He and my mother weren't married. As soon as he learned she was pregnant, he deserted her. When my family couldn't locate him, they were forced to leave their home in Iowa to avoid a scandal. I was born in Los Angeles. I never knew him. I don't even know his real name. I'm hoping, since you obviously had a relationship with him, you'll fill in the blanks."

She studied me for a moment and then spoke softly. "His name was Jacob Quinn Maguire, but everyone called him Quinn."

"My mother said he was an artist."

"Yes, and a very successful one. Have you ever heard of him?"

That was why I couldn't find him in a Google search! I was looking for an artist with the last name of Quinn. If he had married my mother, I would have been named Martha Maguire. Instead, I'd been given my mother's maiden name of Harris. "No, I can't say I have heard of him, but then I've never taken much interest in the contemporary art world." I ignored the slight lifting of her chin.

"I don't know why things didn't work out with your mother. That was long before my time. I only knew him as a devoted husband and father. I'm sorry for you."

The last thing I wanted was her pity. "We survived. Tell me about him. Do you have any photos?"

"Yes." She reached over to a small mahogany end

table next to the sofa and handed me a photo in a silver frame. "This was taken just before he disappeared."

A chill traveled up the back of my neck as I saw my father for the first time. His red mustache and long sideburns reflected the style of the '70s. He wore a short-sleeved shirt in a bright green Hawaiian print and smiled at the camera. I stared at his hazel eyes. Who would've guessed that this affable, handsome man had secrets? "Tell me more about him. Where did he come from?"

"His parents were from Ireland, but he was born in Massachusetts. He studied art at the Rhode Island School of Design in the late forties and traveled the country painting landscapes until the mid-fifties. Then he suddenly switched directions and became a portrait painter. That's when he got noticed and his career took off. His study of Governor Hugh Carey hangs in the capitol in Albany, New York. Another one of his works hangs in the Whitney."

"Did he have any other children that you know of? After all, he could've seduced dozens of gullible young women like my mother. Who knows how many other half siblings we might have out there?"

She wrinkled her forehead. "That's not the father I knew."

"Tell me what you do know."

Giselle picked up a cell phone and typed in a brief text with her thumbs. "I think we should have those mimosas right about now."

Almost immediately, a door opened down the

hallway and the domestic I'd met earlier rolled in a tea cart with a bottle of Dom Pérignon chilling in a silver bucket of ice, a pitcher of fresh orange juice, an assortment of cheese, slices of crusty baguette, and a bowl of plump, green grapes. I reached for the fruit and filled a small plate, placing it on the weathered wooden coffee table in front of me.

Giselle caught me looking at the label on the champagne bottle. "I know what you're thinking. Why ruin an expensive champagne with orange juice? I mean, who does that, right?"

I shrugged. "I thought most people used the cheaper bottles for mixed drinks."

"Well, I'm not most people. Inferior champagne makes an inferior drink. As long as you're going to imbibe, you might as well treat yourself to the good stuff." She poured the bubbly halfway up our crystal flutes and topped it off with the juice. "Cheers." She raised her glass.

"L'chaim." I took a thirsty drink, enjoying how the smooth bubbles seemed to spread through my body and relax my muscles. Almost immediately I sensed a shifting in my mood. It might've been before noon on Napoli Drive, but it had to be evening in the real Naples, and she was right. Those mimosas were the best I'd ever had. I began chewing a crunchy green grape, content to listen to her story.

"My mother's father, my grandfather Eagan, made a fortune in oil and built a beautiful home in

Beverly Hills, which he filled with antiques and works of art. In the mid-sixties, he decided to have everyone's portrait painted. At the time, my mother was a student at Marymount, studying music. She told me that one day she came home from school and there Daddy was, setting up his easel in Granddad's office.

"Daddy lived in the small guest cottage for the next year while he painted all the family members. By the time he finished, he and my mother had fallen in love. When they married in 1966, Granddad built them a house right next to his in Beverly Hills. I came along in '68."

I couldn't believe my father had been in LA all those years, so close to us. What would my mother have done if she knew? The Pico Boulevard area where I grew up was directly adjacent to Beverly Hills. Did their paths ever cross? How would she have felt seeing him with another woman? Another child? "You said last night that you were looking for our father. I take it he disappeared on you, too?"

Giselle poured herself another glass and didn't bother with the orange juice. "When I was twelve, he kissed me good-bye and left for a trip to New York. At first, Mother told me he had gone there for a gallery opening. He'd traveled many times before, but he'd always called to say good night, no matter where he was. This time was different, though. He never called me."

"How did your mother explain it?"

"She didn't really. She just said he must be too busy. But I could tell she was upset, too." Giselle's voice caught in her throat. "We never heard from him again."

"Looking for him couldn't have been that hard. After all, couldn't you trace him through his subsequent work? Especially if he was that well-known in the art world."

She sighed. "As far as we know, he never painted again. It's like he stepped off the face of the earth."

"Did your mother report him missing?"

"Oh yes, but against my grandfather's wishes. Granddad wanted to avoid a scandal, but my mother was determined to find Daddy. The art scene buzzed about it for months. But no clues ever turned up. His case quickly went cold." She took another sip of champagne. "I was very young at the time. I didn't understand what was going on. It's only been recently I've started to understand some of the pieces of the puzzle. I was hoping you could shed some light, but clearly you know less than I do."

"I have to admit, I'm intrigued by the mystery. Maybe my fiancé can help us discover what happened to him. He's a federal agent."

She raised her eyebrows. "Are you saying you'll help me look for him?"

I nodded. "Yeah. I'm pretty good at finding things out." I popped another grape in my mouth and surveyed the paintings in the room. "You own quite a bit of art yourself. Are any of these pictures his?"

She smiled. "Absolutely. I kept all his paintings, including some of his early works. I'll be happy to show them to you before you go. It might help you get to know him better."

I looked at the pristine skin of her hands and manicured fingernails. I saw no signs they had ever held a paintbrush. "Did you inherit any of his artistic talent?"

"Unfortunately, no." She sighed. "I'm more a pianist like my mother. Did you?"

"In a way, but not with paint. My medium is fabric. I'm an avid quilter."

She brightened. "So was my grandmother. I have one unfinished top of hers packed away somewhere. She was in the middle of sewing it for me when she died. I'll dig it out one day to show you."

I finished the last of my mimosa, and Giselle walked me around the room, stopping in front of a group of landscapes. "These are Daddy's earliest works."

Quinn's scenes were misty and bucolic, much in the romantic style of Turner. I could see why an impressionable eighteen-year-old girl would fall under the spell of his talent. The signature at the bottom read *J. Q. Maguire.*

She took me down a hallway into a formal dining room. "These are three paintings he kept for himself.

I've displayed them in chronological order to show the progression of his talent."

Giselle kept speaking, but I stopped listening and became lost in the pictures. The first portrait showed a young girl in a blue dress reclining in soft, green grass with a faraway expression on her face. What was she dreaming of as she twirled the stem of that dandelion? In this picture, Quinn's brush-strokes were tentative, almost shy.

The next painting showed the same woman, a few years older, sitting in a café with an expression of satisfaction, as if she'd just finished a good meal. This time Quinn used rich, jewel tones and his strokes were more confident.

The third portrait showed the woman in early middle age, with sagging eyelids and more flesh around the chin. But the artist treated her with the same careful respect, softening some of the lines with reflected light and others with shadow. His regard for the subject of the paintings was unmistakable in the languid lines of his brush.

"Martha?" I gradually became aware Giselle was still speaking. "I think I lost you for a second."

I blinked back tears, too moved to speak.

She smiled. "I can tell by your reaction that you like them."

"You don't understand," I finally managed to choke out. "These are all portraits of my mother!"

Her mouth flew open. "But how can that be? You said Daddy vanished from your mother's life before you were born." She gestured toward the trio of paintings. "Obviously, these are studies of the same woman done over a period of years. Are you saying Daddy was cheating on my mother?"

I nodded dumbly as the world, as I'd known it, began to spin in my head.

CHAPTER 4

I pulled myself together enough to take photos of the portraits with my cell phone. I reached for Quinn's framed photo. "Can I borrow this?"

Giselle hesitated. "Better yet, I'll scan it right now." She disappeared briefly and returned with a printout of the photo.

"Thanks." I put the print in my purse and promised to touch base soon. Then I aimed my Honda Civic toward Uncle Isaac's house. I needed some answers, and I needed them now. Did he know that leaving Iowa hadn't ended my parents' affair? Those paintings were proof of that. How much more was he hiding from me? To make things worse, I could feel a headache coming on.

"Faigela!" My uncle greeted me with a huge smile and his pet name, which meant "little bird" in Yiddish. "I wasn't expecting a visit. Have you had lunch? I was just about to make a tuna sandwich. Come. Sit. I'll make you one, too."

I kissed him on the cheek and followed him into the kitchen. "Don't bother. I just had a little something at a friend's house." He gestured for me to take a seat at the chrome and gray Formica table, where I had colored pictures and done my homework as a child. This room in the modest California bungalow hadn't changed since Bubbie, my beloved grandmother, was alive. Green tile on the counter, cabinets painted with semigloss ivory, and pantry shelves sagging under the weight of cast-iron pots and pans.

Uncle Isaac moved slowly but efficiently, cutting two sandwiches on the diagonal and placing them on white Corelle lunch plates, with kosher pickle spears. When he finally sat down, he said what my bubbie would've said. "It's only a sliver. Enjoy."

I bit my lip, trying to decide how to begin.

"*Nu*?" he said. "I know that look. Something is bothering you."

"You're right, Uncle. Something big is bothering me."

"So, out with it. What could be so bad?" He bit off the corner of his sandwich.

"Where do I begin? It all started when Quincy sent in her DNA." I told my uncle everything about finding my half sister, Giselle. "Mother was right. His name was Quinn. Jacob Quinn Maguire. Turns out, he also lived in LA. And, a little over thirty years ago, he disappeared again." The more details I revealed about my father, the slower Uncle Isaac chewed. "And here's the most shocking thing of all." I showed him the paintings of my mother on my cell phone. "Did you know about this?"

He swallowed hard. "These look like paintings of your mother."

"That's right. They're portraits Quinn painted right here in LA! She must've been around forty in the last one. Don't you see? Leaving Iowa never stopped their affair. They somehow found each other again."

Uncle Isaac seemed to shrink as he slumped back in his chair. He looked at the table as he spoke. "*Gottenyu!* I knew she was meeting a man, but I had no idea it was your father. Your bubbie, may she rest in peace, had died, so everything was up to me. I was afraid your mamma would get herself into trouble again. You know . . ."

"You mean, like having another bastard child?"

He looked up sharply. "No, *faigela*! Don't ever call yourself that. You were everything to us. But your mamma, she never had much *sechel*. I'm not saying she was stupid, she just didn't have good judgment. So, I followed her one day to Kresky's Kosher Market on Pico, where she met a man with red hair."

I pulled Quinn's photo from my purse. "Is this the man you saw?"

"*Vey iz mir!* It's been a long time, but I think that's the same man. Is that . . . ?"

I nodded. "Go on."

He cleared his throat. "As they walked to his fancy Cadillac, I saw the sun glinting off a ring on his left hand. I followed them all the way to the Sunnyside Motel in Santa Monica."

"Then what?"

"Then I left." He shrugged.

"That's it? Why didn't you try to stop her?" Confusion and anger stirred in my chest.

He stared at his hands. "She was a grown woman. I had no right. If your bubbie was still alive, she'd know how to handle your mamma. But I'd already closed my shop for half a day to follow her. I had to get back to my customers if I was going to put food on the table. I tried talking to her that evening after you'd gone to bed. Find out who he was. Talk some sense into her."

Poor Uncle Isaac. My anger drained away as quickly as it appeared. He'd devoted his life to taking care of my mother and me. What a great sacrifice. The only thing he asked in return was that I be happy. I reached across the table and squeezed his hand.

"She refused to talk," he continued. "That's when I decided if I couldn't stop her, the least I could do was protect her. I took her to the doctor and got her some birth control pills." He shook his head. "Quinn. I had no idea."

"Did she ever mention if he maybe asked about me? Or tried to see me? Did she ever say anything about child support, for God's sake?"

"She never said a word. If he offered to pay, your mamma never took him up on it—at least as far as I know."

"Why didn't you tell me any of this before?"

Uncle Isaac stared at me for a moment. "I wanted to protect you from the truth about your mamma's behavior. It would've set a very bad example for a young girl."

"Well, what about two years ago, when you finally revealed that my father hadn't died in a train accident? Wouldn't that have been a good time to tell me the whole truth?"

"In my day, you didn't speak about such things. You just kept it under the rug."

"*Swept* it," I softly corrected him. "Swept it under the rug." I shoved the sandwich in my mouth, trying to chew away my resentment. "He was my father."

His eyes pleaded for understanding. "How could I know they were still seeing each other?"

A heavy silence settled around us as we finished our lunch. Had my uncle told me everything, or was he still holding back? The pounding in my right temple increased and fibromyalgia pain began to spread through all my muscles. Thank goodness I kept a tiny pillbox in my purse. I walked my empty plate to the sink, retrieved my meds, and swallowed them with a glass of tap water. My uncle remained seated at the table, staring into the distance.

"Please understand, Uncle, I don't blame you for anything my mother did."

His body seemed to relax and he turned his face my way.

"But I'm not stopping until I know the truth."

"What about your half sister? How does she feel about this?"

"Giselle and I are both determined to learn what happened to him."

"I don't want you to get hurt." He spoke so faintly I could barely hear him. "You say he disappeared over thirty years ago? Who knows what you might turn up under that rock? Promise me you'll be careful."

"Aren't I always?"

He didn't have to say anything. The look on his face said, *No.*

I cruised along Pico Boulevard until I found Kresky's Kosher Market. A moist breeze from the west smelled like the Pacific Ocean. I fed the meter and stood on the sidewalk with my hands in my trouser pockets. I closed my eyes and breathed deeply, trying to imagine what my mother felt long ago as she waited for my father to pick her up in his Cadillac. She must've known he was married, because Uncle Isaac said he openly wore his wedding ring. Yet she apparently loved him enough to accept her role as a secret mistress.

Her last words before she died of cancer at the age of sixty had always puzzled me. "Where's Quinn?" she'd asked. Now I finally understood why. Even though he'd disappeared a second time, her whole life had been defined by the hours she waited for him.

And how did Jacob Quinn Maguire feel about her? Was she just a little something he kept on the side? An adoring dog who would come whenever he beckoned? I retrieved my cell phone from my purse and took another look at the photos I'd taken of her portraits through time. I couldn't shake the feeling the artist had feelings for his subject.

A homeless woman wearing several layers of ragged clothes pushed her loaded shopping cart next to me and thrust a dirty hand in my direction. "Spare change for a meal?"

Over fifty thousand homeless people lived in LA, lured here by the warm winter climate and tolerant government policies. They were especially visible in this part of town. I pulled a twenty out of my purse, handed it to her, and smiled.

"God bless." She snatched the bill from my hand and hurried down the street.

That could have been my mother without Uncle Isaac's help.

I stood for several minutes more in front of Kresky's, imagining a world long before cell phones and computers and homeless people. It was easy to do in this Orthodox Jewish neighborhood. A pregnant young woman in a long skirt, long sleeves, and a head scarf pushed a baby stroller into the market just as another emerged with several sacks of groceries. Tomorrow was the Sabbath, and I assumed they needed to get the shopping out of the way today because they'd be busy cleaning house and cooking all day tomorrow.

By the time I got back to Encino, my headache and the fibro pain had disappeared. I opened my computer and Googled Jacob Quinn Maguire. Not surprisingly, I got several hundred hits, including a row of images of his paintings marching across the top of the screen.

Formal portraits stared out from the canvases, men and women sitting in rooms lined with bookshelves or draped with blue velvet. His style tended toward impressionism, using short brushstrokes. But he also borrowed from the Dutch school, relying heavily on the contrast of strong light and shadows. No wonder his portraits had been in demand. His works were a bold and brilliant fusion of styles.

The ringing of the phone pulled me away from the screen.

Lucy didn't waste words. "So, what happened with your sister? What is she like? Does she look like you? What did you find out about your father?"

"Honestly, Lucy, it's been a tough day. There's a lot I learned about both my parents, but I'm just too exhausted to talk right now. Can we save this for tomorrow?"

"*Both* parents? Now my curiosity is killing me. Are you okay? Do you want me to come over?"

"I just need some time to process everything. I'll see you tomorrow. Promise."

I returned to the search results on my computer. Dozens of photos showed Quinn with art luminaries of his day, like Bengston, Warhol, and Leibovitz. I felt a stirring of resentment. How different would my life have been if he'd settled down with my mother? Or, at the very least, if he'd claimed me as his daughter? Would I have been raised Catholic? Gone to private schools? Owned a car at sixteen? Traveled the world? Met famous people? Married someone else?

I spent the next two hours reading accounts of his disappearance in old newspaper and magazine articles. Even Wikipedia devoted a short paragraph about the mystery at the end of his biography. The *Los Angeles Times* had been especially enthusiastic, assigning not one but three reporters to follow the story. Jacob Quinn Maguire, successful member of the LA art scene, had suddenly disappeared. His wife, daughter of prominent oil baron Jerome Eagan, reported him missing after Maguire failed to show up at a gallery opening in New York.

That sudden disappearance certainly jibed with what Giselle had told me earlier in the day.

Subsequent investigation revealed he had never boarded the plane from Los Angeles. One lurid article in the tabloids speculated about gambling debts and Mafia connections. But if the police ever suspected foul play, the papers never reported it. Besides, if someone wanted to get rid of a body, Los Angeles and the surrounding deserts, ocean, and forests had an infinite number of possible dumping grounds. Without any evidence of murder, a search wasn't practical.

A plea had gone out for witnesses to step forward, but none appeared. A reward of $100,000 was offered by the Eagan family, but even that failed to produce any clues. Eventually, the media coverage petered out. As far as anyone knew, this was a simple missing-persons case that had gone cold.

The Beverly Hills Police Department spokesman on the case had been Captain Bela Farkas. The name was familiar. When my friend Harriet Oliver had been murdered, the LAPD detective who worked on her case was Gabriel Farkas. I wondered if the two were related.

I looked up from the computer and drained my glass of wine. I closed my eyes and vaguely remembered reading about the Maguire case all those years ago. But never in my wildest imagination would I have guessed the missing man was my father. How would I have felt if I'd read about my parents' affair in the newspapers? My husband at the time, Aaron, was intent on building a career as a Beverly Hills psychiatrist. He would've been horrified with such a scandal so close to home.

Thankfully, neither the police nor the newspapers knew about the relationship between my parents. Nowadays the tabloids would jump at the chance to exploit a sleazy story about the dead man, his mistress, and an illegitimate child.

An unaccustomed heaviness burned once more in my gut as I realized there would never be a mention of me or my mother in any version of his life. It suddenly dawned on me I still might be dealing with some unresolved abandonment issues. *Get hold of yourself, Martha. That water moved downstream a long time ago.* But the feeling wouldn't go away.

I was still in a bad mood when Crusher came home that evening. He'd hardly had a chance to walk through the front door when I blurted out, "My whole life has been a lie!" Then I burst into a thunderstorm of tears.

CHAPTER 5

Friday morning, I woke up exhausted after spending a restless night trying to switch off my brain. I shuffled into the kitchen, still wearing my blue pajamas printed with penguins on surfboards.

Crusher stood at the sink, already dressed for his job in jeans and a black T-shirt, with a fresh red bandana on his head. He was an undercover agent for the Bureau of Alcohol, Tobacco, Firearms and Explosives. For the last two weeks he'd been part of a stakeout watching a group of terrorist sympathizers suspected of shipping firearms to Syria from the port of Los Angeles. He handed me a steaming cup of Italian roast. "Feel any better, babe? You had a rough night." He should know. He'd listened patiently while I cried my eyes out and dumped everything I'd learned about my parents. When we went to bed, I tossed and turned in his arms most of the night, finally falling asleep at three.

"Sorry if I kept you up." My voice croaked. "I just couldn't stop going over everything in my head.

I've got to find out what happened to my father. Maybe I'll even learn why he denied my existence."

Crusher placed a plate of buttered toast in front of me. "What do you need?"

That question was one of the reasons I loved the man. He never tried to "manage" me or tell me what to do. And he understood me well enough to know I would never abandon my quest.

"To start with, I'd like to see the police files on his missing-persons case. I can't ask Noah Kaplan to get them for me. He's LA, not Beverly Hills. Besides, he might ask something in return for the favor."

"Like what?"

"Like a blessing on his romance with Quincy."

Crusher laughed. "You can't stop love, babe. Listen. ATF often works with local police departments. Let me see what I can do. What else do you need?"

"I'd like to speak to the detective who worked on the case."

"When was that? Thirty years ago? Thirty-two? Chances are the dude's long gone. He probably aged out and retired. Might even be dead."

I frowned and picked up a golden piece of toast, softened in the middle by melted butter. "Yeah, but I'm still going to try. I even have an idea where to start."

He bent down and kissed me. "I'm sitting inside the surveillance van again today, but I'll see what I can do." He headed for the front door, lifting his keys, ATF badge, and gun from the hall table. "Do you want me to pick up anything for Shabbat tonight?"

"No thanks. I've got it covered."

An hour later, I sat in Lucy's kitchen, tracing the squares on the checkered blue tablecloth with my fingertip. ". . . and that's the whole story."

My friend had been listening with her elbows on the table and chin in her hands. When I finished speaking, she sat up straight and slowly shook her head. "Dang. I mean, what're the odds of your parents finding each other in a big city like LA? Sounds like your mother wasn't as out of it as you thought. She was able to hide a huge secret from everyone. For years, no less."

"But why didn't he ever want to see me?" Tears stung my eyes.

"Are you sure he didn't try?" She pointed to Quinn's photo I'd put on the table. "Do you remember your mother ever introducing you to a man with red hair?"

I swiped at the tears running down my cheeks. "No. I've racked my brain a thousand times, but I don't remember ever seeing this man."

"I'm sorry, hon." She got up from the table and came back with a box of tissues. "Do you honestly think you can solve a thirty-two-year-old cold case?"

Good question. What made me think I could succeed where the police had failed? Quinn was a high-profile missing person. Surely the BHPD had been under a lot of pressure to find him. I put the photo back in my purse and stood to leave. "If I can figure out where the investigation failed, maybe I can figure out which rock to look under."

Lucy walked me to the front door and gathered me in a hug. "You know I'll help you in any way I can."

Before walking outside, I remembered another reason I wanted to talk to my friend. "By the way, is everything okay with you? You and Ray went to see your lawyer yesterday."

She swiped the air with a dismissive hand. "Nothing to worry about. We were just bringing our wills up to date."

Why did I get the feeling there was more she wasn't telling me? "Good to know, Lucy. Because if there is something *unusual* going on, you know you can always talk to me. Right?"

"Of course!" she said just a little too brightly.

Instead of driving home, I sat in the car in front of Lucy's house and opened my cell phone. I scrolled through my contacts until I found what I was looking for, the phone number of the man who worked on my friend Harriet Oliver's case a couple of years ago, LAPD Detective Gabe Farkas.

"This is Martha Rose. Remember me?"

"Granny Oakley!" He referred to the name the news stories dubbed me right after I stopped Harriet's killer with his own gun. "How could I forget? It's been how long?" He wheezed like a fat man with asthma and chuckled. "Solved any more murders lately?"

"A couple."

"Really? I was only kidding."

"Really. Anyway, right now I'm looking into a cold case, and I have some questions for you."

"Uh-oh."

"Do you have time to see me this morning?"

"Can't we take care of this over the phone?" His voice turned cautious.

"It's complicated and very personal. I'd rather do this face-to-face."

"I'll be at my desk until noon."

"Thanks, Gabe. I'm driving over the hill from Encino. I'll see you in about a half hour."

I hopped on the 405 south, exited right on Santa Monica Boulevard and headed toward the West LA station on Butler. My watch read eleven-thirty when I checked in at the front desk. I didn't have to wait long.

The extremely heavy forty-year-old lumbered out of his office with a big smile on his face. "Well, if it isn't Granny O!" He zeroed in on my engagement ring and whistled. "Is that what I think it is? Who's the lucky guy?"

"His name is Yossi Levy. He's ATF."

Farkas's brown eyes twinkled. "No kidding! I guess I'm not surprised you ended up with a guy in law enforcement." He led me through a door marked CONFERENCE ROOM and gestured for me to sit. The padded seats were a step up from the solid metal chairs in the cramped interrogation rooms. "Can I get you some stale, bitter coffee?"

"As tempting as that sounds, I think I'll pass."

I looked around for a camera lens on the ceiling and blue walls. "Is anyone else listening?"

"Nah." He shook his head. "You can speak freely." He leaned back, clasped his hands on top of his portly stomach, and his voice softened. "You said this was about something personal?"

I took a deep breath and told him how I found my half sister, Giselle Cole, and the subsequent discoveries I made about my parents. "I want to find out what happened to my father."

"Even if the cold squad reopened this case after more than thirty years, what makes you think they'll find anything new at this late date?"

"For one thing, the police never knew about his affair with my mother. Maybe that'll shed a different light on the facts, open a new line of inquiry." I could tell by his expression he was about to discourage me. I held up my hand like a stop sign. "Look, Gabe. I know I'm grasping at straws, but if I could only get a look at the file, maybe talk to the officers involved. Actually, I've done some preliminary research online. Old newspaper articles about the case often quoted a spokesman for the Beverly Hills Police Department, a Captain Bela Farkas. Is he a relative of yours?"

Farkas sat up straighter and raised his eyebrows. "Yeah? That's my old man. He's the reason I became a cop."

All my senses went on high alert. "Could you give me his phone number and address? I really need to talk to him."

He unwrapped a protein bar from his jacket pocket. "Pops retired to Green Valley, Arizona, an old folks' community south of Tucson."

"I've heard of it."

"Yeah, it's a nice place, but way too hot for me. My wife says if I lose weight, I'd be able to tolerate the heat better. She keeps putting me on different diets, hoping one will stick. Right now, she has me doing Weight Watchers again." He handed me half the bar.

"A fellow traveler." I bit into the caramel-covered nuts and dried cranberries. "How's it working for you?"

He spoke around a bulging cheek. "Fine. If you don't cheat."

"Same here. So, will you help me talk to your father?"

Farkas swallowed the last of his illegal snack. "Unfortunately, no one can reach him right now. He's on what he calls a 'spiritual retreat.'" He made air quotes with his pudgy fingers. "He's done this before, where he leaves his cell phone at home and goes fly-fishing up in Oak Creek Canyon."

"For how long?"

"Usually he resurfaces after a week or so. The best I can do is leave him a text and voice message later this afternoon. He'll pick them up when he's ready to return to the real world. Meanwhile, I know a guy in Beverly Hills. I'll put in a request for the Maguire file. It might take a few days to locate it, but I'll let you know as soon as it comes." He stood looking at his watch. "I'm due in a briefing." He pointed to my left hand and smiled. "Again, congrats on your engagement." Then he surprised me by giving me a quick, one-armed hug.

On the way home, I stopped at Bea's Bakery in Tarzana for a loaf of raisin challah and a twelve-inch-long hunk of apple strudel. Another stop at the kosher market for a brisket, and I was back in my kitchen by one—plenty of time to heat the oven to 275 degrees and slow-cook Shabbat dinner.

I set the table with a white cloth and my bubbie's white china with the blue rim. As I laid down the last piece of silverware, my cell phone buzzed with an incoming text message from Crusher. *Got file. Interesting. C U tonite.*

My heart sped up a little. If Crusher said the file was interesting, that could only mean we were finally onto something.

I called Giselle and told her what I'd learned.

"Set an extra place," she said. "I'm coming to dinner."

Why did she have to be so bossy? "I thought you never came to the Valley."

"I didn't say *never*. I just avoid the place like the plague."

"Oh. Sorry I misunderstood, your highness."

"You don't have to get all snarky. I'm only being honest."

I rolled my eyes. "Whatever. Be here by seven. I'm fixing brisket."

"I don't eat red meat." *Fingernails on a blackboard.*
I sighed. "I'll grill a salmon fillet, then. Okay?"

"Perfect. Shall I bring dessert? Benesh makes divine éclairs."

I didn't have time to give my Gentile sister a lesson on why a kosher meal is either meat or dairy but never both. "Don't! I'll explain later. By the way, we'll be celebrating the Sabbath. My family is very Jewish."

"Fabulous! You're my big sister, Martha. I want to know everything about you. I'm so glad you decided to invite me to a real Jewish dinner."

"Have you forgotten that you invited yourself?"

"Don't get technical. I mean it when I say I'm honored."

Strangely enough, I believed her.

CHAPTER 6

I dressed for Shabbat in my long black skirt, pink silk blouse, and my bubbie's pearls. At six-thirty Crusher walked through the front door with Uncle Isaac, whose dark embroidered Bukharin skullcap sat like a square box over his short, white curls. I settled him in the living room and pulled Crusher into the dining room. His hands were empty.

"Where is it, Yossi?" I whispered. "My father's missing-persons file?"

"Check your messages. I e-mailed you a copy. This is the digital age, remember?" He noticed the fourth plate on the table. "Who else is coming for dinner?"

"Giselle. She invited herself because she also wants to see what's in this file."

"You should prepare Isaac before she gets here."

"Good idea."

"Meanwhile, I'm going to shower. Sitting in that

surveillance van all day was hot and sweaty work." He kissed my forehead and disappeared down the hallway toward the bedroom.

I walked back into the living room and sat next to my uncle. "Um, I wanted to let you know we're having a guest for dinner tonight." I cleared my throat. "It's Giselle Cole."

He pulled back a little and studied my face. "*Nu?* Things seem to be moving fast along those lines."

"It's fine. She says she wants to get to know me better. I'm just concerned about your comfort. I want you to be okay with this. And I should warn you, she can be a little outspoken."

"I'll be okay only if you are." He patted my hands. "I know you want answers. Who could blame you? But after what he did to your mother, I wouldn't care if your father was roasting in Gehennah."

"I know you're angry, Uncle. Me, too. But I'm not giving up my search for the truth."

He sighed. "You may never know the whole truth, *faigela*. Remember what I always taught you—*every answer brings a new question*." How often had I heard him repeat that Yiddish saying?

The ringing of the doorbell interrupted our conversation. Giselle stood on the doorstep in a slinky black cocktail dress with short sleeves and black stiletto heels. A diamond necklace twinkled around her throat. In jarring contrast, a scarf printed with golden horseshoes over a bright blue background was wrapped over her head and tied

under her chin babushka-style. "Here." She smiled
and thrust a bouquet of pink roses and a bottle of
Dom Pérignon toward me. "Happy Sabbath."

My jaw fell open at her curious choice of evening
wear, and I stared at her a beat too long.

"What?" she demanded. "Aren't you going to
invite me in?"

I closed my eyes briefly and stood to the side.
"Sorry. Sorry. Come in."

A cloud of French perfume followed her through
the doorway. She stopped and slowly scanned the
inside of my house. "Well, this isn't the best part
of the Valley, but it's not the worst. You could've
ended up in Pacoima."

I gritted my teeth and made mental apologies to
the North Valley community of mostly blue-collar
Latino and African American families.

She spotted my uncle sitting in the living room
and strode over to him. "I'm Martha's little sister,
Giselle. You must be the brother of Daddy's mistress."

Poor Uncle Isaac! His jaw dropped open and he
looked at me with wide eyes. I could tell he was far
from pleased at the crude characterization of my
mother.

"This is my uncle, Isaac Harris," I said.

She sat next to him on the sofa and smiled. "I'm
happy to meet you, Uncle Isaac."

She called him *Uncle* Isaac and not Mr. Harris, or
just Isaac? What chutzpah. And why was she still
wearing the head scarf? She crossed her long legs,

and the hem of her tight skirt rode up six inches
above her knees, exposing smooth, slender thighs.
If family members were identified by the shapes of
their legs between the hip and the knee, no one
would ever guess we were related.

I asked, "Giselle, what's with the scarf?"

She patted the silk draped over her auburn hair.
"It's Hermès. Do you like it? I'm wearing it out of
respect for your Jewish customs. Don't you people
keep your heads covered on your Sabbath? Like the
Moslems?"

I briefly closed my eyes. "Take it off, G. I appreciate the sentiment, but no, you're not required
to do anything like that in my house. If we're
ever in a situation that dictates otherwise, I'll let
you know."

She untied the knot under her chin, whipped off
the scarf, and smoothed her perfect, straight hair.
"Thank God. This thing was ruining my whole look."
She suddenly sprang off the sofa and hugged me.
"You called me G. I really like that. It'll be our pet
name as sisters, okay?"

Oy vey.

She released me from her grasp when Crusher
came into the room. He wore his usual Sabbath
attire of black trousers, a crisp white shirt, and a
white crocheted yarmulke covering his head. "I'm
Yossi." He stretched his right arm toward Giselle.

She took his hand in both of hers and held on.

"Are you the federal agent responsible for that rock on Martha's finger?"

"Guilty." He pulled his hand away.

She gave the tall giant a slow once-over and then winked at me. "He'll do."

Oh dear God. Doesn't this woman have a filter? "Excuse me, but it's time to put your salmon on the grill." Clearly I wasn't going to have time to look at my father's file before dinner.

Ten minutes later we gathered at the dining room table. "Now's the time for the scarf, G. Me, not you. I cover my head as a sign of humility when I talk to God." I draped the white cloth over my head and lit the candles. "Blessed art Thou, oh Lord our God, King of the Universe, Who has sanctified us by Thy commandments and commanded us to kindle the Sabbath lights." I removed the scarf and sat while Crusher honored me with a reading in Hebrew of the *Eshet Hayil*, the "woman of valor." When he finished, he lifted my hand to his lips and kissed it.

Giselle watched intently. "What was that you just did?"

He said, "It's a passage from the Bible praising the woman of the house. The husband reads it to his wife at the beginning of every Sabbath, as a kind of thank-you for all her hard work the previous week."

"That's beautiful." She sat back as Uncle Isaac recited the *Kiddush* welcoming the Sabbath.

He blessed the wine. "Blessed art Thou, oh Lord

our God, King of the Universe, Who created the fruit of the vine." Then he passed the silver cup around the table for all to partake equally. When the cup finally made its way to Giselle, she picked up her napkin and wiped the rim before taking a sip. "Germs," she said.

Uncle Isaac looked at the table and wagged his head slowly.

Crusher sang the *hamotzi*, blessing the challah. "Blessed art Thou, oh Lord our God, King of the Universe, Who brings forth bread from the earth." He tore off pieces of the soft, yellow bread, sprinkled each with salt, and passed them around the table.

"Why the salt?" Giselle nibbled on the soft part of the bread.

"Originally it was used to add flavor. But it's also a sign of something deeper." Crusher touched his head covering. "Jews no longer have a temple in Jerusalem. So, we treat our table like an altar. Every meal becomes a metaphor for sacrifices on that altar. Since one of the commandments in the Bible is to include salt with the sacrifices, we put salt on the challah to fulfill that commandment."

"Nice. I get it."

"You're a good learner," said Uncle Isaac.

I smiled at Giselle. "Now we eat."

During the meal, the two men discussed the Torah portion for the week as was their custom and the custom of observant Jewish males around the world. Giselle waited patiently, using her fork to slide the last of her salmon around the plate. She eventually buried it under a pile of uneaten roasted potato chunks. Finally, she looked at Crusher. "I want to see the old missing-persons file on my father. Martha said you found something interesting."

CHAPTER 7

"I have the file on my cell phone, G." I retrieved my phone from my purse. We left the men at the table with their hot tea and apple strudel and settled on the living room sofa.

She stared at the screen and moaned, "It's too small to read!"

"Don't worry." I pressed a button. "Come with me." I led her to my sewing room, where my printer began spewing out page after page of BHPD documents.

While we waited, I asked, "Tell me what you remember about the time he disappeared."

"Well, I was twelve. Nobody told me he was missing. I just thought he was away on a long trip. Whenever I asked, Mother would tell me not to worry, he would be home soon. A lot of people I'd never seen before came to talk to my mother. When they did, she sent me out of the room. I remember overhearing a lot of whispering and my mother crying."

"When did you find out the truth?"

"About two weeks after he'd gone. Mother forgot a copy of the *LA Times* on the breakfast table. I sat down for my waffles and saw his photograph on the front page, along with the caption, 'Car of famous local artist found at airport. Foul play or cold feet?' Mother had to tell me then."

"What exactly did she say?"

"I still remember her words exactly. She said, 'Your daddy didn't fly to New York after all. He decided to go somewhere else, but silly Daddy forgot to tell me where. So, right now, we don't know where he is. He's bound to come home soon, though, and I know he'll be very sorry he made us worry because he loves us so much.' I believed her for a while, but after six months, she had to acknowledge he was probably never coming home. We were never the same after that."

"In what way?"

Giselle looked around the sewing room as if noticing for the first time the sewing machine and all the colorful fabrics folded on shelves. She strolled over to my Prairie Braid quilt still in the hoop. "All the fun went out the door with Daddy. The scandal of his disappearance humiliated Mother. She stopped seeing her friends. She rarely left the house." She ran her fingers gently over the bumpy texture of the stitches. "You know, I think that's when my grandmother began making that quilt I told you about."

The printer stopped running and the room became silent. I gathered a sheaf of papers and spread them out on the cutting table. "I think we can sort through these to establish a timeline. We'll pin the results up here on my design board." I pointed to the white flannel sheet hanging on one wall of my sewing room.

When I saw the confusion on her face, I hastily added, "Many quilters use something like this to audition quilt blocks or swatches of fabrics as they work on their projects. Regular cotton fabric easily sticks to the fuzzy nap of the flannel sheet." I pointed to the pages of the missing-persons file on the table in front of us. "Of course, these papers won't stick to the flannel. We'll attach them with straight pins."

"Sounds like you've done this before."

I nodded and gestured toward the empty flannel sheet. "It's called a murder board."

She grabbed my arm. I'd just spoken out loud the word we'd avoided using. "So you think Daddy was murdered?"

"Don't you?"

Giselle and I sat at my cutting table and began to sort the files into three stacks: reports, interviews, and evidence. Then we arranged them in chronological order. The initial missing person's report yielded basic information we already knew. On Sunday, May 25, 1980, Jacob Quinn Maguire left his home in Beverly Hills for a flight to New York on TWA. He was scheduled the following night to attend an opening at the Montmartre Gallery in Manhattan. The family filed a missing-persons report after several days of not hearing from him. Quinn was never seen or heard from again.

A subsequent report indicated his Cadillac had been located two weeks later, parked in the TWA lot at the airport. "Look at this, G. Quinn made it as far as LAX." I read from the page in my hand. "'A preliminary examination of the vehicle by detectives failed to find the subject's luggage, indicating his disappearance may have been voluntary.'"

"Does this mean Daddy might still be alive?"

"Maybe. Or it could mean that whoever abducted him also took his luggage to make it look like he did a bunk."

Her shoulders sagged. "Does it say if they found any other clues?"

"That'll be on the forensic report in the evidence pile."

Giselle picked up a paper. "Here it is." She began to read aloud.

"'A search of the subject's Cadillac, California license plate PAINTR 1, was conducted on June ninth, 1980, by the Forensic Division of the BHPD. The following is a summary of the results.

"'The glove compartment contained the following: a vehicle owner's manual, Thompson street guide, a pair of men's leather gloves, sticks of charcoal, a gum eraser, a small spiral sketchbook, and a package of condoms.'"

She stopped briefly and raised her eyebrows. "Condoms?"

"Keep reading," I urged.

"'The interior of the car yielded seven receipts. Five for gasoline from the Mobil station on Wilshire and Robertson; one for a carton of Marlboro cigarettes from 7-Eleven on Sepulveda; and one for two corned beef sandwiches from Kresky's Kosher Market on Pico Boulevard.'"

There it was. Although the police might not have known why Quinn would be at Kresky's Market, I knew. Uncle Isaac said that was where he used to pick up my mother. That receipt was proof Quinn was seeing my mother right up to the time he disappeared.

"'The ashtray held seven Marlboro cigarette butts, three with red lipstick.'"

"Stop," I said. "Could those cigarettes be your mother's?"

"I don't think so. She smoked, but she never wore red lipstick. She said it looked too garish against her skin. She only wore frosty pink." Her eyes narrowed. "How about your mother? Did she smoke?"

I thought about how she used to sit for hours on the same chair in the living room and gaze out the bay window with a view of the street. I'd watched the smoke from her long Virginia Slims curl upward in a ribbon, dancing in the tiny air currents. I sighed. "She was a heavy smoker, but she never wore lipstick."

Giselle continued to read.

"'The trunk of the vehicle contained the following: standard repair kit including jack and spare tire. Unidentified coarse fibers, possibly from canvas cloth.

"'Fingerprints: Nine full and partial sets were collected. Five were identified as belonging to the subject and his family members: wife Louise, daughter Giselle, mother-in-law Edith Eagan, and father-in-law Jerome Eagan. One set belonged to the investigating detective, and two sets remained unidentified.

"'Trace: No visible traces of blood were found, and an examination with luminol revealed no fugitive traces. Ultraviolet light revealed evidence of multiple semen deposits on the leather of the backseat. Lab tests confirmed the samples were the same blood type as the subject, type A positive.'"

She stopped and glared at me. "The condoms. The semen. Daddy had sex in the backseat of his car? Like some horny teenager?"

I stared at her. "Look, G, I know what you're thinking. He could very well have been with my mother. But since Quinn wasn't exactly the faithful type, he also could've been screwing any number of women. It may be that one of *them* is responsible for his disappearance. After all, there were two unidentified sets of prints and cigarettes with red lipstick that neither one of our mothers wore."

She twisted her mouth and frowned. "When you told me about your mother, I thought it was kind of romantic Daddy had a secret mistress for so many years. But now it turns out he was nothing but a horndog! Do you suppose Mother knew about all his affairs?"

"Why don't you ask her?"

"I can't. She's dead. She always refused to talk to me about him. I think she lied about everything!"

"Now you know how I feel. Go on. What else does the report say?"

She began to read again, skipping over most of it. "Hair samples, blah-de-blah, fibers, soil, plant material. 'In conclusion, no visible indications of a struggle or foul play were found.'"

"Sorry to interrupt." Crusher stood in the doorway. "I came to tell you I'm about to drive Isaac back to West LA and knew you'd want to say good-bye."

Giselle also stood. "I can drive Uncle Isaac back to West LA and save you a trip back and forth over the hill."

There it was again, her use of *Uncle* Isaac. I worried about how he'd respond to being alone with the woman who insulted his sister earlier in the evening. I tried to discourage her. "We're not finished here, G. Besides, it's not exactly on your way. My uncle lives far south of you in the Pico-Robertson area. You'd be taking a big detour from the Palisades to drive him. Yossi can do it."

"Don't be silly, Martha. It's the least I can do for

my big sister! Besides, I've had enough surprises for one night. We can continue this tomorrow."

She leaned over and kissed my cheek, then she turned to Crusher. "Let's go."

She headed toward the living room. Crusher turned to me behind her back and rolled his eyes.

"This will not end well," I whispered.

Uncle Isaac glanced at me nervously then turned to Giselle. "It's very kind of you to offer me a ride home, but you don't have to bother."

"It's no bother, really. I'm happy to help my big sister."

I knew my uncle. He was too polite to keep refusing. He shrugged. "Well, if you say so."

Crusher and I wished them Shabbat shalom and watched as they walked toward her red Escalade parked in my driveway.

"So, why haven't you ever been married, Uncle Isaac?"

"I never found the right one."

She opened the passenger door for him and offered to help him inside. "A cute little old man like you? I bet you've had tons of girlfriends."

To my surprise, he laughed.

She closed his door, walked around to the driver's side, and waved at us before she got in.

As they drove off I asked, "What do you think of her?"

Crusher threw back his head and laughed. He closed the door and took me in his arms. "I think she's a lot like you in a scrawny, unedited sort of way."

"But I'm smarter, right?"

He nuzzled my neck. "Way smarter."

I thought about Giselle's skinny thighs. "What about desirable?"

He began to undo the buttons on my pink silk blouse. "Ten times more desirable."

"Only ten?"

He moaned softly. "A hundred times."

We spent the rest of the evening eagerly fulfilling another lovely Sabbath tradition.

CHAPTER 8

Saturday morning I carried a cup of breakfast coffee to my sewing room and sorted through the pile of witness interviews, beginning with Giselle's mother. The detectives had questioned Louise Maguire more than once. According to her initial testimony, on the morning of May 25, 1980, she'd packed Quinn's suitcase and watched him toss it in the trunk of his Cadillac before heading for the airport. That was the last time she saw or heard from her husband.

Her next interview was conducted two weeks later, after Quinn's missing car was impounded.

When questioned later about the condoms and semen in the car, LM claimed to have no knowledge and appeared to be very distressed. When asked about the red lipstick on the cigarettes, she stopped the interview and refused further discussion.

That seemed to substantiate what Giselle and I suspected last night. Some woman other than either of our mothers had been smoking inside Quinn's Cadillac. The skin on the back of my neck tingled a warning as I read a third interview dated a month later.

LM said she and her husband drove to an isolated spot near Mulholland Drive to "spice things up a bit." She initially denied knowing about the car sex because she'd been too embarrassed. She also claimed the red lipstick had been hers.

Why did she change her story? Louise Maguire was hiding something. The last line of the detective's notes confirmed he also didn't believe her story.

LM seemed agitated and refused to make eye contact. Body language suggests she's lying.

Next I read the interviews with Louise's parents. The initial conversation portrayed them as being perplexed by Quinn's disappearance.

Jerome and Edith Eagan were questioned together. The last time they saw Jacob Quinn Maguire was the evening before his disappearance, when both families had dined together at the Jonathan Club. They said their son-in-law was excited about returning to New York. They never heard from him again.

Stapled to that document were follow-up interviews dated after the Cadillac had been examined.

Edith Eagan denied any knowledge of Maguire's extramarital affairs. She said her daughter's marriage was successful and happy and that Maguire was devoted to his family. He had no reason to leave his wife and daughter and disappear.

In a separate interview, Jerome Eagan didn't seem to be surprised at the forensic evidence.

JE didn't seem disturbed by his son-in-law's flings. But he was disturbed about Maguire's missing luggage. JE said, "<u>If I find out he ran off with one of his little chippies, I'll hunt him down myself!</u>"

The detective underlined the last sentence.

I continued searching but found no evidence of any further interviews with the family. I did read brief interviews of friends, neighbors, and colleagues, both in LA and New York. Quinn was under exclusive contract to the Shiffer Gallery in Beverly Hills. The owner, Eliza Shiffer, was interviewed but denied knowing anything about his disappearance.

Only one artist friend, a potter named Jayda

Constable, was able to add significant information. She admitted to having an ongoing affair with Quinn whenever he visited New York. In the rest of the interview, the artist said she and Quinn made plans to stay together at the Plaza during his week-long stay. She revealed that on the day before he disappeared, he phoned to say he was bringing a lot of money with him to New York. When he didn't show up, she suspected something "bad" must have happened to him. No follow-up interviews were ever made.

The more I learned about my father, the more disgusted I became. He got my mother pregnant and abandoned her. Then he married the daughter of an oil baron, had another child, and made my mother his mistress. Now I found out she was only one of his many lovers. Not everyone was as passive as my mother had been. Could he have been killed by an angry paramour or a jealous husband?

The few remaining papers from the file revealed the BHPD monitored Quinn's known bank accounts and credit card statements but found no sign of cash withdrawals and no activity after the date of his disappearance. One month after he went missing, the investigation died a quiet death.

Now, more than ever, I needed to talk to retired BHPD Captain Bela Farkas. To dismiss a high-profile case like that after only a month seemed strange. When database searches and credit card statements failed to turn up any trace of Quinn, didn't the police suspect foul play? If so, why didn't they expand their probe?

I picked up my cell phone and called Giselle. "I think you should know what I found in the rest of Quinn's file this morning."

"You finished going through it without me?"

"It's eleven in the morning, G. I wasn't going to sit around until you decided to call."

She yawned. "I like to sleep in on the weekends."

"Do you want to know what I discovered or not?"

"Chill out. Why are you such a grumpus this morning? Didn't you get any last night?"

Did I ever, but I wasn't about to tell her that. "I'm not grumpy, I'm just disturbed by what I didn't find in the file." I told her what the witness reports revealed.

"I don't get it. Daddy was famous. How could they forget about him like that?"

"That's what I intend to find out. I'm going to track down the two detectives who worked the case. I'm also planning to talk to the guy who supervised those detectives, Captain Farkas. He's incommunicado right now, but his son, Gabe, is going to help me get in touch. Gabe's kind of a friend of mine. We worked together on a case a couple of years ago."

"Well, I have a right to be there when you talk to all these people. After all, he was *my* father, too."

"Of course. But when I tell you to meet me somewhere, you better show up on time. I don't want to be standing around waiting for you to roll out of bed."

"Stop right there, Sissy. Just because you're older doesn't mean you're the boss of me."

Sissy? I blew out a puff of air. Working with Giselle wasn't going to be easy. "To change the subject, thanks again for taking Uncle Isaac home last night."

"No problem. He really is a lovable little guy. I've decided to adopt him."

"What did you talk about?"

"He wanted to know all about me, my late husband, and my son, Nicholas. He asked most of the questions and I did most of the talking."

No surprise there.

"I asked him what you were like growing up." She chuckled. "He said I reminded him a little of you. Curious, adventurous, and a good learner. Wasn't that sweet?"

"Yossi said something similar last night."

"It must be our DNA, right? Speaking of Yossi, what a hunk! I always thought Jewish men were little and indoorsy. I didn't know they could grow so tall and lumberjacky. By the way, I heard Jewish men are great in the sack. Does he have any friends?"

Oy vey. "As much as I enjoy our conversations, G, I'm going to have to cut this one short. I've got some errands to run."

"Okay, but before you go, I wanted to let you know I think I've located that quilt I told you about. The one my grandmother was making."

"Bring it to my group. We meet every Tuesday morning at ten. My house."

"There you go being bossy again, Sissy. Honestly!"

I ended the call and picked up a notepad. Now that I had a grasp of what was in the missing-persons file, I began writing summaries of the facts. Then I used straight pins with colorful round glass heads to pin each note to the flannel sheet. I lined them up in a horizontal row to establish a timeline that began with Quinn's disappearance on May 25, 1980, and ended one month later. Then I posted a list of questions.

Where did Quinn's luggage go?

What about the cash he was bringing to New York?

Who was the mystery woman with the red lipstick?

Who belonged to the unidentified fingerprints?

Why didn't the police investigate foul play?

Possible motives: jealousy, robbery.

I stood back and studied the murder board, adding one last touch, Quinn's photo and printouts of the three portraits of my mother. There was nothing more I could do until I spoke to Captain Bela Farkas. I hoped he could help me track down the investigating detectives and Jayda Constable, Quinn's artist lover. I also hoped that, after more than thirty years, those people were still alive with their memories intact.

The quiet rumbling in my stomach reminded me it was lunchtime. Something about Lucy's too-breezy attitude the other day bothered me enough that I gave her a call. "What are you doing right now?

We haven't had time to catch up for a while. Come over. I'm fixing brisket sandwiches on challah."

"Good idea. There's something I've been meaning to tell you."

I shook with a sudden chill at the somber tone of her voice.

CHAPTER 9

Lucy sat at my kitchen table, poking listlessly at her sandwich.

I cleared my throat. "You said you wanted to talk to me about something?"

"Ray went in for a colonoscopy last Monday and they found some polyps. We still haven't gotten the biopsy results."

"Don't most polyps turn out to be benign?"

"There's a history of colon cancer in his family. His mother, aunt, and cousin Rocco all died of it." Her perfectly made-up face crumpled in pain. "I couldn't bear it if anything happened to my Ray."

Lucy and Ray Mondello had been together their whole lives. They grew up in the small town of Moorcroft, Wyoming, and became sweethearts in the seventh grade. They got pregnant and married—in that order—during their senior year in high school. At the end of Ray's tour in Vietnam, they moved to Los Angeles, where they raised five sons and built a successful auto repair business.

I moved my chair closer and put my arms around my best friend while she leaned into me and sobbed. "I don't blame you for being concerned," I said, "but this could be nothing at all. Is Ray complaining about any symptoms?"

Lucy picked up her napkin, dabbed at her eyes, and blew her nose. "No." Black mascara smudged the skin under her eyes. "He says he feels strong as an ox and frisky as a fox." She curled her fingers in the air quotes she loved so much.

"Well, then, he's probably fine. If the biopsy results are positive, God forbid, we'll face this together. Do the boys know what's going on?"

"No. We wanted to wait until we knew one way or the other. We should get the results by this coming Monday."

"And this was the reason you updated your wills the other day?"

"Yes." She sniffled. "Just in case."

"I'm not going to tell you not to worry, Lucy, because if I were in your shoes, I'd be sitting on *shpilkes* till I found out. Frankly, I think this calls for some serious chocolate."

She smiled for the first time.

I normally avoided mixing meat and dairy in the same meal, but my Catholic friend wasn't bound by the same kosher rules. When we finished our sandwiches, I prepared a generous bowl of chocolate chunk ice cream with milk chocolate syrup and placed it on the table before her. "As Uncle Isaac would say, *Ess, faigela*. Eat up."

Ten minutes later, Lucy's spoon scraped the bottom of the bowl. She leaned back and closed her eyes and sighed. "I feel better now." She looked at me. "When is Quincy coming to town?"

"She's due to arrive tomorrow, but I won't see her right away. Kaplan's picking her up at LAX and they're going straight to his place. She says they'll join us for Shabbat on Friday, but I don't know if I'll see her before then. I hope she gets good and sick and tired of him by the end of her visit. I've already invited her to stay here if things don't work out."

"Come on, Martha. Is he that bad?"

"Worse!"

"What'll you do if they end up getting married? Having children?"

"Pray that their babies scream all night long with colic and grow up to be rebellious teenagers with earrings in their lips."

Lucy laughed. "So, tell me what's new with your investigation."

I led her to my sewing room.

She stepped closer to the murder board and began to read the timeline I'd constructed. "Where'd you get this information?"

I pointed to the stacks of papers on the cutting table. "Yossi managed to get a copy of Quinn's missing-persons file." I showed her the forensic report.

"Ewww," she said. "Semen in the backseat?"

"I know, right? I mean, if Quinn was fooling around like that, maybe he pissed someone off."

"Like a jealous husband?"

"Exactly! Yet the police never considered foul play."

"Wait a minute. That family was fairly prominent, right? Then why did they make a big stink and demand more? A family like that would've had influence in very high places."

"I don't know the answer to that. The Eagans didn't contribute any useful information. And Louise actually changed her statement to whitewash her husband's infidelities."

"What does your sister say?"

"Half sister. She was only twelve at the time and doesn't remember much. Unfortunately, her mother and her grandparents are gone, so we can't ask any of them. But I did locate the supervising captain at the BHPD. I'm hoping he'll tell us why the case wasn't pursued."

"Well, you certainly have your work cut out for you, girlfriend." She arched her back and stretched. "Thanks for lunch and, you know, the shoulder. I've got to go. My grandson Trey has a soccer game this afternoon. Keep your fingers crossed for the biopsy report on Monday."

"Of course I will. By the way, you'll have a chance to meet Giselle on Tuesday. I've invited her to bring a quilt her grandmother was piecing when she died. Depending on the shape it's in, I thought I'd help her finish."

After Lucy left, I cleaned up the kitchen. As I wiped down the apricot-colored marble kitchen counters, my phone rang.

"Martha? Gabe Farkas here."

"Hi, Gabe. Sorry I haven't been in touch. I meant to tell you I already got a copy of my father's missing-persons file."

"That explains the other request they said they received. My dad finally surfaced and called me just now. I told him about you and he's willing to talk. But he won't do it over the phone. He's insisting he'll only speak to you in person."

I didn't relish a trip to Arizona, especially in July, when the thermometer soared into the triple digits. "You think he knows more than what's in the file?"

"Yeah, but he wouldn't tell me what. He told me to give you his phone number so the two of you can work out the details."

I wrote down the info. "I really appreciate your help."

"One more thing. At some point, this could turn into a homicide investigation. You need to keep me in the loop. Agreed?"

"Of course."

I immediately called the number he gave me. "This is Martha Rose. I believe your son just told you about me?"

The voice on the other end was gravelly but strong. "Southwest has four flights daily from LAX to Tucson. Call me back when you've made your reservations, and I'll pick you up at the airport."

"Okay. I'm bringing my half sister, Giselle. She was twelve when our father went missing."

"I remember her. Smart little girl. Redhead."

"That's the one."

I hung up and immediately called Giselle. "If I can book a flight on Southwest, do you want to fly to Tucson with me tomorrow?"

"Southwest? That Greyhound bus with wings? I'd rather wear retail. We'll use the company jet. It's hangered in Van Nuys, not too far from you. I'll swing by your place at nine. Be ready."

"What company is that?"

"Eagan Oil. My grandfather's company, which is now my company. And pack an overnight bag just in case."

"Just in case what, G?"

"Just in case we decide to do something fun, silly. Like rocking a night in Vegas or spending a couple days in New York."

Sin City wasn't my idea of fun. On the other hand, if we flew to New York, maybe we could locate Quinn's East Coast mistress, the potter Jayda Constable. "What time should I tell Farkas to pick us up?"

"Never mind that. I'll have a limo waiting for us when we arrive. Just get his address and tell him we should be at his house between eleven and noon. We'll even treat him to lunch."

I reeled with surprise in the face of Giselle's efficiency and command. She actually sounded like a CEO. Had I been misjudging her? I called Captain Farkas back and told him our plans.

"Private jet, eh? So, the granddaughter managed

to hang on to Eagan Oil . . ." It was more a statement than a question. "I'm surprised."

You're not the only one.

The following morning I packed a small bag with a change of outfits, a linen dress, pajamas, and extra underwear. My orange cat tried several times to climb inside and curl up on top of my clothes. Ever since Crusher moved in, Bumper had become extra needy and clingy.

"I might not be back tonight." I gently pushed the cat away for the fourth time. "Do I look okay?" I brushed some errant cat hair off the sleeve of my white linen jacket.

Crusher handed me a new toothbrush still in the package and a travel-sized toothpaste and grinned. "You look way too sexy to be on your own. You sure you two don't want a bodyguard? My duffel is always packed and ready."

I tossed the last-minute items in the bag, zipped it up, set it on its rollers, and popped out the telescoping handle. "As appealing as that sounds, I think we'll be okay. It's not like we're flying to Afghanistan."

"No, but you may be going to New York. Same thing."

At eight forty-five, Giselle knocked on my door. She wore a mint green casual trouser suit with wide legs and a flowing jacket over a tank top. Gold hoops flashed in her ears and hammered gold bangles circled her wrist. "I'm a little early. I forgot traffic is much lighter on a Sunday morning. Are you ready?"

Crusher grabbed the handle of my bag and lifted it into the back of Giselle's car. He turned and kissed me gently. "Be careful, babe. Don't take any chances."

Then he looked at Giselle. "Try not to piss anyone off."

At first she frowned and plopped her fists on her hips. Then she threw back her head and laughed. "Why should I quit now?"

We took the 405 north to Sherman Way and headed west to the Van Nuys Airport. The morning sky was still overcast with the marine layer that sometimes cooled the summer mornings. Giselle parked the red Escalade next to the hangar and left her keys in the car. A pilot in a crisp blue uniform carried our bags to a small white aircraft with the words EAGAN OIL painted in blue letters on the side. The backward-slanting wings looked as if they would slice through the air like a pair of fast-moving sickles. "We're cleared for takeoff in a half hour, Mrs. Cole."

"Great. Thanks, Sam." She smiled at me and gestured with her head toward the jet's stairway. "Let's get on board."

We climbed the short distance to the door and stepped inside to a world of beige leather and thick, tan carpeting. A dozen generously upholstered easy chairs faced each other in small groupings around inlaid wooden tables. Individual television screens and USB ports dotted the interior. Giselle commandeered one of the chairs and gestured for me to sit across from her.

A slightly plump, uniformed hostess emerged from a small room toward the front end of the plane, carrying a silver tray with a silver coffeepot and two china cups. "Good morning, Mrs. Cole." She set the coffee service and plates with fresh almond croissants on the table between us and handed us each a white linen napkin with *Eagan Oil* embroidered in blue on the corner. "Would you like me to prepare breakfast?"

While the hostess poured fresh coffee, Giselle turned to me. "What about it, Martha. Are you hungry? Earline fixes a wonderful mushroom omelet."

My watch read nine-fifteen. I hadn't eaten breakfast, and it might be hours before we'd have a chance to eat lunch. "Sure."

"Make that two, Earline. And hold the bacon. My sister's Jewish."

I caught a flicker of surprise before Earline averted her eyes and replied, "Yes, ma'am. It'll be ready before we're airborne."

We were already halfway through our omelet by the time the jet taxied down the runway. It gathered speed and lifted effortlessly into the air, without disturbing the coffee in the cups.

I said, "I could get used to this kind of luxury, G.

I've never flown first class, let alone in a private jet with such personal service."

"It's ironic, isn't it? I mean, you Jews have always been the rich ones. Yet here we are, fortunes reversed."

I glared at her. "You're such a piece of work! Do you even realize how offensive you are?"

She looked puzzled. "Really?"

I crossed my arms tightly. "The image of rich, greedy Jews has been the battle cry of anti-Semites throughout the centuries and it's simply not true! There have always been rich and poor among Jews, the same way there are rich and poor among Gentiles. No religion has a corner on wealth or poverty. As for the notion of Jews being greedy, that's another ugly slander. Generosity and charity are requirements in the practice of Judaism."

"Well, what about that guy David Shapira? He got rich off of a Ponzi scheme."

"And who do you suppose invented that scheme? Charles Ponzi. Not Jewish!"

Giselle raised her hands in surrender. "Sorry! I only said what I've heard all my life. How was I supposed to know you'd take it personally?"

I shook my head. "Well, now you do. I don't ever want to hear that crap come out of your mouth again."

I looked up just then to see Earline's eyes bug out and jaw drop. Apparently, she wasn't used to hearing anyone speak to Giselle in that way. I picked up a *People* magazine, buried my anger in an article about Kim Kardashian's ass, and spent the rest of the trip in silence.

We reached Tucson before eleven-thirty. As soon as we stepped off the plane, a blanket of heat slapped us in the face. We hurried toward the air-conditioned limo and headed toward Green Valley, within ten minutes of landing. Giselle pulled a chilled bottle of Perrier out of a small refrigerator. She poured two glasses with slices of fresh lemon and spoke in a little voice. "Are you still mad, Sissy?"

I sighed. "You managed to push one of my hot buttons, G, but I'm over it."

"Thank God!" She reached over and crushed me in a hug, causing me to spill some of my Perrier on the gray carpet. "We're almost there. What kind of name is Farkas, anyway?"

"Hungarian. So do me a favor and don't make any snide comments about Budapest!"

CHAPTER 10

I gazed at the parched landscape of Southern Arizona as it slipped past the window of our limo. Gradually the cactus and paloverde gave way to green leafy trees—acacia, mountain laurel, and Texas umbrella. Mexican bird-of-paradise bushes with bright orange flowers, salvia with deep purple flowers, and lush Florida bluebells grew alongside barrel cactus and ancient saguaros.

"This is so different from what I expected," Giselle said. "Now I know why they call this place *Green* Valley."

We drew up in front of a small adobe-style house with a red-tiled roof. The front yard was carefully landscaped with gravel, a meandering path of river rock, and two lacy pepper trees. Succulents in bizarre shapes were artfully interspersed between yellow lantana and white rock roses. Obviously, Captain Farkas liked to tend his garden.

Our driver opened the door and helped us out

of the backseat. Another blast of scorching air hit our faces.

I whispered to Giselle, "Is he going to have to sit in a hot car while he waits for us?"

"He's got plenty of AC. Besides, we probably won't be that long."

As we walked toward the front porch, I patted her arm. "Remember, G. Try to be tactful. He wouldn't have asked us to come all this way if he didn't have some sensitive information."

Bela Farkas answered the door in a pair of khaki Bermuda shorts, a white golf shirt, and brown leather sandals. Unlike his overweight son, Gabe, the wrinkled and snowy-haired captain was slender and fit. He greeted us with a nod. "Come in," he rasped in that same gravelly voice I heard over the phone.

The floors were tiled with red adobe pavers and the inside was surprisingly cool. He led us to a living room full of woven rattan furniture cushioned in a print of red hibiscus and green leaves and motioned for the two of us to sit on the sofa. He studied Giselle's face, and a small grin lifted the corners of his mouth. "I met you when you were just a little thing."

"I remember you, too. You gave me a Snickers bar."

He grunted an acknowledgment and sat in a brown leather recliner and nodded toward a frosty pitcher of lemonade and three glasses on a glass coffee table. "Help yourselves. I made it myself this morning. Meyer lemons from my own tree."

I cringed at the next words exploding out of Giselle's mouth.

"You really bungled Daddy's investigation! We've seen the file. He was obviously having affairs, yet you didn't think that was important enough to follow up? I mean, did you ever think he could've been killed by a jealous lover or her husband? And what about the money he was supposedly carrying with him? Those are two motives for foul play right there!" The more she spoke, the deeper Farkas frowned. "Daddy was famous. Another possibility is that someone could've kidnapped him for ransom. Yet there was nothing showing you even considered any of those things." She crossed her arms over her chest and sat back, glaring at him. "I'm surprised you were smart enough to make captain."

I gave Giselle a sharp nudge with my elbow and quickly said, "Please forgive the emotional outburst. It's just that she was very close to our father. To be honest, we've been puzzled and frustrated by the lack of information in his missing-persons file. On the surface, it seems the Beverly Hills police didn't take his disappearance seriously. But I suspect there's more to it. Otherwise, why would you ask us to come all this way? Am I right?"

He nodded.

I poured two glasses of lemonade and shoved one into Giselle's hand. "Drink this and let's have the courtesy to hear what *Captain* Farkas has to say."

I thought I saw a flicker of amusement pass over his face.

He cleared his throat. "When Jacob Quinn Maguire first disappeared, we thought he was just another celebrity jackass messing up. We figured he'd surface in Fiji with some little hottie. But when the LAPD found his car abandoned at the airport, the investigation turned serious. What little evidence we had pointed to foul play. But without a ransom note, a body, or a suspect, any of that was going to be difficult to prove."

Giselle gasped. "You believe Daddy was murdered?"

"Absolutely."

"Yet you did nothing?"

"On the contrary. As soon as I said as much, Chief of Police Rex Nelson ordered me to stop the investigation."

My stomach tightened. "Is that what you couldn't tell me over the phone? What exactly did he say?"

"Nelson said we didn't have the luxury of spending a lot of time on a dry investigation, no matter how famous the guy was. He said we should—and I quote—'deploy our resources for more pressing cases.'"

"What could be more pressing than a murder?" I took a big gulp of the tangy lemonade.

He looked at Giselle. "His friendship with your grandfather Jerome Eagan."

Oh my God. Is he suggesting a deliberate cover-up?

Giselle briefly closed her eyes. "I think I remember someone named Mr. Nelson coming to parties at my grandparents' house. Was he really tall with blond hair and a mustache? Loud voice?"

"That's him. I believe Chief Nelson conspired with Eagan to obstruct the investigation."

Bingo! Corruption at the very top.

Giselle frowned. "Why would he do that? Grand-dad loved Daddy like his own son."

"You were only twelve. Grown-ups don't always let little kids know what's really going on. The fact is, your grandparents were uncooperative and"—his voice softened—"your mother changed her story and lied to us. In my experience, you don't do that unless you have something to hide."

"You may be right." Giselle slumped back against the cushion. "I think they tried to hide what a rat Daddy turned out to be. To avoid public humilia-tion. Appearances meant everything to my grand-father. He ruled our family. He would never have tolerated a scandal. That's probably why Mother lied in her last interview. He must've made her change her story to protect the family honor."

"That's one theory," he said.

Or maybe someone in Giselle's family was more deeply involved than they wanted to admit.

"There's something else important that's not in your file." I told Captain Farkas about the ongoing affair Quinn had with my mother. "Their affair, the testimony of his East Coast lover Jayda Constable, and the forensic evidence from the backseat of his car all prove he was a womanizer. Do you think that led to his death?"

Farkas raised his eyebrows and nodded. "I wish we'd known about your mother at the time. Maybe she could've given us something important. But it wouldn't have mattered. Nelson stopped us from tracking down any of your father's lovers outside that artist woman in New York. And she had an alibi."

Giselle spoke in a little voice. "Do you think my mother knew the extent of Daddy's fooling around?"

"If she hadn't suspected before he disappeared, she certainly knew by the time we were through."

"Why do you think she lied and said she was the one having sex in the back of the car with Daddy?"

He shrugged. "You said it yourself. Probably to avoid scandal. There's one more thing you should know. One of the detectives heard rumors that your father had gambling problems, and maybe that's why he disappeared."

I remembered reading about that in one of the tabloid articles. "Are you saying he was killed because he couldn't pay his debts?"

"That's not the way it works. You can't collect money from a dead man. Your father was worth more alive because he made a lot of money off his paintings. And if the witness Jayda Constable was telling the truth, he was bringing a lot of cash to New York. That doesn't sound like a man with money problems."

"Captain Farkas," I said, "I'd like to talk to the detectives who worked the case. Do you know where we can find them?"

"Last I heard, Meredith Gomez had to go into one of those whatchamacallits—memory care—in the San Fernando Valley. I can give you the info, but I doubt you'll get much from her. Eric Rohrbacher divorced his third wife five years ago and moved to Vegas. I can look up their contact information. Just give me a minute."

He left the room briefly and returned with the numbers written on a yellow sticky note and pasted to the front of a manila envelope. "Inside you'll find copies of all my personal notes on your father's case." He handed me the envelope. "I kept them as a kind of insurance. In case my guys' handling of the investigation was ever questioned. Aside from documenting the interference from the chief of police, it's mostly my personal thoughts and observations of the family." He grinned at Giselle. "I think I called you a precocious little redhead who'd be a knockout one day."

Giselle smiled back. "I'm sorry for earlier. How about letting us make it up to you and take you to lunch?"

"Rain check. I have a class to teach in about forty-five minutes. Criminology at Pima Community College."

I stood and offered Captain Farkas my hand. "Thank you so much for your time and for these notes. Could you please do me one more favor? We want to interview Detective Rohrbacher as soon as possible. Would you phone him right now to smooth our way?"

"Done. So tell me again how you know my son Gabe."

I briefly explained that we worked together on the investigation into the murder of my friend Harriet Gordon Oliver. "I think your son is not only a brilliant detective, he's a very nice person. Now I see where he gets that from."

Captain Farkas puffed out his chest and laughed. "He said some of the same things about you." He leaned toward me. "Are you single?"

I smiled and held up my left hand with my engagement ring. "Spoken for."

"He's a lucky guy. If things ever change, you know where to find me."

As we climbed into the limo, Giselle said, "Does that kind of thing happen to you often?"

"What?"

"The flirting, silly."

"Often enough."

"I would never have guessed." After a moment, she shrugged and said, "I guess I shouldn't worry so much about maintaining a perfect figure. You seem to do all right."

I wondered how she'd managed to live this long.

On the way back to Tucson, I read the information on the sticky note. Detective Meredith Gomez lived in Thanks for the Memories Assisted Living facility on Bob Hope Drive in Burbank. Captain Farkas was right. Interviewing her would probably prove to be fruitless. Nevertheless, I'd visit her when we got back to LA.

Detective Eric Rohrbacher, on the other hand, lived in Las Vegas. I showed the note to Giselle. "We should visit this guy next."

"Let's call him right now," she said. "I'll tell Sam to file a flight plan for Vegas."

God must've been smiling on us, because Rohrbacher agreed to see us that afternoon. Before we left Tucson, we stopped at La Migra Grill for a lunch of authentic Mexican carne asada tacos, guacamole, and a chilled rice and fruit drink called Adios Arpaio. An hour and a half later we were airborne, heading for Nevada.

Air traffic on a Sunday afternoon in Las Vegas was super busy with weekend vacationers flying back home. We circled for ten minutes over a brown landscape with garish hotels punching the skyline. Another white limo waited for us as we taxied to the hangar. I'd hoped to escape the oppressive Arizona heat, but Las Vegas was just as miserable as Tucson.

This time Giselle ordered our bags to be transferred to the car. "By the time we're finished with the detective, it'll be way too late to fly to New York. Let's stay and have a little fun tonight. What do you say, Sissy?" An expectant smile sparkled on her face as we settled in the backseat.

"I'm not keen on staying here, G. I don't gamble, and I don't really drink."

"We don't have to go to the casinos. We could take in a show or sit in bed and watch movies with a huge bowl of popcorn and a box of Milk Duds.

Come on, Martha. It'll be a chance to bond." Her face suddenly turned serious. "Aside from my son, Nicholas, you're the only family I have."

For the first time, I realized Giselle might be lonely. Her tactless behavior probably didn't win her many real friends. In addition, her husband was dead and her only child lived three thousand miles away. I knew how that felt. Besides, I couldn't resist the eager, puppy-dog look in her eyes. "Yeah, okay."

She reached over and hugged me—yet again. "I'm so happy. We really are becoming best friends."

Oy vey. What next?

CHAPTER 11

At four that afternoon, our limo pulled up in front of a rambling, ranch-style home in an upscale neighborhood. I unbuckled my seat belt. "How does a retired detective afford a house like this?"

"Captain Farkas said Rohrbacher moved here five years ago." Giselle counted backward on her fingers. "That was at the height of the great recession when property values were in the toilet. He probably paid way under market for this place. Even now you can get a good deal on Vegas properties."

"Maybe. But it's still Las Vegas, and it's still in the middle of the desert."

As we approached the front door I said, "I'm begging you, G, to keep your mouth shut. You only manage to piss people off and make things harder."

Eric Rohrbacher was pushing sixty. He had a two-day growth of beard and a sparse, gray ponytail. "Welcome to Vegas," he said as we stepped inside a living room full of black leather, chrome, and a shaggy white area rug. A deer's head with dusty antlers and sad, black marble eyes hung on the wall over a glass-enclosed fireplace.

He grinned at Giselle. "I didn't think I'd ever see you again. Yet, here you are, all grown up. Can I get you girls something to drink? Beer? Soda? Martini?"

"No thanks. We're good." Giselle shrugged off her jacket.

"Actually, I'd love some water." I was annoyed she had tried to speak for me again.

When he left the room, I made a zipping motion across my lips and steered her toward the sofa. "Remember, be nice."

Rohrbacher returned with tall glasses of ice water, relaxed in his chair, and placed one ankle across his knee. "When the captain phoned and asked me to see you, he told me what you were up to. I don't know what more I can add."

"Maybe you could begin by telling us what you think happened to our father." I took a sip of the icy water.

Giselle sat on the edge of the sofa.

"There were rumors he had a gambling problem and owed a lot of money to the wrong people. My sources also said Jerome Eagan had to bail out his son-in-law several times. Maybe Eagan got tired and refused to pay off the debt. The theory was your father was desperate and scared and disappeared to save his own skin."

"That's a lie! Daddy would never leave me like that."

I closed my eyes. So much for keeping quiet. I put

a restraining hand on Giselle's arm. "Why wasn't any of this noted in the missing-persons file?"

Rohrbacher frowned. "I'm sure I wrote it in one of my notes. I remember rejecting the gambling debt theory because it didn't make sense. Especially in the face of testimony that he carried a lot of cash on the day he disappeared. If my notes are missing, someone removed them."

Oh my God. How far has the cover-up extended?

I told him about Quinn's affair with my mother. "We know our father was a philanderer. Captain Farkas believes he could've been killed by a jealous lover or husband. What do you say?"

"I say anything's possible. And we would've followed up on that angle, too. But since you've spoken to the captain, you know we were ordered to drop the investigation." He directed his next remarks to Giselle. "Powerful people live in Beverly Hills, and your grandfather was one of them. The powerful get to live by different rules than the rest of us."

"What about your partner, Meredith Gomez?" I asked. "What did she think?"

"Merry? She always said your father was still alive. She believed he'd skipped town with a bankroll big enough to start over somewhere far away from his troubles in LA."

"After time passed without any trace of him, did she ever change her mind?"

He looked apologetically at Giselle. "She said if he was dead, someone in the family must've killed him." Giselle opened her mouth to object, but I squeezed her arm.

"Did she point to anyone in particular?" I asked.

Rohrbacher shrugged. "Not seriously. Merry joked that the killer always turned out to be the spouse."

Giselle crossed her arms. "I refuse to believe anyone in my family could've killed Daddy! Especially my mother. She loved him too much."

"Then why did your grandfather stop the investigation?" Rohrbacher asked.

Giselle repeated the explanation she'd given Captain Farkas. Her grandfather wanted to protect the family from scandal.

The detective shrugged skeptically. "Maybe."

Didn't Captain Farkas react the same way?

"What else could it be?" she demanded.

"Like my partner said, maybe he absconded to another country with enough cash to start a new life. Or someone who knew about the cash robbed and killed him before he could leave town. Or . . . I hate to repeat myself . . . but someone close to him killed him in a moment of rage. It happens."

Back in the limo, Giselle said, "Can you believe that guy? What a nerve to accuse my family like that!"

"I'm proud of you, G. You showed remarkable restraint."

All the traveling and running around had made every muscle in my body tense and the nerves in my right hip felt like fire. I helped myself to some bottled water from the tiny refrigerator built into the side of the limo, swallowed my pain meds, and rubbed my hip. "I hope we're headed for our rooms now. I could do with a nice, hot bath. Which hotel are we staying at?"

"Hotel? Those sleazy germ factories? Oh no. No way. We're going to my house."

My jaw dropped. "You have a place here?"

"On the links at Anthem. It's a private club. There's a wonderful restaurant where we can either go to eat or order in."

"You also live off the links at the Riviera Country Club in LA. You must be an avid golfer."

She waved her hand. "No way. But my husband, Ryan, was. And he taught our son, Nicholas. That's why I hang on to all of our places. For Nicky's sake."

"*All*? How many houses do you own, anyway?"

"My main house is the one you visited in the Palisades. It's where I feel most comfortable. Then there's Granddad's estate in Beverly Hills, where I sometimes entertain clients, this one in Vegas, an apartment in Manhattan, and a house in Hilton Head. Oh, and I bought a loft for Nicholas near Harvard."

"Who looks after all these places when you're not there?"

"If I'm going to be away from LA for longer than a couple of days, I take Isabella along with me. She's the woman you met in the Palisades. Otherwise, I employ one full-time caretaker for each residence and hire extra staff if I'm having guests."

Must be nice.

I noticed the houses we passed kept getting larger and larger, with lush, green lawns spreading over acres. Where did all the water come from to sustain this thirsty landscaping in the middle of the desert? At last we pulled into the driveway of a stone-clad three-story mansion with a fountain in the middle of a circular driveway. Giselle smiled. "Home, sweet home. You'll have your pick of eight different bedrooms, not counting Nicky's or mine."

The interior space soared under the tall ceilings. Plush fabrics in neutral grays covered the king-sized overstuffed furniture—in sharp contrast to the riot of color and prints in her French-inspired LA home.

"This was my husband's favorite retreat," she said. "He chose all the furnishings for the downstairs."

"Judging by the size of everything, he must have been a big man."

Her eyes misted over. "Yes. He was six-four. I really miss him."

"What happened?"

"He died four years ago. Heart attack at the seventh hole." Her lips trembled and she blinked back tears. "He was only forty-five."

"I'm really very sorry, G." I put my arm around her and gave a little squeeze.

We took an elevator to the second floor, where

Giselle showed me four bedrooms in addition to her own giant suite of rooms. "There are five more bedrooms upstairs, but I thought it would be more convenient if we camped out on the same floor."

"I'd hardly call it *camping*."

Each room was beautifully appointed with antique furniture and fine linens and had its own luxury bathroom.

"Have you decided which room you like the best?"

"I like the one with the robin's-egg blue walls. There's a big Jacuzzi tub in the bathroom that's calling my name. I also noticed a framed pencil drawing on the wall that looks an awful lot like my mother."

"Hmm." She tilted her head. "I know which one you mean, and I'm pretty sure that drawing was one of Daddy's. You should take it."

A plump woman in her fifties, wearing an apron over a cotton dress, stepped off the elevator with our luggage. "Where shall I put this, Mrs. Cole?" She pointed to my small suitcase with her chin.

"In the blue room, Parker. And please make sure there are fresh hot towels and a fluffy robe for my sister."

The woman looked at me with curious, wide eyes and quickly recovered. "Yes, ma'am."

I spent the next half hour making good use of the bubbling spa in my bathroom. Then I wrapped myself in a plush terry-cloth robe and settled against the crisp white pillows on the queen-sized bed and dialed Quincy's number. "Did you arrive okay?"

"Yes. Noah picked me up at LAX two hours ago. We're at his house in Sherman Oaks now."

I heard a male voice murmuring in the background, and Quincy giggled.

"I've gotta go, Mom. Talk to you later."

I didn't want to think about what they might be doing. To distract myself, I opened the manila envelope and pored over Captain Farkas's notes.

At six-thirty I changed into a gray linen dress and my grandmother's pearls. Giselle said I could have the pencil drawing of my mother. I lifted it off the wall and turned it over. The back had been left open in order to expose a message written by the artist on the reverse side of the drawing: *For the love of my life. Your Quinn.* Really? He declared my mother was the love of his life? So, what was Giselle doing with her picture?

At seven that evening we sat at a table in La Grenouille with a pink linen cloth and lots of crystal glasses. Dark wood paneling covered the walls and a dozen waiters scurried around like black beetles wearing white gloves. Thanks to the hot soaking and the meds, the pain in my hip had subsided.

Giselle picked up the menu. "This restaurant is famous for their frogs' legs. They're my favorite. You should try them, Sissy."

Was I ready to give her a long explanation about why frogs weren't kosher? "No thanks, G. Frogs are on the list of forbidden foods for Jews. I'll have the poached sea bass instead."

"What list is that?"

I decided not to give her the talk about why certain animals were "unclean," because I didn't want to spoil her enjoyment of the meal. "It's in the Bible, actually. I'll show you one day if you're interested."

The waiter took our order and left as silently as he'd appeared.

Giselle buttered a hot roll. "I told you before, I'm very interested in everything you do. You're like some exotic bird who flew into my garden. But it seems like being Jewish is awfully complicated. So many rules."

"You're right. There can be a lot of rules. Especially if you're Orthodox. But there's also great comfort to be found in ritual and clear boundaries. Especially in today's world, where social media has blurred the lines of privacy."

Ten minutes later the waiter placed our hot plates on the table. Giselle cut into a crispy piece of breaded meat that looked like fried chicken. "Where do we go from here? We're pretty sure there are two reasons why Daddy could've been murdered. Womanizing or gambling."

"It could be either, or both. Don't forget, we also have one detective who imagined our father could still be alive somewhere far away."

"Do you believe Captain Farkas? That it was Granddad who stopped the investigation?"

"I read the captain's notes this afternoon. You're not going to like this, G, but he said after Chief Nelson ordered the investigation to stop, Quinn's missing-persons file was sanitized. Someone in the department removed a statement from a witness close to the family, along with Detective Rohrbacher's notes on the possible connection to gambling or robbery."

"Oh my God," she gasped. "Did he say who the witness was?"

"Your housekeeper, Anna Figueroa. Do you know where she is after all these years?"

"Figgy? Yes! I kept her on as the caretaker for the estate in Beverly Hills. It's an easy job for an older woman, especially since I'm rarely there."

"We should talk to her as soon as we get back to LA. Find out what she told the police that was so bad it had to be scrubbed from the file."

"Okay, but first thing in the morning we're flying to New York. While you were resting this afternoon, I found Jayda Constable."

CHAPTER 12

We left Las Vegas at eight Monday morning, right after an early breakfast. Giselle wore a blue pantsuit, but I dressed comfortably in my jeans for the five-hour flight to New York.

I felt a stab of pride as I watched Giselle on her laptop efficiently conducting company business. She spoke to someone on her computer screen.

"I'm sorry, Harold, but you'll have to find another way to handle our Arab friends. You need to grow a pair. Tell them they can lower their price to zero dollars per barrel, but we won't give in. We'll simply stockpile current production until they begin to choke. I refuse to blink first."

She ended the call and closed her laptop. "My grandfather almost ran this company into the ground by surrounding himself with his old cronies. Once I took over, I got rid of all the deadweight and replaced them with really smart people. Harold was my study partner at Wharton, back in the day.

Together we've managed to pull the company from the brink and make it profitable again."

"You studied at Wharton? I'm impressed."

"Yeah? Well, Jews aren't the only ones who can be shrewd in business." She stopped when she saw the expression on my face. "What now?"

I decided her insensitive remarks were made out of ignorance, not malice. "I'm amazed at some of the things that come out of your mouth, G. Not all Jews are in business. We're involved in every aspect of life. You name it, there's a Jewish person who does it. The only generalization you can make about us as a group is that we place a high value on education. That's why we're called the People of the Book."

"I've never heard that expression."

"Why am I not surprised?"

Three hours in, the hostess, Earline, served a lunch of chicken Caesar salad along with fresh, hot rolls she'd baked in the galley. Airplane food never tasted this good. Another great thing about traveling in a private jet was that there were no lines to wait in. We landed in Teterboro, New Jersey, at four, Eastern time and went straight from the plane to the backseat of a town car waiting for us on the tarmac. Giselle gave our driver the address and we headed for Jayda Constable's apartment in Brooklyn Heights, fifty minutes away.

"What did she say when you called her yesterday?"

I asked as we traveled toward the New Jersey Turnpike.

Giselle rolled on a fresh coat of lip gloss and rubbed her lips together. "She said, and I quote, 'It's about damn time. I've been waiting years to tell someone all the crap I know.'"

"Good. It sounds like she's more than ready to talk."

The artist's apartment was a third-floor walk-up in a building next to a small produce market. The large windows were thrown wide open to let in the sultry summer air. I could see why Jayda chose the apartment; it was full of light and over-looked a small garden slowly going to weeds in the back of the building.

A plush, purple velvet sofa shared the small living room with an old-fashioned phonograph and tall bookshelves overflowing with everything from paperbacks to oversized art books. An unfinished canvas stood on an easel near the windows, featuring an elephant painted with primary colors in a primitive, folk-art style.

Jayda Constable wore a T-shirt under white painter's overalls stained with droplets and smears of every pigment in the rainbow. Her waist-long gray hair hung unrestrained around her face and down her back. High cheekbones and wide, dark eyes hinted at the beauty of her younger self. I understood why Quinn had been attracted to her.

She studied us for a moment, searching our faces.

"You both have his eyes. And you"—she pointed to Giselle—"have the same red hair." She walked across the room to a small efficiency kitchen and came back with a bottle of merlot. She handed us each a generous serving of the ruby red wine in ceramic mugs with an iridescent glaze. "I don't like glasses with stems. They tip over too easily."

I knew what she meant. I preferred to drink my wine from a Moroccan tea glass. "These mugs are beautiful. Did you make them yourself?"

She nodded and glanced at her hands, knobby and distorted from arthritis. "They're some of the last things I did before my hands got too weak to work with clay."

"So you switched to painting?" asked Giselle.

Jayda's mouth moved into a smirk. "What was your first clue?"

Giselle laughed and took a sip of wine then explained to Jayda why we'd come to see her. While she spoke, I took mental notes of the details in the room. Threadbare red Persian carpet on scuffed hardwood floors and various glazed ceramics sitting on every flat surface. A substantial round oak table stood near the kitchen with a vase of yellow freesias and a bronze sculpture of a vagina.

I switched my attention to the art hanging on the walls and stopped at a framed pencil drawing of a young woman. "You have a lot of nice art." I set my mug on the wooden chest that doubled as a coffee table and moved toward the drawing. A signature in the corner read *J. Q. Maguire.* "Is this a picture of you?"

Jayda smiled. "Yes. Quinn drew that for me one

year. There's a message on the back. Go ahead and look."

I removed the small drawing from the wall and turned it over. *For the love of my life. Your Quinn.* It was identical to the message he wrote on the back of my mother's pencil portrait. *What a jerk!*

I hung Jayda's picture back on the wall and sat down. "What did you do when he failed to show up for the gallery opening?"

"I freaked out, that's what. Especially since he said he was bringing a lot of cash."

"Do you know what the money was for?"

Jayda blinked and took a slow breath. "The whole gallery opening thing was just an excuse to come to New York. We were really going to Atlantic City. He liked playing at the new Resorts Casino Hotel but couldn't let his family know. He'd lost a lot of money in Las Vegas once and had to ask his father-in-law to bail him out."

"Where did the cash come from?"

She shrugged. "I think he'd just sold a painting. He had an exclusive contract with the Shiffer Gallery in Beverly Hills. We didn't always discuss those details, and I never asked. Anyway, two LA detectives actually flew to New York to question our circle of friends. I told them about the money and swore something terrible must've happened, but they blew me off."

"Didn't anyone ever contact you after that first interview?"

Jayda shook her head rapidly. "I tried to keep in touch with that woman detective, what was her name? Marilyn? Meredith? But every time I called her, the answer was the same. 'No new developments.' She eventually stopped taking my calls. In the end, I gave up trying to make anyone listen to me and just got on with my life."

"What do you think happened to Daddy?" Giselle spoke for the first time, gripping the mug tightly.

"Isn't it obvious? He wouldn't just stop painting and disappear. Art was his whole life. Someone robbed and killed him and got away with it."

"Did Daddy ever talk about his wife and family? Did he ever talk about me?" Giselle asked in a tiny voice.

Jayda paused for a few seconds, as if deciding what to say. "Quinn was a passionate guy. He lived in the moment. When he was in New York, he belonged to the art scene here. His West Coast life didn't exist for him. He liked to keep the two things separate."

"If you were the love of his life," I said, "how did you feel about his being married and living on the West Coast?"

"Our relationship was open." She wagged her finger. "If you're thinking I was jealous enough to kill him, you're way off base. We both had other lovers. We were exclusive only when he was in town. The jealous one was his wife, Louise."

Giselle's eyes narrowed. "Are you saying my mother knew about Daddy's affairs?"

Jayda shrugged. "Of course. That's one of the

few things Quinn did talk about. He said she would fly into a rage whenever he came to New York."

Poor Giselle. This wasn't looking good for her mother. Louise not only lied to the police about having sex with her husband in the car, she lied about ever knowing he was unfaithful. I wondered if she also knew about the gambling. "Jayda, you said there were other lovers. Do you know who? Did he ever mention my mother, Shirley?"

"Like I said, he had a big ego and an appetite to go with it. He had more than one woman in LA. I don't know any of their names. He did mention a daughter he never met. I guess he meant you?"

I just had to ask. "Did he ever say anything more about me or my mother?"

Jayda tipped the mug and took a long drink of wine. "I know what you two are really asking. You want to know if your father loved you. All I can say is, it's hard for a man like him to see beyond his own needs. But to the extent he could feel affection, I'm sure he felt something toward the two of you. If you were beautiful, he was beautiful. If you were talented and successful, he was talented and successful."

"What you're describing is a total *narcissist*!" Giselle spat out the word in disgust. "That's not at all how I remember Daddy."

Jayda sat back and smiled sadly. "Quinn was the most charming man I ever knew. He had great charisma. I'm glad you have some good memories

of him. Even though he fought with his wife, I'm
sure he enjoyed being around his kids."

*Not! He never even bothered to meet me, let alone spend
time with me.*

I swirled the wine in my cup. "Is there anything
else you can think of that might help the two of us
find out what happened to him?"

"Are any other family members involved in your
search?" Something about her expression set off my
internal alarm.

"No, both our mothers are dead. Why do you ask?"

She cleared her throat. "No other siblings are
involved?"

Giselle and I looked at each other, and I could
tell she was thinking the same thing I was. I grabbed
her hand and squeezed.

Jayda took a deep breath. "You also have a brother.
You didn't know?"

"No," I said, "but I'm not surprised. Until two
weeks ago, I didn't know about Giselle, either. And
now you're telling me we have a brother? God knows
how many more of us may be out there."

Giselle reached for the bottle of merlot. "For God's
sake, Jayda. You don't strike me as the motherly
type."

The older woman shook her mane of gray hair.
"Not me. Someone in LA. Quinn loved the idea of
having a son. He talked all the time about the boy."

"What is his name?" I asked.

"She wanted to give the baby his name. But Quinn
didn't want to take the chance that his in-laws would

find out. So, she named him after her own father, including the last name. Quinn only ever referred to him as Junior."

"How old is he?"

"The boy was born in LA in 1971. Quinn was in New York at the time. I remember, because that's the first night we slept together."

I did the math. "That would put Junior in his early forties, only a couple of years younger than you, G."

Giselle took a long gulp of wine. "Can you believe him? A young wife waiting for him at home with a toddler, your mother waiting at home hoping for him to call, and a third woman in the hospital having his baby. And all the while, he's here in New York screwing Jayda."

"What else can you expect?" Jayda asked. "Men like Quinn demand to be adored."

"Clearly," I said, "there was one person who didn't adore him."

We took our leave of the artist and headed down three flights of stairs.

"Crap!" Giselle's voice echoed in the stairwell. "The more I find out about Daddy, the angrier I get."

I clung to the handrail and looked down, concentrating on not tumbling down the steps. "Men cheat. That's been my experience, anyway." *Well, maybe not all men. I didn't believe Crusher would ever cheat on me.* "What really grabs me the wrong way is what Jayda said about Quinn liking the idea of having a son. I mean, what are we? Chopped liver?"

"Exactly! We need to find this Quinn Junior."

"It won't be easy, G. We don't even know his name."

"Is there a way to find out?"

"Maybe." I twisted my engagement ring. "I know just the person who can help."

CHAPTER 13

The town car waited for us at the curb, with the motor running, and the driver opened the rear doors. "Where to, Mrs. Cole?"

"Manhattan." She turned to me. "We'll spend the night at my apartment."

"Wait! I need to get back to LA. Tomorrow is Quilty Tuesday, and people are scheduled to show up at my house at ten a.m. Remember? You were going to bring your grandmother's quilt to the group."

"I've given the crew the night off, so you'll just have to reschedule. Besides, I've planned a girls' night out. We're going to have fun, Sissy. We have tickets to see one of the hottest shows on Broadway, *The Best Man*. You don't want to miss a chance to see Eric McCormack and James Earl Jones, do you? Afterward, we're dining at Un Deux Trois, a great little French place."

"I haven't missed a Tuesday in seventeen years.

Besides, I didn't bring the right clothes for a fancy night in New York City."

She waved her hand. "Not to worry. What size do you wear?"

"Sixteen petite. Why?"

"What about shoes?"

"Seven and a half. Wide."

She punched a couple of buttons on her cell phone. "Hello, Simone? This is Giselle Cole. I'm staying in Manhattan tonight and I'd like a huge favor."

Giselle's west-facing apartment overlooked Central Park and received the afternoon sun. A smiling woman with latte skin greeted us with a Jamaican accent. "Welcome home, Mrs. Cole." She took our luggage from the driver, who had followed us upstairs, and disappeared toward a hallway.

Giselle led me to the living room, painted in soft lavender with a plush gray velvet sofa and peach silk chairs. A purple and pink area rug with a Chinese cherry blossom design covered the hardwood floors in the center of the room. Crystal chandeliers and a couple of antique French regency pieces completed the elegant space.

I walked over to a generous bank of windows and gazed at the green canopy in the park across the street. "This is breathtaking, G."

Just then the doorbell chimed and the maid

hurried to the foyer. I glanced at my watch. It read twenty after six.

A cheery voice with a French accent called, "Giselle? I came as soon as I could, *chérie.*"

A petite older woman in a black dress and severe bun breezed into the apartment, followed by a younger man pushing a clothing rack and rolling a suitcase. Giselle introduced the woman as Simone, her personal stylist.

Simone took one look at my stretch denim jeans, T-shirt, and Crocs and screwed up her face. "Yes, I see what you mean. But I think I can fix this." She removed the tarp from the clothing rack and uncovered several fancy dresses. She waved her hand back and forth in my direction. "Take off your clothes, *chérie.* We have to hurry if you're going to make the theater."

"Don't I have anything to say about this? I can't afford designer clothes."

Giselle crossed her arms. "This is my treat, Sissy. Just strip down and stop complaining."

Simone removed a floor-length beaded red sheath with spaghetti straps and a slit up the side, several sizes too small for me. "This just came in. I thought you'd look fabulous in it."

To my relief, she handed the gown to Giselle, who immediately removed her blue linen pantsuit and slipped the gown on. The skinny dress clung to her slender, athletic figure. Her bare shoulders and arms were tight and well defined, without any hint of flab. Every time she took a step, her slender thigh peeked out from the slit in the skirt.

"You look stunning, G."

"I love it. I'll wear it tonight."

Simone smiled with satisfaction and handed her a pair of scarlet-colored four-inch heels. Then she returned to the rack and handed me the same dress in a much larger size. "I also brought one for you." She handed me the replica. It definitely wasn't designed for a short, overweight fifty-something with huge thighs, flabby arms, and an ample bosom."

I stared at the both of them. "You're joking, right? No way! Uh-uh. I'd look like a gilded tomato in that thing."

"But Martha!" Giselle pleaded. "Wouldn't it be fun for us to dress alike? Absolutely no one else does it."

"Not only no, but *heck*, no." I turned to Simone. "I hope you brought something more appropriate for my size."

For the next half hour, I tried on beautiful floor-length designer dresses. In the end, I rejected the sleeveless ones and the chiffon tent printed in white and brown like a reticulated giraffe. I settled on a long-sleeved, low-cut black crepe number that accentuated the girls but covered the rest of me down to my ankles. Simone finished off my outfit with some strappy black heels, a beaded clutch, and dangling crystal earrings. "There you go, *chèrie*, almost perfect. You need to wear Spanx, though.

I brought some in your size." She handed me a pair of XXL panty hose.

I could be so insulted, except they *were* my size.

Finally, she studied my face for a moment and then handed me some jeweled combs. "Use these."

When Simone left, Giselle looked at her watch. "It's nearly seven. We have ten minutes to get ready if we hope to make an eight o'clock curtain."

I hurried to the bedroom with my new outfit and struggled into the mercilessly tight panty hose. I turned slowly in front of the mirror. Simone was right. My silhouette under the dress was a lot smoother with the Spanx. I slipped into the high heels and pinned my long curls on top of my head with the sparkling combs. The only other jewelry was my engagement ring and glittering earrings that dangled provocatively against my bare neck. I dashed on some pink lipstick and met Giselle in the living room at ten after seven. She waited for me, armed with a bottle of perfume.

"Wow!" Her eyes widened when she saw me. "You look much better when you want to. If you lost some weight and worked out a little, you'd be really fabulous for someone your age."

I did an internal eye roll and closed my eyes while she spritzed expensive fragrance all over me.

On the way to the theater, I called Lucy on my cell phone. "I'm in New York and won't be home until tomorrow. I'm afraid I'll have to miss quilting. Can you call Jazz? Did you get the results of Ray's biopsy yet?"

Lucy's voice tightened. "I'll call Jazz. I was going to cancel, anyway. The doctor wants to see us in his office tomorrow. They don't do that unless there's bad news. I'm so afraid, Martha. I don't know what I'll do if anything happens to Ray."

"Maybe it's something minor, Lucy. Try not to panic. I'll call you as soon as we get back."

Next I called Crusher.

"Babe." He sounded relieved. "I was wondering when I'd hear from you. I miss you. When will you be home?"

"We're in New York right now but we're coming back tomorrow. I have a lot to tell you. Meanwhile, can you do a search of birth records for me?" I told him about my half brother.

"A brother, huh? Your old man was one randy dude."

"That may be what got him killed."

"Do you have any info I can go on?"

"He was born in 1971 in LA. Name unknown. But I'm thinking maybe Quinn is listed on the birth certificate as the father."

"I'll get on it tomorrow."

My daughter, Quincy, was my last call.

"I can't wait for you to come back, Mom. Noah and I have a big announcement to make."

My stomach sank. "Does this mean things are serious between the two of you?" *Please God, make it not true.* "Why can't you tell me now?"

Her laughter tinkled over the phone. "You'll find out when everyone else does. Hurry back."

As soon as the curtain went up, my stomach rumbled loud enough for the woman sitting in front of me to turn around and stare. At first Giselle poked me with her elbow. Then she reached in her purse and shoved a protein bar in my hand. The crinkle of the paper unwrapping echoed throughout the orchestra seats.

All during the play I kept trying to think of ways to derail my daughter's romance with Noah Kaplan. I even briefly considered not going back to LA in order to forestall their big announcement. I also worried about Lucy's husband, Ray. Over the years, he'd been like my protective big brother. What if something was seriously wrong with him? I decided that no matter what the crisis, I would put my own life on hold to help my closest friends. *Please, God, make him okay.*

Later that evening, we sat at a linen-covered table in a charming French restaurant near the theater.

"I'm starved, G. I'm not used to eating this late."

"The trick is to remember to eat a snack beforehand."

As we sat waiting for our first course, a bottle of Cristal champagne chilling in a bucket of ice arrived at our table. Giselle looked questioningly at the sommelier.

He pointed to a table across the room. "Compliments of the gentleman."

The man looked at our table and raised his glass and smiled. He appeared to be in his early sixties, handsome, silver-haired, and impeccably dressed in a black tuxedo. Giselle smiled at him and primped her hair.

The wine steward cleared his throat and flashed a business card in his white-gloved hand. "The gentleman asked me to give this to you, madam." Giselle reached for the card, but the steward handed it to me.

A note was scribbled on the back. *Please, may I introduce myself?* The card belonged to Andrew Goldman, Esq., of Goldman, Perren and Sage. I showed it to Giselle.

"Good Lord. Goldman Perren is one of the biggest law firms in the city. What could Andrew Goldman possibly want with *you?*"

I glared at Giselle and snatched the card back. "Why don't we just find out?" I smiled at Goldman and nodded once.

He immediately crossed the room and stood by my chair while I introduced myself and offered my hand.

"I'm Martha Rose, and this is my sister, Giselle Cole."

He bent over to kiss my hand, and I caught him sneaking a closer look at my cleavage.

"Forgive me for being blunt, but at my age I don't believe in wasting time. You are a beautiful woman, an enchanting creature. And I'd like to know you better."

"Thank you for the champagne, Mr. Goldman. I'm terribly flattered, but I'm already spoken for." I raised my left hand to show him my engagement ring, glad for once that Crusher had given me an impressive three-carat stone.

"I'd like a chance to change that. May I take you to dinner sometime? We could fly to Paris in my private jet tomorrow."

"Again, I'm flattered. But I'm flying back home to LA in *my* private jet first thing tomorrow."

Giselle kicked me under the table.

"What a shame. Still"—he pointed to the card in my hand—"you have my phone number. Call me if you change your mind, Martha Rose. I'm your devoted admirer." He made a courtly bow and walked back to his table.

Giselle sat with her mouth open during the whole exchange. When Goldman returned to his table, she said, "Do you realize that was the first time you ever called me your sister?"

She was right. Without realizing it, I had slowly come to accept her as family. At first the thought of having a half sister, who had lived with the father I never knew, stirred painful feelings of jealousy and abandonment. But the more I got to know her, the more I realized we shared a common loss. Jacob Quinn Maguire had disappeared from both our lives. I smiled at those hazel-green eyes that looked just like mine. "You're beginning to grow on me, G."

Giselle sighed. "And this is the second time in two days I've seen guys flirting with you. First Captain Farkas, now Andrew Goldman. Did you see the way he checked out your ta-tas?"

"It happens more than you think," I chuckled. "Men can't help it. Their reptilian brain draws them straight to the comfort of the mother's breast."

"That does it!" she said. "I'm getting a boob job as soon as we get back to LA."

CHAPTER 14

Tuesday morning, we landed at the Van Nuys airport at ten, Pacific time. Sam, the pilot, removed our luggage and garment bags with our brand-new dresses and carried them from the aircraft to Giselle's red Escalade.

"Thank you, Sam." She passed him what looked like a few Benjamins. I'd seen her do the same thing with the hostess, Earline, a few moments earlier. Giselle may be bossy and tactless, but she is also generous.

"Pleasure as always, Mrs. Cole."

"Come on, Sissy," Giselle said. "Let's get you back home." As we drove toward Encino, she asked, "Do you think your Yossi's had a chance to search for Quinn Junior's birth records yet?"

"He said he'd get on it this morning. But I've learned you can't expect instant gratification with these things, G. Sometimes it takes a while. You have to learn to be patient."

"I don't see why. Aren't all those records in some sort of database? Seems to me, all you need to do is plug in the search parameters and voilà! There's your info."

"Unfortunately, the government doesn't run as efficiently as private business. Who knows if those old records are even digitized?"

When we pulled into my driveway, Crusher's Harley was already gone. Giselle helped me carry my garment bag and suitcase inside the empty house. My orange cat, Bumper, greeted us with a loud meow and rubbed his cheek hard against my ankle. I used to think it was a sign of affection until I learned he was merely marking his territory with the scent glands on his jaw. I picked him up anyway and scratched him behind his ears. He purred like the motor on a sewing machine.

Giselle looked around the space slowly, as if seeing it for the first time. "It looks so much different in the daytime. I love how the light filters through those cheap white curtains on your front windows. It makes the inside feel peaceful and beachy."

"Was that supposed to be a compliment?"

"Oh, look!" She pointed to a crystal vase of pink roses on the glass coffee table. She picked up the envelope propped against the clear container and handed it to me. "Yossi is such a romantic."

I had a sinking feeling the roses might not be about romance at all. I slid my finger under the flap and opened the envelope. The short note read: *Sorry, babe. On assignment. Love you.*

I blew out a puff of air and handed her the note. "Remember what I said about the process occasionally being slow? Well, this is one of those times. Yossi's job comes first. He won't be available to help us until his assignment is finished."

"When will that be?"

"Days, weeks, months. I never know. We may have to ask someone else to help look for those birth records. Meanwhile, we still have stuff to investigate."

"Like?"

"Like interviewing your old housekeeper, Anna Figueroa, and visiting Detective Meredith Gomez in the memory care facility."

Bumper wiggled out of my arms and jumped to the floor.

"Do you really think we should bother with Meredith Gomez?"

"You never know. Sometimes, people with dementia have brief, lucid episodes. Maybe we'll get lucky and find her during one of those moments."

"Well, then, what are we waiting for? I'll drive. Let's talk to Figgy, then we'll go see the senile woman."

"Slow down. I have to call my friend Lucy first." I worried about their visit to the doctor's office this morning.

"Fine. While you're doing that, I'm going to look at your murder board again." She walked toward my sewing room.

When Lucy didn't answer her phone, I figured they must still be with the doctor. So, I left a message and called Quincy. "Hi, honey. Giselle and I just got back. We're at my house right now. I didn't have a chance to tell you yesterday that I have a half brother somewhere."

"Get out of town!"

I told her what little I knew about him. "He was only nine at the time our father disappeared. It's a long shot, but it's possible he might remember something that could help us."

"Can I do anything?"

Quincy was a journalist, and I knew our search would tweak her nose for news. If she were alone, I'd consider taking her with us. But I couldn't risk the chance she'd bring Kaplan along. All I needed was for that little weasel to lecture me on interfering in police business, even if it was a cold case, and even if it was my own father who had gone missing.

I took a calming breath. "Won't that take time away from Noah? After all, he's cashing in vacation days to be with you. That's not easy to arrange with the LAPD."

"We could both help. He is a detective, after all."

But not a very good one. "I'd hate to interfere with your vacation, honey. I'll let you know if anything comes up. Meanwhile, when am I going to see you?"

"This Friday night at Shabbat. We'll make our big announcement then."

"I can hardly wait." I resisted the urge to grind my teeth.

I found Giselle studying the murder board and

tapping her lips with her fingers. "You know, Sissy, we have a lot more information to add."

"You're right. Let's log all the new stuff we've learned and pin it up." I handed her a handful of blank note cards and a pen. "You write."

We attached several more notes to the white sheet using straight pins with colorful glass heads: information we learned from Captain Farkas, Detective Eric Rohrbacher, and Jayda Constable. Giselle had drawn a huge question mark on one of the cards, with a heading that read *Quinn Junior.*

Our next stop was Beverly Hills. We took Coldwater Canyon from the Valley to Readcrest Drive. The two-story Italian villa built by Giselle's grandfather, Jerome Eagan, stood like an elegant lady in a pink stucco gown. Wide white trim bordered generous groupings of windows. A lacy white pediment crowned a window in a three-story tower standing sentinel over the entrance. An arched colonnade marched across the front of the house all the way to the end, the top of the colonnade forming a balcony that served the second floor.

I did a 360 turn, taking in the beauty of the estate. The vast landscape featured broad green lawns, fruit trees, and formal gardens filled with fountains, roses, and a myriad of colorful blooms. A smaller version of the main house stood next to the villa on the same property.

Giselle seemed amused at my reaction. "This is

where I grew up. The main house belonged to my grandparents. The smaller one is where we lived."

"For once, I'm speechless, G. The Eagan estate is quite grand."

"I know. I hang on to it because I can't bear to think of anyone else living here. Figgy stays in the main house now. Shall we go in?" She didn't wait for an answer but turned abruptly and headed up the broad stone steps to a pair of tall wooden doors carved with an odd combination of gargoyles and cupids.

Just as we reached the entrance, one door swung open and a tiny elderly woman in a blue dress with a white apron stood smiling on the other side. "Welcome home, Mrs. Cole."

That made three different employees who had greeted my sister the same way in as many days. One in Las Vegas, one in Manhattan, and now Beverly Hills.

Giselle bent over and gently hugged the wrinkled Anna Figueroa. "So good to see you, Figgy. This is the sister I told you about. Martha Rose."

Anna Figueroa stretched her mouth into a smile, showing a set of new porcelain teeth, but her eyes broadcast suspicion and disapproval.

"We'll be in the living room. Is the coffee ready?" Giselle asked.

"Yes'm. And those favorite almond croissants of yours. I'll get them now."

"Bring three cups, Figgy. I want you to join us."

The older woman raised her eyebrows in surprise, nodded once, and bounced down a hallway in a pair of blue and silver Nike trainers almost as big as she was. Giselle led me into a living room the size of a hotel lobby, furnished with antique Italian and French pieces. Pink silk damask covered most of the upholstered chairs. I would've declared the space gaudy and pretentious, except it somehow worked perfectly with the architecture.

We settled on the deep cushions of one of the six sofas covered in lavender velvet as Anna Figueroa reappeared, pushing a serving cart with coffee and croissants. Before taking a seat directly across from us, she poured three cups and laid out a plate of pastries on the green marble top of the coffee table.

Her eyes darted back and forth between my sister and me while she waited, curiosity and concern deepening the wrinkles.

As Giselle explained what we had learned over the previous two days, the old woman drew her arms closer to her body, eyelids drooping.

"We discovered your statement to the police went missing from the file. This is very important, Figgy. I want you to try to remember exactly what you told them."

"It was a very long time ago . . ." Figgy wove her fingers together and squeezed, pleading with her eyes for Giselle to stop asking.

"If you're trying to protect me, don't bother.

I'm not a child anymore. I know all about my father's behavior. What I want more than anything is to find out what happened to him, no matter where that leads me."

Figgy took a deep breath. "I told them I kept myself to myself. If your father was having any affairs, I certainly didn't know about it."

Giselle put down her coffee cup. "But you knew more than you told the police?"

She nodded. "I used to hear your parents arguing when you weren't around. He swore he wasn't cheating, but I found perfume on his clothes, lipstick on his shirt, and once, oh Lord, on his underwear. Then, about six months before your father disappeared, your mother started getting phone calls. After those calls, she'd cry for hours. Once I went to another room and picked up the telephone extension and listened in." Color crept up her cheeks. "I'm not proud of it, but I felt so sorry for your poor mother." Figgy seemed reluctant to continue.

"Go on," Giselle urged gently.

"It was a woman. She said she was the mother of Mr. Maguire's son. She told your mother to stop standing in their way, that he didn't love her anymore."

G frowned deeply at the revelation. "And why didn't you tell this to the police?"

"Because I didn't want Mrs. Maguire to find out I'd listened in on her private conversation. She would've fired me for sure, and I couldn't let that happen." She blinked back tears. "You needed me more than ever, *querida*."

Giselle also teared up at the use of the endearment. Clearly, she had a closer bond with the housekeeper than I'd imagined. "You always looked after me, didn't you, Figgy? Did my grandparents know about my father? About his son?"

The old woman nodded slowly. "I think so. Your grandmother caught your mother carrying on something awful after one of those phone calls and spent hours trying to calm her down."

Things were looking grim for Giselle's family. No wonder the grandfather, Jerome Eagan, stopped the investigation and tried to cover up Quinn's infidelity. They all had plenty of motive to kill him. The question was, which one of them might have done it?

"What do you remember about the morning he disappeared?" I asked.

"I went to fetch Mr. Maguire's suitcase to carry it out to the car. Mrs. Maguire was yelling and crying. 'You think I don't know about your whore in New York?' He told her she was imagining things again. 'We'll talk about it when I get back,' he said. Then he kissed her on the forehead like nothing was wrong, got in his car, and drove away. That's the last we ever saw of him."

"Did you know he was carrying a lot of money with him?" I asked.

"No." She licked her lips nervously. "Why would I know something like that?"

Giselle leaned toward the old lady and spoke softly. "Tell me honestly, Figgy. What do you know about his gambling?"

"Not much." She sighed. "He had a problem that your grandfather had to fix a few times. Their arguments were pretty loud. But for several months before he disappeared, things quieted down, and I assumed he'd stopped gambling."

"So, what do you think happened to him?" I asked.

"I'm sure someone killed him. Maybe someone he owed money to. Maybe someone who was jealous. It wasn't Mrs. Maguire, because right after he left, she locked herself in her room and refused to eat for two days. And it wasn't Mrs. Eagan, because she took care of both Mrs. Maguire and Miss Giselle during that time."

"What about Jerome Eagan?"

Giselle threw me a harsh look but kept her mouth shut.

"Do you think he could've killed his son-in-law or hired someone to do it?"

Figgy looked at Giselle as if to ask for permission to speak.

G gave a slight nod of her head. "It's okay. We just want the truth."

The old woman blinked rapidly and pushed her shoulders back. "I always thought it could've happened that way. Mr. Eagan was a powerful man."

"How do you mean?" I asked. "Physically powerful or politically powerful?"

"Both."

CHAPTER 15

"Will that be all, Mrs. Cole?" The housekeeper reverted to their formal relationship and stood before her employer.

"Thank you for being honest, Figgy. I've always been able to count on you, haven't I?" Giselle's voice caught in her throat. "You were like a mother to me, especially after things got so bad. I'll always love you for that." She sprang up off the sofa, reached the old woman in two steps, and hugged her for several seconds.

Figgy murmured, "I promised when you were a little girl that I would never leave you, *querida*. And I never will."

Giselle pulled away and swiped the corners of her eyes with the back of her hand. "Can you bring me that bag I asked you about, please?"

"I'll get it for you now." She turned on her Nike

trainers and left the room. Moments later I heard the whir of an elevator taking her to an upper floor.

"It seems you and Figgy have a very special relationship," I said. "I can see why you continue to take care of her."

Giselle fetched a tissue from her purse and blew her nose. "After Daddy disappeared, my mother turned into a basket case. She was more than happy to let someone else take care of me."

"I can relate, G. My mother did the same thing. From the moment I was born, she handed me over to Bubbie, my grandmother, and Uncle Isaac."

"My grandmother tried," said Giselle, "but she wasn't very good with the day-to-day details. So Figgy stepped in. She was the one who comforted me when I cried. She was the one I went to when I first got my period. She guided me through those awful teenage years. My grandparents' only ambition was for me to make a good marriage. But Figgy pushed me to go to college. I owe her more than I could ever repay."

A new idea started nibbling at the back of my brain. How far would Anna Figueroa go to protect Giselle and her mother?

The housekeeper returned with something wrapped in a large plastic bag. "I found this in your grandmother's sewing room. I gathered all the pieces I could find."

"Is this the quilt you were telling me about?" I asked.

"Want to see it?" Giselle opened the bag and removed a half-finished quilt top.

I recognized the pattern immediately. "This is a gorgeous example of a Grandmother's Flower Garden, G. It's one of the most labor-intensive quilts to sew."

I explained that the Grandmother's Flower Garden is made entirely of small hexagons measuring one or two inches in size and hand sewn together on the edges to form an overall mosaic design. In the classic configuration, a single hex forms the center of a "flower." It's typically yellow, like the center of a daisy. Next, hexagons in colorful prints are fitted together in a circular shape around the center, usually two rows deep. The colorful rosettes are then separated from each other by plain hexagons, before being joined together. The overall effect, when completed, looks like a field of blooms scattered on a solid background.

Giselle unfolded the top and it crackled. "Are all quilts made with paper?"

"No," I said. "But this design calls for a method called English paper piecing. Each fabric hexagon is wrapped around a slightly smaller paper of the same shape and basted into place. That stabilizes the edges and makes them easier to sew together. Here, let me show you." I flipped the top over to the back side to reveal the thin paper templates underneath. "After the whole top is assembled, the paper templates are removed from the back side, leaving a nice, soft quilt top."

"You mean you have to cut each of those shapes by hand?"

"Not necessarily. Your grandmother, like women

before her, may have cut everything by hand, but nowadays you can purchase precut paper templates by the hundreds. Traditionally, our foremothers cut individual hexagons out of old newspapers, magazines, and any other bit of paper they could get their hands on. Making quilts used to be all about using up scraps—fabric leftovers and, with English paper piecing, whatever paper was at hand."

I refolded the top and placed it in the sack. "Bring this to our next quilting group. We'll figure out how much more we need to add to the top. Then we'll piece it, quilt it, and you'll have a beautiful remembrance of your grandmother."

"But I don't know how to sew."

"You will by the time I'm done with you."

We left Readcrest Drive and drove to Spago in Beverly Hills for a quick lunch of artichoke pizza and mixed green salad. Then we headed over Coldwater Canyon to the Valley and our interview with former BHPD Detective Meredith Gomez.

Our destination turned out to be a one-story beige stucco building in a largely residential area on Bob Hope Drive in Burbank. The facility sat on two lots behind a neat lawn bordered with clumps of purple campanula. THANKS FOR THE MEMORIES ASSISTED LIVING was written in discreet gold letters on the glass of the locked front door.

We pressed a buzzer and almost immediately heard the release of the electronic lock. A blowsy blonde sat behind a counter to our right in the small reception area. She wore green scrubs with the word *Smile* embroidered in white on the left side of her chest. Directly in front of us was another locked door.

Just as I was about to speak, I heard the loud warbling of a songbird. When she saw the look on my face, she jerked her thumb over her shoulder. "It's the clock." The numbers on the wall clock behind her were missing, and in their place were pictures of twelve different species of birds. "Every hour we get to hear a different birdcall. It gives the patients something to look forward to. Can I help you?"

"Yes. We're here to see Meredith Gomez."

She typed something on a computer keyboard and frowned at us. "Are you relatives? It says here all her visitors have to be on the guest list approved by her next of kin."

Giselle began to say "Nnnn" when I pinched her arm. She stopped and waited for me to speak.

"Yes. We've traveled a long way to see her."

The receptionist scrolled down the screen. "Hmm. I have only one name on the list. Are you Fabiola Lamonica?"

I nodded vigorously. "That's right. We came all the way from Italy."

"Well, I can only let you in, Miss Lamonica. Your friend will have to get approval from the family."

"Oh no, you don't understand." I pointed to Giselle. "*She's* Fabiola. I'm Martha, her translator. Fabiola's deaf, poor thing, therefore, I help her communicate with the outside world. Wherever she goes, I have to accompany her."

I had to hand it to Giselle. She didn't miss a beat. She turned to me, screwed up her face, and threw out her arms in a gesture of confusion as if to say *What's going on?* I began waving my hands in the air and elongating each vowel. "This niiice lady says we can go insiiide and see your aunt Mer-e-dith."

Giselle nodded an *Aha*, and smiled at the receptionist, touching her forehead with her thumb. God knows what that really meant in sign language.

"Fabiola says 'thank you.'"

The receptionist smiled and in a loud voice said, "You-Are-Welcome."

"Uh, one more thing. Fabiola hasn't seen her aunt since she was a little girl. She's not sure she'd recognize her. Can you tell us where to find her?"

"Our patients tend to wander off. For their own safety, we have them wear ankle monitors. Let me see where she is right now." The blonde turned to the computer once more. "She's in the TV room. She likes the afternoon soaps."

"Thank you," I said.

Giselle put thumb to forehead again, and the receptionist touched hers in return. I sent a profound mental apology to all the hearing-impaired people in the world.

The inner door buzzed open and we stepped into a large lounging area with sofas and chairs upholstered in blue faux leather. Speckled vinyl tiles covered the floors. A strong pine scent permeated the air, and I guessed every surface had been chosen to be easily cleaned. Signs high up on the walls pointed to the TV room, the dining room, and the private rooms of the residents.

Giselle whispered under her breath, "How awful to end up in a place like this!"

I noticed a woman in green scrubs with a mop and bucket over to the side watching us. "Hands," I hissed out of the corner of my mouth as I wiggled my fingers in the air.

We found Meredith Gomez sitting in a recliner alone in front of the television. Her head slumped forward on her chest and soft whistles came out of her nose as she slept. Her long black hair was streaked with gray and fastened at the nape of her neck. Her peaceful face hinted at her former beauty. I guessed she was barely into her sixties, tragically young to be suffering from dementia, and not that many years older than me. I breathed a silent thanks to God that I still had all my marbles.

I gently shook her shoulder. "Detective Gomez?"

She stirred and opened her eyes, looking at us with a blank expression.

"You don't know us," I continued. "I'm Martha and this is my sister, Giselle. Our father went missing thirty-two years ago, and you worked on his case. His name was Jacob Quinn Maguire, but everyone called him Quinn. Do you remember?"

The detective stared at us, appearing not to comprehend a word I'd said.

Giselle leaned in closer so Gomez could clearly

see her face. "I was a little girl at the time Daddy went missing. Don't you recognize me?"

Meredith smiled, but her eyes remained vacant. "Did you bring my chocolate pudding?"

"Please try to remember," I urged.

A severe woman in a navy blue business suit and militant posture approached us from the lounge area. "Right after lunch in the afternoon is probably the worst time for a visit. Our patients tend to get drowsy and foggy by then. The best time to visit is in the morning when they're fresh." She gave a quick shake of her straight, blond bob. "I'm Miss Leathy, the administrator. And you are?"

I turned to Giselle and began gesturing rapidly.

"What are you doing?" demanded the woman.

"I'm translating. My name is Martha and this is Fabiola Lamonica, Mrs. Gomez's niece. She's come all the way from Italy to see her aunt. Since Miss Lamonica is deaf, she relies on me to help her communicate with the hearing world."

The woman frowned at us. "It's called interpreting, not translating." Then she began signing in the smooth, elegant gestures of real American Sign Language. She didn't speak but watched us carefully.

We were so screwed.

When neither of us responded, she frowned and slapped the side of her right hand into the palm of her left. "Just as I suspected! You don't know how to sign and you're not deaf. Just who are you and why are you here?"

I began gesticulating again and turned toward my sister, enunciating. "She thinks we are lyyying. She doesn't know we're using *Itaaalian* sign language."

Giselle responded with a brief ripple of her fingers, until Miss. Leathy shouted, "Stop pretending! Answer me right now, or I'm calling the police."

"Fine!" My sister drew up to her full height and stared into the administrator's eyes. "I actually know Meredith Gomez. She was one of the detectives investigating my father's disappearance thirty-two years ago. The case was never solved, but my sister, Martha, and I have uncovered new information. We're here to ask Detective Gomez some questions."

"Do you know where you are?" Miss Leathy gestured toward the room. "This is a memory care facility, and Mrs. Gomez is an inpatient. Even if you did have permission from the family to talk to her, it would be futile. Her disease is too advanced."

"Still," I said, "we'd like to come back in the morning and try. How can we contact the family for permission?"

The frowning administrator crossed her arms. "You can't. That information is confidential."

"But you can contact them, right?" Giselle reached into her purse and handed the woman a business card. "Tell them why we'd like to speak to her and get back to me."

Miss Leathy reluctantly took the card and read it.

She looked at Giselle and narrowed her eyes. "Right. Like I'd believe you were the CEO of an oil company. Anybody can have business cards printed. You're nothing but a con artist."

"You're partly correct. I'm not just the CEO, I'm the *owner*. And here's a sign you will understand."

My half sister, the oil tycoon, raised an elegant fist and extended her middle finger.

CHAPTER 16

Giselle drove me back to Encino and promised to call the minute she heard back from the administrator at Thanks for the Memories Assisted Living. I went straight to the murder board in my sewing room and reviewed our notes.

Bela Farkas—captain BHPD 1980, now retired
Ordered by Chief Nelson to stop investigation
Quinn's missing-persons file sanitized

Eric Rohrbacher—detective BHPD 1980, now retired
Notes on Quinn's gambling missing from file

Jayda Constable—Quinn's NY lover
Quinn traveled to NY to gamble in Atlantic City
Quinn carried a lot of cash when he vanished

I still had nothing to write on Detective Meredith Gomez's card. We had to get permission from the family to interview her in the morning hours on the off chance she might be more lucid. It was a long shot that probably wouldn't pay off. Still, we had to try.

The conversation with Anna Figueroa had been much more helpful. She'd not only overheard arguments between Jerome Eagan and his son-in-law over gambling debts, she'd witnessed Louise and Quinn arguing over his infidelities. She also confirmed that Louise knew about her husband's illegitimate son. Once again, I wondered: Just how far would Figgy go to protect Giselle and her mother?

Next, I erased the question mark my sister had drawn on the card for our half brother and wrote:

"Quinn Junior" (real name unknown)—
Quinn's secret illegitimate son
Born in LA 1971
His mother (name unknown) harassed Quinn's wife, Louise Maguire

Then I added the new information to the rest of the cards, hoping to see a pattern emerge.

Louise Maguire—Giselle's mother, Quinn's wife
Jealous and angry about husband's affairs and Quinn Junior
Lied to police

Jerome Eagan—Quinn's father-in-law
Influenced chief of police to stop investigation.
Argued with Quinn over gambling debts. Bailed him out.

We knew very little about Quinn's mother-in-law, Edith Eagan, except that, like her daughter, Louise, she relinquished the day-to-day care of Giselle to the housekeeper, Anna Figueroa. I'd be surprised if she didn't know everything about Quinn's transgressions.

We now had enough new information to seriously suggest homicide. Suddenly I remembered Lucy never called me back. I called her for the second time that day but got only voice mail. It wasn't like Lucy to avoid my calls. The fact that I was leaving another message scared me. What if Ray's biopsy was positive for cancer?

"It's me again, Lucy. What did the doctor say this morning? Please call me."

I phoned Jazz Fletcher next. He answered on the first ring, voice low and flirty. "Hello, tall, dark, and delicious."

"Huh?"

"Oh my God! I thought you were someone else." His voice fluttered.

"Sorry to disappoint. It's only short, delicious me. Have you heard from Lucy lately? She hasn't returned my calls."

"No. Should we be worried?"

"Ray's going through a health crisis, and they were supposed to talk to the doctor today."

"Shall we go to her house? I can be there in forty-five minutes."

I understood Jazz's impulse to rush to Lucy's aid. When you loved a friend, that was what you did.

But I also knew Lucy must have her reasons for not responding right away to my phone calls. "Not yet. If the doctor gave them bad news, we should respect their privacy until they're ready to talk about it."

Jazz sighed. "Now you've made me so nervous, I'm going to have to take a Xanax—even though it makes me drool. By the way, how was your trip with your sister? Lucy said you flew all over the country in a private jet."

He listened quietly while I brought him up to date.

"Our biggest challenge right now is to find our half brother."

"A brother? My, my, your father certainly kept himself busy. I'm afraid to ask, but what did you wear on this trip?" Jazz the clothing designer was constantly trying to rehabilitate my wardrobe.

"You'll be thrilled to know that while we were in Manhattan, Giselle bought me a designer dress, and we went to the theater and dinner afterward."

"No! You really bought a *designer* dress? Which house?"

"The dress is a Rachel Zoe, and I actually looked pretty good. In fact, during dinner some big-shot New York lawyer hit on me."

"Wait. What about shoes?" he teased. "Please tell me you didn't wear your Crocs."

I laughed. "I bought a very expensive pair of black stilettos that only pinch a little."

"There *is* hope for you! Zsa Zsa and I are coming over tomorrow morning to see this famous dress.

And if we haven't heard from Lucy yet, we should pay her a visit."

After I spoke to Jazz, a tsunami of fatigue washed over me. I was too exhausted to cook dinner. Instead, I nuked two Trader Joe's frozen chicken tamales in the microwave. Five minutes later I removed the steaming corn husks and tucked into the taste of masa, cumin, and chicken.

Tamales were an especially important tradition in the Latino culture. Families cooked for days, preparing dozens of handmade tamales for their Christmas feast. Masa, a paste made from cornmeal and lard, was spread on the inside of corn husks. Then a filling made with chilies, cheese, cooked chicken, or beef was spooned onto the masa. The whole thing was rolled up, sealed inside the husks, and steamed in a huge pot until cooked through. Fortunately for me, the Trader Joe's tamales weren't made with lard, so they became my go-to food when I needed a meal in a hurry.

I finished eating at six-thirty and headed for a hot shower and a clean pair of pajamas. Then I settled on the sofa, wrapped my blue and white quilt around my legs, and turned on *Jeopardy!* I barely heard the answers as I went over the events of the last few days one more time. It was clear Quinn's disappearance wasn't just a missing-persons case anymore. Jacob Quinn Maguire had been murdered. Worse, his killing had been covered up at the highest levels of the Beverly Hills Police Department and the file had been sanitized. I'd have to convince my outspoken sister to be careful. Poking into that kind of corruption and wrongdoing might prove dangerous.

Wednesday morning at ten, Jazz showed up wearing a butter yellow linen suit and a white shirt with a mandarin collar opened at the neck. He kissed both my cheeks, sat on the sofa, and opened a yellow tote bag. Inside, his little Maltese, Zsa Zsa, wore a pastel pink and yellow floral pinafore, with a pink butterfly barrette in her topknot.

The six-foot-tall man bent over and cooed, "Who's Daddy's little girl?"

The dog licked his face, jumped out of the bag, and headed straight toward my cat, Bumper, who was stretched out like a fluffy orange pillow in a patch of sunshine on the floor. Bumper raised his head briefly to touch noses with his tiny doggy friend then closed his eyes again and resumed his nap.

Jazz gave me the once-over, silently disapproving of my jeans and T-shirt. "Okay, Martha. Show me the dress!"

I retrieved the garment bag from the closet, unzipped it, and removed the long-sleeved black gown.

My designer friend gasped approval. "It's gorgeous. The draping is masterful. And the décolleté— it shows off your best feature. No wonder the guy hit on you."

While he examined the dress more closely, I

poured two cups of fresh Italian roast. My phone rang and I recognized the caller ID.

"Good morning," Giselle said. "I just heard from Miss Leathy at Thanks for the Memories."

"That was fast."

My half sister giggled. "She said she Googled me and found out I was telling the truth about who I was. I knew she'd cave when she saw the dollar signs. They always do."

"And here I thought she was mesmerized by your charm. You know, when you flipped her the bird?"

"She gave my phone number to Meredith Gomez's son, Carlos, and he's going to call me this afternoon at two."

"I'll come to your place."

After another unsuccessful attempt to reach Lucy, Jazz left. I spent the rest of the morning doing laundry from my trip and giving the house a general cleaning. At twelve-thirty, I changed my clothes, jumped in the car, and headed south on the 405 toward the Palisades. As I neared the Sunset Boulevard off-ramp, a new idea hatched in my head. I could barely wait to run it by Giselle.

When I arrived, the housekeeper showed me to the living room, where my sister sat gazing through the mullioned windows to the golfing greens beyond her large yard. She cradled a cell phone in both hands and turned to greet me with a serious look on her face. "I hope we can talk the son into letting us interview Detective Gomez."

I plopped down next to her on the sofa. "You

know, G, it just occurred to me on the drive over. Quinn had an exclusive contract with that gallery in Beverly Hills. Yet the file never mentions an interview with the owner, Eliza Shiffer. Don't you find that suspicious?"

She nodded rapidly. "You're right, Sissy. You know, the Shiffer still exists. It's been taken over by Eliza Shiffer's son. He contacts me every once in a while to ask if I'm ready to sell Daddy's paintings. He claims to know serious collectors who'd pay a fortune for any one of them. Apparently, they're worth a lot more because of Daddy's mysterious disappearance."

"Is Eliza Shiffer still alive?"

"I don't know. But we should definitely find out."

At precisely two, Giselle's cell phone rang. She took a deep breath and answered, "Giselle Cole." She listened for a moment and then said, "Thank you for calling, Mr. Gomez. My sister is with me, so I'm putting you on speaker." She pressed a button and held the phone between us.

I leaned toward the phone. "Hello. My name is Martha Rose, and we appreciate your taking the time to call."

"Actually, I only have a few minutes before I have to leave for the studio. What is it that you want, Mrs. Cole?"

Studio? His voice sounded familiar. Where had I heard it before?

Giselle explained who we were and why we wanted to interview his mother. "Miss Leathy says that sometimes memory care patients are clearer in the mornings."

"I'm afraid I can't allow you to question my mother. She won't remember a thing. She doesn't even recognize me anymore. I'm sorry, but I won't risk your upsetting her."

Suddenly I realized why his voice was familiar. "Are you *the* Carlos Gomez? The weatherman on ABC Eyewitness News?" I pictured the handsome Latino, with dark hair, standing in front of a weather map, always dressed in dark suits and brightly colored neckties—blue for stormy weather, green for mild weather, and yellow to red for the hotter days.

He answered with a terse "Yes."

I tried to think of a way to establish some rapport in the hopes he might relent. "Well, I just love your reports. I listen to you every night. I live in Encino and appreciate that you always feature our local weather. You know," I chuckled, "maybe you should hire me. I have fibromyalgia, which is more accurate than your Mega Doppler thingy. I can always tell days in advance when it's going to rain."

When he didn't respond, I tried a more direct approach. "Look, I understand your wanting to protect your mother. I'd feel the same way. But what if you were present when we talked to her? You could stop the interview if you felt she was becoming upset."

"The answer is no. You'll have to get your information elsewhere. Now, if you'll excuse me, I have to get to work." The phone went silent.

Giselle said, "Now what?"

"You know, G, I promised to update my friend Gabe Farkas on our investigation. I think it's time to make that phone call. Gabe can help us search for Quinn Junior's birth records, since Yossi isn't available. Plus, as a police detective, he might be able to interview Meredith Gomez."

"Well, what are we waiting for?"

I retrieved my cell phone from my purse and dialed Farkas's number. "Hi, Gabe. Remember when you said to call if my father's disappearance turned into a homicide investigation?"

CHAPTER 17

An hour later, Giselle and I sat across the desk from Detective Gabriel Farkas. "You have an actual office now? With doors?" I asked.

The forty-year-old shifted his considerable bulk in the chair. "Just happened. You're looking at the youngest guy to make chief of detectives in West LA. History."

"Congratulations!" I smiled at the portly man. "Your dad must be proud. He's a nice person, by the way, and extremely helpful."

Farkas looked at my sister. "He remembered you from when you were a child, Mrs. Cole." Then he turned to me. "And he was very taken with you. Am I in danger of one day having to call you Mom?"

I threw back my head and laughed. "You're safe for now."

"So, tell me what you got." He leaned back and clasped his pudgy fingers behind his neck.

I took a deep breath and related everything we'd found out. "The Beverly Hills chief of police,

Rex Nelson, stopped the investigation the minute your father reported Quinn was likely dead. Your dad also told us Quinn's missing-persons file had been sanitized, and we found plenty of evidence to support that. This screams conspiracy, Gabe, and your dad said as much."

"That's why my old man insisted on speaking to you in person. I know him. He didn't want to take the chance that anyone would be listening in on your phone conversations."

Giselle pulled out her cell phone and stared at the blank screen. "Oh my God, are you suggesting our phones have been hacked?"

"It's easier than you think." Farkas frowned. "I admire what the two of you have done up to this point. You've exposed an unsolved murder and possible cover-up. But if the BHPD chief was involved, who knows how much higher this thing went. What you're alleging is very serious."

He paused, tapping his fingers on the desk. "It's unlikely after thirty-two years, but suppose the players in this drama are still alive. If they heard you were poking around, they might feel threatened. And depending on who was involved in the conspiracy, you could be in danger. Now's the time to back off and let the pros take over."

"Will you help us, Gabe?"

"Jeez." He raked his fingers through his hair. "Technically, your father's case is out of our jurisdiction. It belongs to Beverly Hills."

"You can't turn it over to them yet." Giselle

strained forward. "We don't know why they hid Daddy's murder or who was involved. You said it yourself. If the Beverly Hills bad guys are still alive, they'll just squash the investigation again."

"I agree," I said. "We can't hand over the case until we have more information. Listen. Jayda Constable said Quinn was close to his son. Our half brother was nine at the time of Quinn's disappearance. We'd like to find him. My fiancé was going to help me look, but he got called away on assignment, and I don't know when he'll be back."

Farkas took a hit from his inhaler and looked at the ceiling. "Why me, God?" He slid a pen and a yellow tablet across the desk toward me. "Write his name."

I screwed my face into an apology. "I wish I could. The only thing we know about him, is that he was born in LA in 1971."

"Are you kidding me? I'll need more than that. There are one hundred fifty thousand babies born in the county each year."

"Sorry."

"Can you at least narrow it down to the month?"

"Well, the night our brother was being born in LA, Quinn was in New York," I said.

"Screwing Jayda Constable," Giselle added. "She said it was their first time. Maybe she remembers."

"He sounds like father of the year," Farkas scoffed. "Write down this Jayda's phone number."

Giselle scrolled through her cell phone contacts and showed me the number stored there. I copied it on the tablet, double-checking to make sure there were no mistakes. "Our only other possible lead is Detective Meredith Gomez. Can you question her?"

"I can try. But don't get your hopes up."

"Don't forget to ask her about the cover-up by Chief Nelson." Giselle waved an imperious hand.

Farkas ignored the commanding gesture. "I didn't make chief of d's by accusing neighboring city officials of crimes I have no way of proving." He stood with a grunt and ushered us to the door. "For now, let's just concentrate on finding your brother."

"Thanks, Gabe."

He sighed. "I'm going to regret this. I just know it."

Back in the car, my stomach growled.

Giselle said, "You hungry? Really? It's only five."

"I could eat." What I really meant was, *I'm starving, but I don't want you, oh slender one, to judge me.*

We ended up at El Indio on 26th Street and San Vincente in Santa Monica. The bar was crowded with happy hour, but we walked straight past the noise into a half-empty dining room. We slid into the red vinyl seats of a small booth with a wooden table made glossy by a thick layer of hard resin. Corona and Tecate labels peeked up through the transparent coating.

Almost immediately, a blond waitress wearing a yellow halter top and long floral skirt placed a basket of warm corn chips and a bowl of chunky guacamole in the middle of our table.

Giselle said, "This place is so popular, you usually

have to wait for hours to be seated. But since it's only five, way before the time most *normal* people have dinner, I knew we wouldn't have a problem."

I ignored the snarkasm and looked at the menu. "What's good to eat here?"

"Almost everything. Because it's totally vegetarian, you don't have to worry about pork or shellfish or anything made with lard." When she saw my surprise, she snapped a corn chip in half, raked it through the guacamole, and shoved it into her mouth. "Welcome to West LA, Sissy."

During a satisfying meal of bean and cheese burritos, we made plans to visit the Shiffer Gallery the following afternoon. I drove Giselle back to the Palisades, then I made my way back to the 405 Freeway north toward Encino. I took the Balboa Boulevard off-ramp, but instead of turning right to go to my house, I made a left and aimed my car toward Lucy's place. I was no longer willing to let my best friend face her problems alone.

It was seven-thirty by the time I arrived at Lucy's front door. I steeled myself for hearing the worst possible news and pushed the doorbell. Almost a minute later the dead bolt made a metallic click and Lucy opened the door with very wide eyes and a flushed face. She clutched a white terry-cloth bathrobe around her body, one hand at the neck and one at the waist. Her feet were bare.

"I'm sorry, Lucy. Did I get you out of the shower?"

"Not exactly." She sounded slightly guarded.

"I'm sorry for the intrusion, but I couldn't wait

any longer for you to call me back. I decided to drop by on my way home. How's Ray?"

A familiar male voice approached from down the hallway. "Just fine until you showed up." Ray emerged, smoothing his disheveled hair, clad only in a short navy blue bathrobe. He stood next to Lucy, who was two inches taller in her bare feet.

"Oh my God." I stammered, mortified when I realized I had just interrupted an intimate moment. "Sorry. Sorry. I'll come back another time." I turned on my heel to go when Ray's laughter boomed.

"Come on in and have a glass of champagne. Lucy and I can pick up where we left off later."

Lucy wrapped her robe tightly around her waist, tied the belt, and moved aside. I stepped indoors. We headed for the kitchen table as Ray went back to their bedroom.

Lucy said, "We've been celebrating."

"I take it then, the news is good?"

Lucy nodded. "We're in the clear. His polyps were benign, but they're the kind that could turn into cancer if allowed to grow. So, because of his family history, he needs to have a colonoscopy every two years."

Ray returned wearing striped blue pajamas under his robe and holding a bottle in his hand. He grabbed a glass from the cupboard, poured my drink, and raised his glass. "*Cin cin!*"

I took a sip and noticed that a little bit of Giselle had rubbed off on me. The champagne wasn't as perfect as the Cristal Andrew Goldman sent to our table at Un Deux Trois, nor as smooth as the Dom Pérignon my sister preferred. Nevertheless, their celebration bubbles tasted like relief and gratitude mixed with joy.

Sitting next to Lucy, Ray put his arm around her shoulder and pulled her close. She let her body melt into his and turned her head to gaze into his eyes. Together since childhood and now in their late sixties, they smiled that secret smile of soul mates, communicating an encyclopedia of love.

I thanked them for the drink. "I can let myself out."

They barely noticed me leave.

I fell into bed that night missing Crusher and wondering when I'd see him again.

Thursday afternoon I took Coldwater Canyon over the hill. Giselle had warned me to wear something good, so I dressed in my white linen suit. She waited for me in the driveway of her Beverly Hills estate wearing an expensive-looking dark suit, white silk blouse, and lots of diamonds.

I pulled up next to her and rolled down the window. "Hop in, G. I can drive us to the gallery."

"No way. If we want to make an impression, we can't show up in something only the help would drive."

"Could you be more rude?"

"I'm only being honest. We'll take my car." She pointed to a midnight blue Jaguar parked near the six-car garage.

"What's wrong with your Escalade?"

"Too soccer mom. And too red. If you want to command respect, you either have to be chauffeured or drive something dark, sleek, and expensive."

I heaved a sigh and parked next to her car.

As soon as I got out of the Civic, she said, "You're wearing that thing again? We've got to get you some new clothes!"

"I was wrong. You *can* be more rude."

I opened the passenger door of the Jag and buckled myself in. I closed my eyes and took a deep breath. Giselle was right. The interior smelled like new leather, expensive perfume, and power. She turned the key and the engine sounded like my cat Bumper when I scratched him under the chin.

We purred our way down Wilshire Boulevard and passed stores I could never afford to shop in: Barneys, Saks, and Neiman Marcus. I had to admit, riding in style made me feel special, even entitled. These last few days with Giselle had given me a glimpse into her world of luxury and privilege. I could easily imagine how a rich person might want to cover up sordid family secrets in order to preserve their social position.

I Googled the Shiffer Gallery on my smartphone and scrolled through old publicity pictures. "Crap. Did you ever meet Eliza Shiffer?"

"I don't think so. Why?"

"According to this old photo, she was quite glamorous. Knowing Quinn's weakness for beautiful women, I think we'd better prepare ourselves."

"Oh my God. Not another one."

The Gallery occupied a space on the first floor of a four-story glass office building on the corner of Wilshire and Doheny. We found street parking in front and headed toward the door.

"Let's hope Eliza Shiffer will talk, G. She held an exclusive contract to sell Quinn's paintings. Surely she'd be in a position to know about his finances. Depending on how close they really were, maybe she can tell us some of his other secrets."

CHAPTER 18

Abstract paintings dominated the white walls of the Shiffer Gallery. One canvas five feet square featured a textured swirl of bright colors emanating from a dark center. On closer examination, it appeared the paint had been slathered on with a palette knife by an artist high on speed or low on lithium. The title on the label read *Black Hole* and the asking price was $125,000.

"Isn't it marvelous? It's a brand-new Pedro Ayala. We have him under exclusive contract. This won't last long, so if you're interested, you should grab it soon."

We turned to look at the owner of the voice. A man in his early forties stood hands on hips, dark purple hair hanging over one eye in studied nonchalance. He wore a black turtleneck T-shirt with long sleeves and skinny black jeans tucked into soft leather half-boots.

Giselle took one step toward him and offered

her hand. "We're looking for Eliza Shiffer. I'm Giselle Cole and this is my sister, Martha Rose."

The man raised his visible eyebrow and accepted her hand, gushing. "You're Mrs. Cole? Oh my God. At last we finally meet. We've spoken on the phone many times." He nodded once in my direction. "I actually knew your father. I'm Wolf Shiffer, Eliza's son."

Giselle reclaimed her hand. "Is she here?"

"Alas! My mother passed away five years ago and left the gallery to me. You must be here about Quinn's paintings. I'd be honored to handle the sale. I have collectors who would pay top dollar to own one."

Giselle held up her hand and gave a quick shake of her head. "Actually, we're here to gather information about our father's disappearance."

Shiffer tilted his head. "What could I possibly tell you? Mother never talked about him, really. And I was only a kid when he went missing."

The same alarm bell that went off in my head must have also clanged in Giselle's, because we looked at each other at the same time. I knew she was wondering the same thing I was.

I placed my hand gently on Shiffer's arm and spoke in a hushed tone. "I wonder if we might enlist your help, Wolf." I leaned closer and whispered, "We believe Quinn was murdered. You may be able to help us solve the mystery."

He raised his eyebrows and placed his hand on

his chest. "Me? I don't get it. Why don't you go to the police?"

"Because right now, he's just a thirty-two-year-old missing-persons case. But if we can collect enough new evidence, we might be able to compel the authorities to reopen the file. We're not asking you to do anything dangerous. We just want you to check your records."

He took a step backward and frowned. "Why?"

"For one thing, we're trying to get a picture of Quinn's finances," I said. "Do you still have the sales records from when he was under contract?"

Shiffer nodded, disturbing the purple curtain of hair on his face. "Of course. Keeping track of provenance is crucial in our business. We preserve all those accounts. What do you hope to find?"

"On the day he disappeared," I said, "Quinn was headed for Atlantic City and carried a large amount of cash. We need to know where the money came from and who might've known about it. Will you help us?"

"I don't know . . ." He crossed his arms and looked back and forth at our faces.

Giselle made a face. "One of Daddy's early landscapes recently sold at auction for two-point-two million. So, if you want to be the one to collect a commission when I decide to sell Daddy's paintings, you'd better man up, Wolf. Show us the records."

Shiffer turned and headed toward a door in the back of the gallery. "Follow me."

I had to hand it to Giselle. She knew just when to throw her weight around. We passed more frenzied Pedro Ayala paintings, each with a six-digit price tag. Two of the labels had a SOLD sticker. Ayala couldn't have spent more than a day on each of those paintings, a week if I was being generous. Yet, if I were to sell one of my quilts, a work of art that required hundreds of hours to sew by hand, I'd be lucky to get a few hundred dollars—barely enough to cover the cost of materials. I bristled at the thought that women's art, like everything feminine, went undervalued and unappreciated.

Giselle motioned for me to slow down and whispered, "He said he knew Daddy, and he seems to be the right age. Do you think he's . . . ?"

"Maybe. But let's not give too much away right now."

Beyond the door was a huge work area with a full kitchen.

Shiffer said, "You look surprised. Don't be. We have frequent events and a kitchen makes it easier for the caterers." He swept his arm in a circle. "The rest is workspace for framing, storage, and shipping. My office is just over here." He pointed to another door on our right. "My assistant is working on some brochures."

A girl with Malibu highlights in her blond hair also wore black from head to toe. She stared at a computer screen, moving text and graphics with a mouse. "Have a look, Wolfie. What do you think?"

She pushed her chair away from her desk and looked up. "Oh. Sorry. I didn't know we had company."

Shiffer waved her away with a small gesture of his hand. "I'll look later, Phee. Right now I need you to bring us some tea and then cover the front."

Without a word, the young woman popped up and headed for the kitchen.

Shiffer directed us to sit in upholstered wingback chairs arranged around a circular inlaid wooden table, an elegant space to conduct the sale of high-priced art. Some photos and small paintings hung in this private space. A small diorama featuring a tree made out of plastic forks sat in a greasy box from a Happy Meal on a side table. I pointed to a framed head shot of a glamourous blond woman with diamond earrings and scarlet lips. "Is this your mother?"

He smiled sadly. "Yes. She was beautiful, wasn't she?"

"Very."

He sat in a third chair and placed a laptop on the table. "All our records have been digitized."

Giselle nudged me under the table with her foot. I looked to see what she wanted. She jerked her head slightly to the wall behind my chair. I swiveled my head and saw it. A pencil drawing that resembled the woman in the photograph. My pulse quickened.

The assistant carried in a silver tea service with three bone china cups on a chased silver tray. She poured the tea then disappeared into the front of the gallery. Shiffer clacked on the keyboard and didn't notice me get up from the table to examine the drawing on the wall. The signature was unmistakable.

"Wolf, my father drew this. Is it a picture of your mother?"

"Yes, but it's not for sale. She cherished that drawing." He sipped his tea and turned back to the computer. Giselle made a circular signal with her finger.

I nodded, removed the picture from the wall, and turned it over. Written on the back were the now-familiar words, *For the love of my life. Your Quinn.* I rolled my eyes at Giselle, nodded once, and sat back down.

Shiffer swiveled the screen to give us a clear view of an Excel spreadsheet then picked up his teacup again. "Here it is. A record of every J. Q. Maguire painting sold."

The spreadsheet recorded the name of the painting, date sold, price, and buyer's information. We learned that Quinn's paintings fetched as much money thirty years ago as Pedro Ayala's did today.

"How was Quinn paid?" I asked.

Shiffer put down the cup. "Don't let the sales price fool you. He didn't get all of that. A thirty percent commission comes off the top of everything we sell." He pointed to a column on the spreadsheet with coded symbols. "Quinn was paid in two different ways. See the letters *BA*? That's when his cut was deposited directly into a local

Bank of America account. Where you see the dollar sign is when we wrote a check for cash. Where you see both symbols at once is when we split the payment. Part deposit, part cash."

"Are there any entries around May twenty-fifth, 1980? The day he disappeared?"

"Let me see." He scrolled down a list and stopped. "It looks like Mother gave him a check on May twenty-fourth for sixty thousand dollars."

"That's the day before he disappeared!" What if Quinn hadn't been killed? He had a cozy deal with the gallery. What if he arranged to receive cash from the future sale of his paintings in order to finance a new life? "Just out of curiosity, were there any sales after that?"

"No. That was the last one. Wait. There's a note here. It says three remaining paintings were returned to his wife. There were legal problems about who to pay if they were sold. Something about Quinn having to be declared legally dead first."

"Now we know where the cash came from." Giselle squinted at the screen. "Does it say what that last payment was for?"

"It was . . . here it is. An advance for a portrait he was supposed to paint of Mrs. Rex Nelson. Of course, the portrait was never done." He peered at the screen. "It says she was eventually reimbursed. The family had to cover the loss."

"I don't believe it!" Giselle snapped. "The wife of the police chief? Where does a cop get that kind of money?"

"Can you print a copy of this document for us?" I asked.

"Sure. But I just want to say that if Quinn was doing something illegal with his money, it wasn't our fault. It was up to him to pay taxes on the cash we gave him."

"Don't worry. Nobody thinks you did anything wrong. Just one more thing. You said you knew our father." I glanced at Giselle. "What do you remember about him?"

My sister sat at full attention in her chair.

Shiffer closed his eyes and paused for a moment. "Let me see. He had bright red hair. He used to come to our house to see Mother. He gave me money for ice cream and she sent me away with the nanny."

"Were your parents divorced?" Giselle asked.

Shiffer crossed his arms, looking like a spider in his long black sleeves. "I never knew who my father was. Mother always said conventional families were overrated. She was a free spirit who belonged to no man."

I stood and began replacing the tea service on the silver tray.

He saw me fussing. "Please don't bother with that. My assistant will clean up."

I smiled sweetly. "No problem. You've been quite helpful to us. I'm glad to return the favor." I carried the tray to the kitchen on our way out.

Back in the Jaguar, Giselle started the engine and pulled into traffic. "You were right, Sissy. Eliza

Shiffer turned out to be yet another one of Daddy's mistresses."

"Yeah. The pencil drawing on the wall proves as much. And did you notice the color of her lipstick? Red. Just like the cigarettes found in the ashtray of Quinn's car. Too bad she's gone. I'll bet her fingerprints would be a match for one of the sets found in the Cadillac."

"Wolf Shiffer is looking more and more like our half brother."

"You might be right, G. But we need to be sure before saying anything. At least now we have a name to give Chief of Detectives Farkas. Hopefully, he'll be able to locate Wolf's birth certificate. Of course, we could be absolutely certain if we had a sample of his DNA to compare with ours."

"Obviously." Giselle snorted. "We'd just have to figure out a way to persuade him to send a sample to Deep Roots. And, by the way, why on earth did you have to act like the help back there? Nobody ever cleans up after tea. Really, I was quite embarrassed."

"Calm down, your highness. I'm way ahead of you. I figured we might not get Wolf to agree to Deep Roots, so I took a sample of his DNA."

She whipped her head around. "What?"

I reached into my large handbag and pulled out a napkin wrapped around one of the bone china cups.

CHAPTER 19

We made slow progress through the afternoon traffic on Wilshire Boulevard.

While we sat at a red light, I called Detective Farkas and put him on speaker. "Giselle and I have a possible lead on our half brother." I told him about the pencil drawing at the Shiffer Gallery. "His name is Wolf Shiffer."

"Like I said before, your old man sounds like father of the year."

"One more thing, Gabe. Wolf doesn't know it, but I managed to get a sample of his DNA to compare to ours."

"Jeez. Do I want to know how?"

"I sort of 'borrowed' a cup he drank out of. He won't miss it. Can you send it to the lab to be tested?"

"Hell, no. First of all, that cup is stolen property. Second, he's not a suspect in a crime. Third, that DNA would have such low priority, it might be months before we get the results back."

Giselle kept her hands on the wheel but leaned

toward my phone. "We're not giving up, Detective. If you won't help us, I'll take the cup to a private lab myself."

"Don't say any more!" Farkas barked. "I don't want to know. Understand?"

"What about Detective Gomez?" I asked. "Have you talked to her yet?"

"What. You think I have nothing else to do than chase your leads? Gimme a break. It's only been twenty-four hours since you dumped this thing in my lap."

"It's just that the longer we wait, the more brain cells she's losing. I think we should talk to her as soon as possible."

"There's no 'we' in this equation. Stay away from Meredith Gomez. You agreed to back off and let me do the investigating, remember?"

"Fine. But you will tell us what you find out?"

"When I've gathered significant information, yes."

"What does that mean?"

"It means you have to be patient and trust me."

There it was again. Trust. My biggest issue. My experience told me that trusting men could be dangerous; but my instinct told me to give Detective Farkas the benefit of the doubt. Hadn't he always been straight with me? "Okay, Gabe. I'll try."

Instead of heading toward Readcrest Drive, Giselle pulled under the porte cochere in the parking lot of Saks Fifth Avenue.

"What are we doing here?" I hadn't forgotten her previous dig about getting me some new clothes.

She opened the door and tossed the keys to the valet. "Come on. I have to pick up a pair of pants I had altered. It won't take long."

Saks occupied a solid, gray stone building on the corner of Wilshire and Peck. Two neatly trimmed palm trees, iconic symbols of Beverly Hills, grew in front. The inside of the store smelled like perfume and hundred-dollar bills. Light glittered off glass and mirrored surfaces, creating a glamorous palace of luxury and style.

My sister knew her way around Saks like I knew the frozen tamale section of Trader Joe's. She strode straight to the register near the Alexander McQueen display.

"Hello, Mrs. Cole," said a middle-aged saleslady with an eager smile. "I'll just go in back and get your slacks now."

As we waited, Giselle pointed to a bright red jacket on a rack across an aisle. "Look at that! Isn't it pretty?" Without waiting for an answer, she grabbed my arm in a vise grip and pulled me into the plus size section. "This would look great with your coloring. Try it on."

I yanked my arm away and turned over the price tag, which read $900. "I can't afford these clothes."

"Let me treat you, Sissy. Face it. You need a complete makeover, and God knows I can afford it."

First Jazz, now Giselle was determined to take away my comfortable stretch denim jeans and imprison me in clothes that had tight waistbands and needed dry cleaning. "I appreciate the offer, G.

But you already paid for an expensive dress I'll probably never wear again. I'm not interested in being made over. Grab your trousers and let's go." I walked back to the register where the saleslady waited.

Giselle pouted all the way back to her estate on Readcrest Drive. She finally said, "You know, Sissy, if we're going to hang out together, you'll be needing that dress we bought in New York. And more. Appearances are everything in my world."

"So you keep telling me. But what's important in *my* world is comfort. Maybe you should try it sometime."

We got out of the Jag and she walked with me toward my Honda Civic.

She wrapped her arms around me and squeezed. "I love you, Sissy."

Had we come this far in our relationship? To my surprise, tears stung my eyes and I squeezed back. "Come to Shabbat dinner again tomorrow night, G. Six o'clock. You'll get to meet your niece, Quincy." I reached in my purse and handed her the napkin with the bone china cup and Shiffer's DNA. "It shouldn't be that difficult to find a lab."

"I'll do it tomorrow."

I thought about the hug all the way back to Encino. Our worlds couldn't be more different. Yet, underneath all that ostentation, my sister was not only smart but canny. She'd managed to pull Eagan Oil back from the brink of collapse and make it hugely profitable again. Her manner was abrasive and tactless at times, but maybe those were the very qualities that contributed to her success.

Nevertheless, I sensed a deep sadness that I could relate to. She'd grown up with an absent father and dysfunctional mother, just as I had. Unlike me, however, Giselle Cole was alone. Her husband had died young and her son lived on the East Coast. I could tell she was starved for a meaningful connection. Since I was her only other close relative, she seemed determined to become part of my family.

I smiled to myself when I realized she already had. And like a good sister, I would fix her the way she wanted to fix me. Only instead of focusing on an external makeover, I'd help her fill that particular hole in her life. After all, she was only forty-four; time to step out of her expensive widow's weeds.

When I got back to Encino, my heart sped up at the sight of Crusher's Harley. I parked my car next to the bike and hurried to unlock the front door. "Yossi?" I called out as soon as I entered.

Even though it was only five, my fiancé strolled out of the bedroom wearing pajama bottoms. He grinned and lifted me off the ground in a hug, smelling like lemon verbena soap from a recent shower. "Babe. I just got back." He gave me a long, searching kiss that tasted like toothpaste and set me back down on my feet.

"What's that?" I pointed to a huge bruise blossoming on the left side of his bare chest.

"During the takedown, the perp closest to me booked it. I went after him. We exchanged fire."

"Oh my God!"

"He was a lousy shot but got lucky once and caught me in the vest." I silently thanked God for inventing bulletproof vests. "Unlucky for him I was a better shot."

"Are you sure you're okay? I hate that you have such a dangerous job."

He took my hand. "I've missed you, *neshama*."

My heart melted when he used the Hebrew expression meaning "soul."

He led me down the hall to our bedroom. "Let me show you how okay I am."

Two hours later we sat in the kitchen eating tuna on rye and potato salad. The hungry giant downed his sandwich in six bites and reached for a second one. "Tell me what you've been up to."

I reviewed all the facts we gathered from Anna Figueroa and Wolf Shiffer. He laughed at the account of our attempt to interview Detective Gomez.

"We gave all this information to Gabe Farkas, who agreed to unofficially take over the investigation."

Crusher helped himself to more potato salad. "I know you, babe. Are you really satisfied to sit back and wait for Farkas?"

I shrugged. "We're not exactly sitting back." I told him about stealing a DNA sample from Shiffer. "It's possible we could know before Gabe does whether Wolf is our brother."

Suddenly I remembered something I'd brought back from Las Vegas. "Wait right here." I hurried to my sewing room to fetch the pencil drawing of my mother. "I found this hanging in the bedroom of Giselle's Las Vegas house. She told me to keep it."

"Who is it?"

"My mother. Read the back."

He reached for the small drawing and turned it over. "Your father wrote this?"

I nodded. "It seems Quinn liked to leave an artistic calling card for each of his women with the same message on the back. *For the love of my life. Your Quinn.* Jayda Constable had one, and so did Eliza Shiffer. God only knows how many more are out there. Quinn was a prolific womanizer."

Crusher looked up, pressed his lips together, and frowned. I knew that look. Something bothered him and he was trying to decide what to say

"What?" I plopped my hands on my hips.

"You say you found your mother's picture in Giselle Cole's house? With this love note on the back?"

"Yes."

"What was it doing there?"

"I know. That's been bothering me, too." Why didn't Quinn give this to my mother? And why would Giselle keep and display a portrait of her father's mistress? "Giselle maintains several houses. They're all filled with beautiful things. This portrait is such a small item, maybe she didn't notice it."

"Maybe. But I think you should ask." He cleared

his throat. "There's one more person you should ask about the portrait. Isaac."

"Uncle Isaac? What could he possibly . . ." I stopped myself mid-sentence. Exactly one week ago, my uncle revealed stuff about my mother I never knew. Could he still have more to tell?

I blew out my breath. "Tomorrow. They're both coming for Shabbat. I'll ask then."

CHAPTER 20

By Friday afternoon, the house was filled with the savory smells of brisket cooking in a marinade of sweet wine; roasted whole chicken rubbed with olive oil, garlic, and rosemary; and the oniony smell of potato kugel. I smoothed the white cloth and set out six plates of my bubbie's white china with the blue rim. The Sabbath table sparkled with silver: flatware, twin candle holders, and a sparkling cup of wine near Uncle Isaac's plate. I covered the challah with a special linen cloth Bubbie hand-embroidered decades ago, featuring clusters of grapes and flowers. Her hand-stitched Hebrew letters spelled out the words *Likavod Shabbat v'Yom Tov*—"In honor of the Sabbath and holidays."

At five, I changed into my long black skirt and a white sweater knitted with fine silk yarn. I fastened my curls on top on my head with the jeweled combs from New York and spritzed a flowery perfume on my neck. I was just slipping my feet into my new strappy black heels when the doorbell rang. Yossi was still in the shower, so I hurried to the living room.

The first thing I saw when I opened the door was my daughter's copper-colored curls.

She stood, grinning in a green dress that made her green eyes sparkle and a face aglow like the Mona Lisa. "Hi, Mom!" She gathered me in a tight hug. I wrapped my arms around her and held her a beat too long. She finally pulled away and stepped inside.

"Why did you ring the doorbell? Did you lose your key?"

"Well, since Yossi moved in, I didn't know if you'd want us just showing up in your living room unannounced."

"This is still your home, Quincy. You are always welcome here."

The dark-haired Noah Kaplan stood slightly behind her, wearing slacks and a shirt without a tie.

I met his brown-eyed gaze for the first time since they'd arrived and offered my hand. "Hello, Noah."

He shoved a bouquet of pink roses into my out-stretched hand and sprang forward to hug me, pinning my arms at my sides. "Shabbat shalom, Mom!"

Crap! My stomach sank as my worst fears were realized. If Kaplan called me Mom, that could mean only one thing.

I patted his back twice with my free hand and pulled away. "Shabbat shalom, Noah. How are you?"

He drew Quincy toward him and gazed, besotted,

at her face. "Over the moon. I've never been so happy. We're . . ."

Quincy put a finger to his lips. "Shh, honey. Not yet. Let's wait until everyone is here."

Well, that cinches it. I glanced at my daughter's naked ring finger and frowned. *What a little cheapskate. Where is the engagement ring?*

Crusher came out of the bedroom in his Sabbath clothes: black trousers and a white shirt. He welcomed the young couple with a hug and a friendly handshake and ushered them into the living room.

Giselle arrived next with a merry-looking Uncle Isaac. She helped him over the threshold and he smiled. "Thank you, *faigela*."

Wait! Why are you calling her by *my pet name?*

He noticed my frown, cupped my face gently in his hands, and kissed my wrinkled forehead several times—just the way he used to do when I was a child. "Good *Shabbos*, *faigela*."

Everyone stood to greet the old man.

"Oh, Zadie, I'm ecstatic to see you." Quincy had to bend down to embrace him. Even though he was technically her great-uncle, she'd always had a special relationship with him and called him Grandpa in Yiddish. "Say hi to Noah."

Uncle Isaac beamed at the young couple and nodded his approval. After all, he was the one pushing the two of them together. "*Nu?* Kaplan. Good *Shabbos*."

"You must be my niece, Quincy!" Giselle exclaimed. "I'd know you anywhere by your red hair and green eyes. We get that from Daddy." She grinned. "I see I worried for nothing. You're not at all heavy like your mother."

Quincy's face went white and glanced at me with a deer-in-the-headlights expression.

I rolled my eyes. "This is your Aunt Giselle, sweetie. She can be rude and tactless, but she means well."

My sister laughed. "Sissy's right. Don't worry, you'll get used to me." She turned to Kaplan and gave the handsome young detective the once-over. "You're Noah?"

He nodded.

"You seem cute enough. My sister tells me you arrested her once."

Not only had he arrested me and thrown me in jail overnight, he smirked when he did it. Every time our paths crossed after that, he'd copped a snide and threatening attitude. Such deliberate nastiness was hard to forgive.

The skin on Kaplan's olive cheeks turned pink and he pressed his lips together. He cleared his throat. "A misunderstanding."

"And a stupid one on your part," she said.

I could've kissed her.

Crusher clapped his hands once to break the tension. "Let's welcome the Sabbath."

I squeezed my sister's hand on the way to the dining room. She squeezed back twice in response. We took our places at the table and I asked Quincy to bless the candles.

I watched with pride at the graceful motions of her hands and her perfect Hebrew diction. A tinge of melancholy secretly tugged at my heart with the realization she and Kaplan would eventually preside over their own Sabbath table.

After Crusher and Uncle Isaac recited the prayers, I brought out hot platters of food. While we ate, I kept waiting for Quincy to speak. But she was too busy scarfing down her favorite dishes. She even took second helpings of everything, which was unusual for her.

When the time came to clear the table for dessert, I'd run out of patience. "Don't keep us in the dark another minute, sweetie. What is your big announcement?"

The couple grasped hands and she took a deep breath. "You're going to be a grandma."

First, I could no longer feel my lips. Then my head filled with a thousand bees, and a black circle closed in on my vision. The sensation of strong arms grabbing me was the last thing I remembered as I slid sideways into darkness.

I woke up stretched out on the sofa, where Crusher must've carried me.

I blinked open to a sea of concerned faces staring down from above. "What happened?"

Giselle helped me sit up and handed me a glass of water. "You've had a shock, Sissy. But a good one, right?"

Tears slid down Quincy's cheeks. "Oh, Mom,

I'm so sorry. I guess I should've prepared you first. I know this is kind of sudden, but you are happy, aren't you?"

"Who wouldn't be happy at the prospect of a grandchild?" *But with Kaplan as the father?* I gulped down some water. "I just wasn't expecting this particular news. I thought you were simply going to announce your engagement. When are you due?"

Quincy placed a protective hand on her belly. "The end of February. I'm only seven weeks along."

My very traditional uncle Isaac looked less than pleased. For him, the child should follow the marriage, not the other way around. He grabbed Kaplan's shoulder and squeezed firmly. "So *nu*? When is the wedding?"

Crusher grabbed Kaplan's other shoulder. "Soon, right?"

Kaplan swallowed and nodded. "We need to find a rabbi."

"Done!" both Crusher and Uncle Isaac said at the same time.

Giselle gave Kaplan a withering look. "I see you haven't even given her an engagement ring. What's the matter with you?"

Kaplan's eyes widened and he looked quickly at Quincy. "I . . . I was going to shop for one on Monday."

Giselle crossed her arms. "Don't be a cheapskate. Two carats at the very least."

Kaplan seemed relieved when she turned her

attention to Quincy. "Let me do the wedding at my house in Beverly Hills. I've got people who do beautiful events for me. They can pull together something spectacular in as little as two days if we have to."

So fast? "It's really up to the kids, G."

Crusher helped me to my feet. "Let's talk about it over dessert."

For the next half hour, we sat at the table eating strudel and discussing the wedding.

Then Quincy yawned. "I'm really tired these days. I think I need to call it a night."

Now I understood her increased appetite, sleepiness, and contented glow.

Kaplan jumped up, concern and tenderness written on his face. "Come on, baby, I'll take you home."

I reluctantly acknowledged, as I watched him help her out of the chair, that Kaplan might've been a jerk to me, but he certainly seemed to love my little girl.

After they left, Crusher leaned over and whispered, "The picture."

"Right!" I brought the pencil drawing of my mother in from the sewing room and handed it to Giselle. "I've been wondering, G. Since we now know Quinn drew one of these for each of his women, how did my mother's picture end up hanging on your wall?"

She shrugged and shook her head. "I found it years ago in a stack of drawings my father left in his studio. I had all of them framed and hung them in my various houses. How could I know this one would turn out to be significant?"

"Weren't you curious about the inscription on the back? I mean, this obviously wasn't a drawing of your mother, yet he called her the love of his life."

"To tell you the truth, I thought it was something he did before he met my mother. I didn't give it a second thought. Remember, until Deep Roots, I never knew he'd been unfaithful, let alone fathered any other children. Who knows why he didn't give it to your mother. Maybe he intended to but disappeared before he could."

I handed the drawing to Uncle Isaac. "Have you ever seen this?"

He adjusted his glasses and peered closely at the drawing. "This is your mama, all right." He turned it over and read the inscription on the back. "*Vey iz mir.* I'm pretty sure that if your mama had this drawing, she would've kept it a secret, just like she kept their affair a secret for all those years."

When I cleared the last plate from the table, the men recited the *birkat hamazon.*

Giselle said, "I forgot to ask you last week. What are they singing?"

"It's called the Grace after Meals. You Christians bless the food before you eat, but we Jews bless God when the meal is over."

"Potaytoes, putahtoes. By the way, I found a lab that'll test for Wolf Shiffer's DNA. I took the cup in today. I also gave them a sample of my DNA for them to compare. We should have the results in a few days."

"I've been thinking, G. I've got the weekend free. Do you want to bring all the pieces of your grandmother's quilt over tomorrow? We can decide how to finish it."

"Sure. But remember, I sleep in late on Saturday and Sunday."

Giselle left soon after with Uncle Isaac, and Crusher immediately poured us each a glass of wine. "You okay, babe?"

"I'm still in shock. This whole thing happened so fast with Quincy and Noah. I was hoping the affair wouldn't last, but now . . ."

"Do you know what I think?"

"What?"

He raised my hands to his lips and kissed it. "I fell in love with you the moment we met. Why can't the same thing happen to them? It's obvious they love each other. No matter what went down between you and Kaplan in the past, you need to get on board this train, Martha. Or it'll leave without you."

CHAPTER 21

Giselle arrived in her Jag at eleven Saturday morning, wearing dark glasses and a dark business suit. She carried two sacks: a large one with her quilt and a smaller one bearing a logo from Western Donuts. "You mentioned last night that you both liked these." She shoved the white paper bag in Crusher's direction.

Inside were a half-dozen glazed apple fritters, each the size of a lunch plate. "Great!" He headed for the kitchen.

A moment later we heard the whirr of the coffee grinder—another reason I loved this man. Living with Yossi was like living with a huge, domesticated bear.

Giselle and I spread the Grandmother's Flower Garden quilt top on the cutting table in my sewing room, where we'd sorted the documents from Quinn's missing-persons file one week before. This was the first chance I'd had to really examine the quilt top closely. Each flower mosaic started with a yellow hexagon in the middle. A ring of six hexagons were stitched together at the edges to form a circular shape around the center yellow hexagon. A second ring of twelve hexagons was stitched to the outside of the first, to form a larger circle or flower.

Edith Eagan, Giselle's grandmother, had grouped printed fabrics in the same color family together to form each flower. She used darker hues in the smaller circle, like deep reds or purples, and lighter hues on the outer circle, like pinks and lavenders. The flowers featured bright combinations, such as indigo with sky blues, kelly green with mint green, orange with gold, and teal with turquoise, among others.

I stretched a fabric tape measure across the width of the ten-inch flowers and the plain muslin hexagons that separated them. "This is approximately eighty inches wide. I think your grandmother intended to make a double-bed quilt." I measured the length. "To complete the top, we need to lengthen it by about four more rows, which means we need about thirty-two more flowers."

She opened the large bag again and dumped the rest of the contents on the table. We counted an additional twenty-five flowers, a whole pile of fabric hexagons in colorful prints waiting to be assembled into ten-inch flowers, and hundreds of plain muslin hexagons to sew in between the flowers.

"I think we have enough. If not, we can always reach into my stash." I waved my arm toward the floor-to-ceiling shelves lining one wall, groaning with stacks of fabric folded and divided into color families.

Giselle opened a plastic Baggie that had also fallen onto the table. "Looks like these are some extra paper shapes if we need them."

Crusher carried a tray into the room, with two mugs of steaming Italian roast and two apple fritters served on paper napkins. "I'm leaving now. Isaac and I are going to visit the rabbi to discuss Quincy's wedding."

I reached for one of the mugs of coffee. "Thanks. Listen, Yossi, I thought about what you said last night, about not being left behind. You were right. I'm totally on board."

He smiled and kissed my cheek. I smelled apple fritter on his breath.

After he left, Giselle handed me one of the six-sided bits of paper. "Take a look at this."

The two-inch hexagon had been cut out of blue stationery with three lines of handwriting on it. I could just make out the words *Dear Quinn, You promised y . . . , eave your wife. Do . . . , our son to . . .* My hand flew to my mouth and I looked at Giselle. "Oh my God. This looks like . . ."

"A note from Quinn Junior's mother." She finished my sentence. "And we know who that probably is. Maybe Grandmother found it among the papers Daddy left behind."

"Figgy said she definitely knew about the boy, G. But why would she cut up the note and hide it in your quilt?"

Giselle was silent for several seconds. "Grandmother was completely under Granddad's thumb. Like we all were. I think this might've been an act of rebellion. I can just picture her discovering the letter and hiding it from him."

"What good would that do?"

Giselle shrugged. "Maybe keeping secrets gave her a sense of power and independence from such a domineering man."

"If she didn't want your grandfather to know about Quinn Junior, why didn't she just destroy the letter?"

"Maybe she thought Daddy was coming back someday. Who knows what she intended? But putting it in the quilt was a way to keep it and hide it."

I regarded my sister with a new respect. What she said made perfect sense. "If you're right, then the rest of the pieces must be around here someplace."

We turned all the fabric pieces to the back, found five more blue paper hexagons, and carefully removed the basting stitches holding them to the fabric. Then we cleared a space on the table, taped the pieces back together, and pinned it up on the murder board. The note read:

5/20

Dear Quinn,
*   You promised you'd leave your wife. Do you want our son to grow up without you?*
*   Money is not enough. I'll take him far away. You can't treat us like this.*

"That conniving witch! Not only did Eliza Shiffer make my mother's life hell, she threatened Daddy right where it hurt. According to Jayda, he loved being with Wolf."

"Take a step back, G. Men like Quinn are incapable of feeling hurt. Thwarted? Yes. Angry? Yes. But feeling hurt requires empathy. As for being threatened, who was playing whom? Quinn managed to deceive and manipulate everyone in his life. Save your pity for his victims."

Encouraged by our discovery of the letter, we searched the quilt for other papers that might hold clues. We found fragments of newspaper articles, bank statements, and an accounting ledger. But without reassembling the pages, they made no sense. More promising were pieces cut from what looked like a desk calendar, with snippets of handwriting.

"We're going to have to separate all these hundreds of papers from the fabric, G. Then we need to fit them together. It'll take a lot of work."

"But what about the quilt? Won't removing the papers ruin it?"

"No. Remember what I said? You can buy precut paper templates to replace the ones we take out of the quilt. We don't have to worry about the part of the top that's already sewn together, just the loose parts, the pieces that aren't attached to anything else." I smiled. "You'll love Lucy and Jazz. They'll help us sew everything back together again. Quilters coming to the aid of another quilter—an old American tradition."

Giselle looked at her watch. "Darn! I have a meeting in an hour. Harold finally brought the Saudis to the table. I hate to leave you with all this, but my office is on Wilshire in Santa Monica. I'd better go. Call you later."

As soon as she left, I called Quincy. "How are you feeling, sweetie?"

"A little nauseated. Does it ever go away?"

"You should feel better after the first trimester. Try eating saltine crackers or drinking seltzer."

"Have you recovered from the shock of finding out about the baby?"

"Truthfully? I'm still processing the happy news. I've never seen you look this beautiful, and Noah seems to be overjoyed."

She laughed. "Totally. He went with Yossi and Zadie to visit the rabbi. We'll get married as soon as the rabbi has space on his calendar."

I cringed at the mention of Kaplan in the same breath as the two most important men in my life.

Accepting him as part of my inner circle wasn't going to be easy. The two of us needed to have a heart-to-heart before that could happen.

"Do you think Aunt Giselle was serious about hosting the wedding?"

"I'm sure she was. And she'll make it an event to remember."

"There's one more thing, Mom."

I immediately picked up a caution in her voice. "What's that, sweetie?"

"Noah asked his partner to be his best man."

"Arlo?" My gut tightened at the mention of Detective Arlo Beavers. My ex-boyfriend and Crusher's old rival. Only three months ago, Arlo had asked me to marry him and I turned him down. "Did he say yes?"

"He said he'd be honored. Will you be okay with that?"

The answer was a resounding *NO*, but, for my daughter's sake, I'd have to suck it up. "We're all grown-ups here, Quincy. I'm sure everything will be fine."

Just shoot me. Not only will my ex-husband be standing under the wedding chuppa with me, but so will my ex-boyfriend.

"What did you think of Giselle?" I asked.

"She's different from you physically. No one would ever know you were related."

I could be so insulted.

"But her personality is a lot like yours. She strikes

me as being a very smart, independent, and generous woman. I admire that. In both of you."

Okay, I was no longer insulted.

"Uh," she hesitated. "Do you think your friend Jazz could make me a wedding dress on short notice?"

"I'm pretty sure he'd jump at the chance." *And stop bugging me about making my gown.* "Have you talked to your father?"

My ex-husband, Aaron Rose, was a Beverly Hills psychiatrist and a blatant social climber. I wasn't sure how he'd react to the news of his daughter marrying a cop, let alone having a baby with him.

"Yes. When he learned the wedding would be at the Eagan estate, he insisted on inviting several of his friends. I think he wants to impress them. I really don't want that to happen, Mom. Noah and I want to be surrounded by people who care about us, not strangers."

And thus it begins. The challenges of planning a wedding. "Don't worry, honey. I'll handle your father."

Before we ended the call, I promised to call Jazz about the wedding dress.

Detective Farkas called at five. "I've just been to Thanks for the Memories Assisted Living. What the hell kind of name is that?"

"I forget."

"Very funny."

"Why are you working on a Saturday, Gabe? Don't you ever take a day off?"

"I was on my way back from a day at Universal

Studios with the wife and kids. I figured since we were in the area, I'd make a short detour and save myself a long trip to Burbank during the week."

"What happened?"

"Gomez's son, Carlos, was visiting her, and he wasn't happy about my being there. Did you know he does the weather on TV?"

"Yes. Don't keep me in suspense, Gabe. Did you interview Detective Gomez?"

"If you can call it that."

"And?"

"Nada. Zip. Zilch. Nobody was home."

"Maybe you should try in the morning. Miss Leathy, the administrator, said she's sharper then."

"Not wasting my time. Gomez is in an advanced stage of dementia. We won't get anything out of her."

Darn! Another dead end.

I told him about the note Giselle and I discovered hidden in the quilt. "The dynamics in her family were complicated. Judging from what she told me, there could be more evidence buried in those pieces of paper Edith Eagan cut up."

"How many pieces are you talking about?"

I groaned. "Almost three thousand."

"Good luck with that. Let me know if your hunch pays off." He ended the call.

CHAPTER 22

"I can hardly wait." Jazz's voice rose an octave over the phone. "I'm thinking yards and yards of ivory silk. High waist to hide the baby bump. And I'll make you a mother-of-the-bride dress. Green brocade to bring out your eyes."

"I don't think we have time for both. They're getting married as soon as the rabbi's available. Just concentrate on Quincy. I'll wear the Rachel Zoe I bought in New York."

"But don't you want something *nyew*?"

"I hate it when you whine, Jazz."

"Fine." His voice returned to his normal baritone. "Just give me her phone number."

"See you tomorrow. Lucy's coming, and you'll finally get to meet my sister." I ended the call and turned to the chore waiting for me on my cutting table.

With a silent apology to Giselle's grandmother, I began to undo all her hard work. A little tug on the knotted end of the thread was all it took to pull out the temporary stitches holding the fabric to the paper. I hunched in my chair as I worked. Less than thirty minutes later, a throbbing rose from the tightness in my neck and shoulders and landed with a thump in my right temple. I closed my eyes against the hammering in my head and rolled my neck in a circle. With a sigh, I realized that working on the quilt would have to wait until the following day.

I stumbled toward my migraine meds and a cup of tea in the kitchen. Twenty minutes later the pounding in my head became fainter, but the cramping in my stomach got stronger. The only thing I'd eaten since breakfast was an apple fritter. As I pulled out the dish of leftover potato kugel from the refrigerator, Crusher's Harley roared to a stop in the driveway.

He bounced through the front door with a huge grin. For a six-foot-six-inch guy wearing size-fourteen boots, he was surprisingly light on his feet. "It's all settled, babe. The rabbi will perform the ceremony at the end of August, right after Tisha B'Av." Crusher referred to the end of a three-week period of religious mourning during the summer, in which Jewish marriages were prohibited.

"That's good news," I said. "That's more than a month away. That gives us a little extra time to plan things." I placed the kugel in the microwave.

"Uh, there's just one thing." He combed his fingertips through his beard and raised an eyebrow. "Noah brought his father to the meeting. The Kaplans want to invite three hundred of their closest friends. They're members of Hillcrest and insist on having the wedding and reception there." He referred to the country club in West LA formed in 1946 by wealthy Jews who had been barred from membership in the Gentile clubs of LA.

"But I thought the kids agreed to let Giselle host the wedding at the Eagan estate."

"Eli Kaplan's exact words were, 'My son deserves much more than a backyard wedding.'"

Oy vey. "What kind of *mishugas* is that? Has he ever seen the Eagan estate? It's magnificent."

He shrugged. "What can I say? Eli Kaplan is a jerk."

"Well, that explains a lot." A twinge of pity sparked in my mind as I imagined a little boy growing up with a heavy-handed father like Eli. "What did Noah say?"

"Not much. Mostly, he seemed disappointed the wedding couldn't happen sooner. Like right away. I think Noah's just anxious to close the deal with Quincy. He's ass over teakettle in love. Says he hopes the baby is a little redheaded girl."

I thought sadly about my own father and how he—when he learned my mother was pregnant—ran in the opposite direction. Maybe Noah Kaplan wasn't such a total loss after all.

"Giselle and I found something important today." I told him about the hidden papers on the back of the quilt. "Pulling everything apart, however, will take a lot of work. There are almost three thousand pieces. Everyone's coming over tomorrow to help."

"Then what? Fitting together a puzzle with thousands of pieces will take time. Is all this work worth it?"

I twirled one of my curls around my finger. "I hope so, because according to Gabe Farkas, Meredith Gomez is too far gone to be any help, and we've interviewed everyone else."

The microwave dinged. I removed the steaming kugel and divided it into two servings.

Crusher loaded his fork, closed his eyes, and made contented noises while he chewed. "I've got confidence in you, babe. If anything's hiding in all those little papers, you'll find it."

By one on Sunday, the summer temperature had soared to the mid-nineties. Lucy and Jazz were the first to arrive. They settled at the dining room table, which I'd expanded with two leaves to increase the working surface.

Giselle waltzed through the front door dressed casually in gray linen pants that hugged her slender hips and thighs. A white silk tank top showed off her firm shoulders and arms. How fair was it that she got all the slim genes?

"This heat is atrocious! I hate the Valley, especially this time of year." She stopped speaking when she noticed Lucy and Jazz sitting like bookends on either side of the table. She marched toward them, smiled, and stuck out her hand. "Don't tell me. You must be Martha's best friend, Lucy. And you've got to be Jazz. The gay one."

Lucy's mouth fell open, but Jazz merely regarded Giselle with a cool eye. "Only on Sundays and holidays."

My sister tossed her head back and laughed. "I've heard so much about you both, I feel like we're friends already. Thank you for volunteering to work on my grandmother's quilt."

"You're welcome." Lucy seemed to recover from her initial shock. "Martha's told us a lot about you, too."

"Really? Like what?"

From the look on her face, I could tell Lucy hadn't expected to be pinned down to specifics. I jumped in. "Like the fact you can appear a little abrasive at times but you mean well."

Giselle's face fell. "Is that all?"

I put my arm around her waist and gently led her to a dining room chair at the far end of the table. "I also told them how smart, generous, and capable you are. And how glad I am we found each other."

A shy smile played on her lips. "Me, too."

I handed her a red and peach "flower" and showed her how to carefully remove the basting threads without tearing the paper. Then I poured everyone a cup of coffee, set out a plate of cookies, and sat down.

A curious Zsa Zsa pranced into the dining room followed by Bumper, who sauntered at a more regal feline pace. The Maltese sported a lavender pinafore that matched the lavender shirt Jazz wore today.

"Well, aren't you the cutest thing!" Giselle reached down to pet the dog.

Zsa Zsa licked her hand, signaling that the newcomer was now an acceptable member of the pack.

The four of us worked more than three hours to liberate all the paper templates. The partially finished quilt top, the loose flowers, and the extra hexagons had all once been stiff with paper that crinkled when handled. Now they fell limp and soft and silent. We placed the fabric back in the plastic bag. Then we spread the thousands of paper pieces across the tabletop. Each hexagon had tiny puncture marks around the edges, where Edith Eagan's needle had pierced them decades before.

"Now what?" Jazz gave me an *I can't believe you're serious* look.

Without hesitation, Giselle went into CEO mode and took charge. "First, we divide them into obvious categories—newspaper, lined paper, plain white paper, paper with typing, paper with handwriting— that sort of thing." She pointed at me. "It would help if we had some sort of containers to put them in."

I hurried to the closet in my guest room and emptied the shoes out of six plastic shoe boxes with lids. I placed them on top of the dining table. "There's more if we need them."

The sorting took over an hour. Halfway through, I had to retrieve another shoe box to hold all the pieces cut from a ledger and what looked like bank statements. "There are two whole boxes of these accounting pages. That's too much. Numbers aren't like words. How will we know we're matching them correctly? We should put them aside for now." When nobody objected, I snapped the plastic lids on the boxes and set them on the sideboard. Then I gestured to the four containers remaining on the table, some of them less full than others. "These look more promising."

Lucy checked her watch. "I wish I could stay longer to help, but I'm already late. Richie's bringing over my newest grandchild tonight."

"Me, too." Jazz picked up Zsa Zsa. "I've got a hot date on Skype in about an hour."

"Thank you for your help!" Giselle gave first Jazz then Lucy a strong hug.

Lucy hugged her back. "Don't worry, hon. We'll help you sew everything back together again."

When we were alone, Giselle said, "Lucy and Jazz are so nice. You're lucky. I've never been able to find close friends like that. Everybody I meet has an agenda. They're either after my business or want a favor—usually involving money. I always have to be on my guard where people are concerned."

"Maybe you've been looking in the wrong places, G."

A strand of red hair had fallen in her face and she tossed her head slightly. "I wouldn't know where to begin looking. Besides"—she smiled—

"I have you now. Shall we get started with the puzzle pieces?"

"Frankly, I'm cooked. It's after five. We can pick this up again tomorrow. Besides, we have to talk."

"About?"

"I've been thinking about the money Quinn carried on May twenty-fifth, the day he disappeared. We know he was paid sixty thousand in cash the day before. That money came from a commission to paint the portrait of Chief Nelson's wife. Where does a cop get that kind of cash? Especially in nineteen-eighties money? If there were notes in the missing-persons file about the sixty thou or where it came from, we have to assume they were removed, along with Detective Rohrbacher's notes on gambling debts."

"But neither Captain Farkas or Detective Rohrbacher mentioned any of that. Shouldn't we talk to them again?"

"Yeah." I nodded. "And there's one more thing. I'm also wondering just how much more information Figgy might still be hiding."

Giselle pressed her lips together. "Hiding? Why would you think that?"

"Hear me out. Figgy admitted to listening in on your mother's telephone conversations. It occurred to me that she might've spied on other family members, too. For instance, did she ever monitor Quinn's calls? It would've been easy to do back then, before the age of cell phones. She could've overheard everything just by picking up one of the landline extensions and listening in. We really should go back and ask her."

"That never occurred to me, but you might be right. You know, Sissy, Figgy's old. We have to be gentle with her. I don't want her to think she's in trouble or anything." Giselle consulted her cell phone. "I have appointments all day tomorrow, but I'm free Tuesday afternoon. If you can meet me at my office at one, we can drive to Beverly Hills together."

I took a deep breath. "I'm afraid there's no 'we' this time, G. I should talk to Figgy alone."

She frowned. "She won't talk if I'm not there."

"I'm not sure that's true. It's obvious she's still fiercely loyal to you and your family. Figgy sees herself as your protector. The thing is, she may not feel comfortable talking about certain things in front of you. She might be more forthcoming if you're not around."

Giselle hesitated. I reached out and grasped her hand. "I understand how protective you feel about Figgy and how much you need to feel in control. But you have to trust my judgment on this. I promise to be gentle with her. Please call her now and set up the interview."

CHAPTER 23

By the time I woke up Monday morning, Crusher had already gone and left a note propped against the coffeemaker. *Don't wait up for me tonight. Working late.*

I sighed. At least he hadn't been called out of town again. I took my coffee to the dining room and sat in front of the four containers full of paper hexes we'd removed from the quilt the day before. I started with the shoe box holding the ones with handwriting, spreading them out on the table before me. I sorted them according to color: white, cream, gray. The largest of those piles was white and would take a lot of effort to sort through. So I pushed them aside and focused on the smaller piles of the cream and gray.

The gray hexes appeared to be cut from a note like the blue one Giselle and I had reconstructed. I matched the six pieces. It read:

Quinn,

When are you going to leave your wife??? Maybe I should tell her about our son. Maybe she'll do me a favor and throw you out.

I need more cash. Do you doubt I'll go straight to your in-laws? I'm sure they'll pay to keep me from going public.

Wow! Eliza Shiffer was pissed off for two reasons: money and jealousy. Both strong motives for murder. Had I just stumbled across our prime suspect?

The doorbell disturbed my train of thought. I opened up to see Lucy wearing the sky blue cotton blouse she favored because it made her orange hair look more "authentic." I stepped aside to let her in.

I led her to the dining room, showed her the note on gray stationery I'd just taped together. "Giselle and I believe Eliza Shiffer was the mother of Quinn Junior, Wolf Shiffer. We're just waiting for the DNA results to prove he's our half brother. What I can't figure out is why Eliza made Quinn give her cash when she could've just disguised the payments as extra commission."

"How often did your father sell a painting?"

I went to the murder board in my sewing room and returned with the document Wolf had printed out. I ran my finger down the column labeled *Date of Sale*. "It looks like he averaged two to three sales a year."

"There's your answer," said Lucy. "If this Shiffer woman relied on child support from your father's commissions, then she'd only get paid two to three times a year. Maybe that wasn't enough."

"But those sales were in the six figures. Her thirty percent commission would've amounted to well over one hundred thousand. In 1980, that was a huge income for anyone, let alone a single mother."

"You can't always tell from the gross income how well a business is actually doing," said Lucy. "I helped Ray grow from his one-mechanic garage to the string of full-service auto shops we own today. And I can tell you there were months we ate hot dogs and beans when our expenses exceeded our income. But we always met payroll and never got behind on the rent because we lived on a budget and saved."

"You're right. Eliza may have owned her own gallery, but who knows how successful she was? She certainly *looked* successful and very high maintenance. She was plastered with diamonds in the photo of her I saw."

"So, you think money is the reason she could've killed your father?" she asked.

"That and the fact he wouldn't leave his wife, Louise." I spread out the cream-colored hexes. "Are you ready to tackle this pile?"

A few minutes later, we had another note written by a different hand.

4/23/65

> *Quinn dearest,*
>   *Here is the picture you asked for. She's in the*
> *fifth grade. I can't accept any money from you*
> *without my family finding out. Go ahead and*
> *open the account in her name. But she can't know*
> *where the money came from. She thinks you're*
> *dead, and we agreed to leave it that way until she*
> *turns 25.*
>
>   *Yours forever,*
>   *Shirley*

I clutched the edge of the table to steady myself. My breathing sped up with each increasing heartbeat.

Lucy's voice pierced the fog that covered my brain and I felt her arm around my shoulder. "Are you okay, hon?"

"No! I'm not okay." Tears stung my eyes. "My mother wrote this. The note is about me!"

"Yeah. I gathered. Sounds like he was more interested in you than you thought. He asked for your photo and set up an account for you."

"Well, if he did deposit any money in my name, I never saw any of it."

Lucy paused in thought, drumming her fingertips on the table. "Get your laptop, girlfriend. We're going to find that money."

Her fingers sped across the keyboard. She typed *unclaimed property California* into Google's search engine and got nearly a half-million hits. She clicked on the URL for the state controller's office home page then tapped the button for unclaimed property. "Go ahead, make your day." She slid the laptop in front of me.

I typed in *Rose, Martha Rivka.* Finding a bank account wouldn't merely be about coming into some money. Finding a bank account would prove that my father had cared about me, after all. Was I prepared to have the world as I knew it turned upside down yet again?

I knew Bubbie and Uncle Isaac loved me. They were the ones who actually raised me. My mother, on the other hand, had been distant. Disconnected. But this note suggested she didn't always live in her fantasy world. She'd made some very self-serving but practical decisions about my welfare. If an account did exist, it would challenge all my assumptions about my father; it would prove Jacob Quinn Maguire had taken responsibility for me, after all.

I held my breath and hit search. Five results popped up for Martha Rose, but none of them were me. I flopped against the back of my chair and blew out a puff of air. It seemed like I didn't have to worry about my world being toppled after all. "This was stupid."

Lucy grasped my shoulder. "I'll tell you what's stupid, Martha. You typed in the wrong name. Quinn set up that account when you were in the fifth grade. What was your name *then?*"

"You're right. What was I thinking?" I went back

to the screen and typed in *Harris, Martha Rivka*. I took another deep breath and clicked the search button. This time, one result popped up. A savings account at Bank of America on Pico Boulevard in my old neighborhood had been escheated back to the State of California in 1983, three years after Quinn's disappearance. I followed the link to the next screen giving the details.

"Ha!" Lucy whooped and threw her hands in the air. "You just won the lottery!"

I had to blink several times to make sure I saw what the screen revealed. One-point-eight million dollars waited for me in Sacramento. I did the math. If Quinn opened the account when I was ten years old in 1965, he had fifteen years to make deposits before he disappeared in 1980. The account would've accumulated interest from B of A all those years until it was handed over to the state as required by law—three years after they lost contact with Quinn. The interest payments would've stopped once the funds left the bank, but the principal remained intact.

So, it was true. Quinn did think about me. He asked for my picture and tried to provide for me. I really did have to reevaluate everything I'd believed about my parents. As if on cue, the muscles in my back tightened with stress and squeezed my neck and shoulders, creating the seeds of a headache.

"You know what this also means, Lucy?" I rubbed the side of my neck. "It means that, besides Quinn, at least one other person in Giselle's family knew about me. Her grandmother Edith Eagan."

"I wonder . . ." Lucy picked up another shoe box and began riffling the contents.

"What are you looking for?"

"Yesterday, when we were sorting the hexagons, I came across a piece of a black-and-white photograph and tossed it in here with the newspaper clippings. Now I'm wondering if anyone else turned up more pieces and what the photo might show."

I made room on the table, and hexes drifted out of the upended container like black-and-white snowflakes. Sections of the picture were easy to detect because the photo paper was thicker than newsprint.

We found twelve hexes and taped them together. A partially assembled head shot stared back at us from the table. The pieces had been cut out of the middle portion of an eight-by-ten-inch photo of an infant—my daughter, Quincy, born in January of 1980.

So Quinn knew about his granddaughter! Was he pleased? Did he want to know us? He disappeared in May 1980. My twenty-fifth birthday was the following month, in June. If he had lived, would he have contacted me on the day I turned twenty-five?

My heart felt like a rock in my chest. "I feel cheated, Lucy."

"I'm sorry, hon. This has been a real shock. You look like heck, girlfriend. What can I do?"

I reached inside the pink box from Bea's and

grabbed an apricot Danish. Maybe I could make the headache go away with some sugar. "Could you please research how I go about getting that money back from the state?"

"Sure. But I'm going to do that at home. You look like you need to rest right now."

"You're the best, Lucy. I think I'll take a walk. Try to process everything."

After she left, I grabbed my keys, locked my front door, and headed toward the park down the street from our housing tract. The homes were built in the 1950s on land that used to belong to the old RKO movie studios. Fifty-five-year-old liquid amber trees lined the parking strip. Their mature roots had pushed up portions of the sidewalk until it resembled a fallen deck of cards. I carefully navigated the rough parts until I reached the rolling green of the parkland at the end of the street.

A cement path wound around silent soccer fields that would vibrate later in the afternoon with the sound of children playing. Resting on a wooden bench under a tall eucalyptus tree, I tried to corral the thoughts swirling in my head.

Something bothered me about the $60,000 from the Shiffer Gallery Quinn was supposedly taking to Atlantic City. Was he really going to wager all of it? Or was some of that cash given back to Eliza Shiffer and some of it deposited for me? Did Quinn keep a record of the money he paid out? What did he do with the B of A statements for my account? Did the answers lie buried inside that mountain of hexagons cut from ledger sheets and bank statements?

I thought about Giselle's repressed grandmother, who cut up evidence of Quinn's secret life and sewed it into the back of a quilt. Who did that? Did she tell anyone else in the family about my daughter and me? About my bank account? Would the knowledge that Quinn made payments for his illegitimate children make someone angry enough to kill him? Like the creepy old grandmother, or Giselle's angry mother?

Maybe Figgy had the answer. I'd ask her the hard questions and pray she'd feel freer to answer without my sister present.

I closed my eyes against the swirling in my head and pretended to sit on the banks of a river. Breathing slowly, I imagined that the swoosh of traffic on the nearby 101 Freeway was the sound of clear water rushing downstream from melting snow in the mountains. A cool breeze pushed the curls off my forehead and calmed the ache in my skull.

I inhaled deeply, opened my eyes, and headed back to my house. Time to contact Giselle.

CHAPTER 24

"I just saw your text, Sissy. I meant to call you earlier, but my meetings are taking longer than anticipated. As a matter of fact, Harold and I are about to take the Saudis to lunch, so I only have a minute to call Figgy. When do you want to talk to her?"

"This afternoon, if possible."

"Fine. I'll set it up and text you. Anything else?"

"Plenty! Call me later when you have time, G. Lucy and I discovered something *really big* this morning."

I wound my way over Coldwater Canyon from the Valley to Beverly Hills at two in the afternoon. Figgy must've heard me drive up to the big house because she opened the door as soon as I mounted the stone steps.

"Would you like some tea, Mrs. Rose?" She wiped her hands on a white apron.

"Yes, I'd love some tea, but only if you'll join me. And please, call me Martha." I wandered into the living room and sat on one of the six lavender velvet sofas.

The old woman returned from the kitchen in five minutes, holding a tray. Her blue and silver Nike trainers squeaked on the hardwood floor. "I brought a plate of those croissants Miss Giselle loves." She set the tray on the marble-topped coffee table in front of me.

I didn't hesitate to help myself to tea with milk and one of the flaky curved pastries topped with slivered almonds and filled with ground almond paste. I considered the sugar to be necessary medicine today for fighting my dull headache. "Should I call you Anna?"

"Everyone calls me Figgy." The housekeeper regarded me cautiously and perched on the edge of a straight-back chair. She poured herself a cup of tea. "Miss Giselle said you have some questions?"

"Yes." I gave her a reassuring smile. "You know we're trying to find out what happened to our father, right?"

She wobbled her head. "Not a good idea. The past is gone."

"Figgy, I think you know secrets about the family that could help us solve Quinn's murder. I also believe you didn't say anything in front of Giselle because you wanted to protect her from being hurt. And maybe you thought you'd get in trouble. Am I right?"

She lowered her eyes but said nothing.

"I know this can't be easy, and I appreciate your

cooperation. You told us the last time I came that you once listened in on a phone call from the mother of Quinn's son to Giselle's mother, Louise. Was that the only time?"

"No." She pressed her lips together.

"Did you ever eavesdrop on anyone else? You won't get in trouble for telling the truth."

She squared her shoulders and jutted out her chin. "Yes. All of them."

Bingo! Just as I suspected.

"Thanks for your honesty. Did you ever hear Quinn talking to any of his lovers?"

"That horrible woman who tormented poor Mrs. Louise about Mr. Quinn's son." The skin tightened around her eyes as she spoke. "She used to call him at night. At first, she just begged him to come to her place. After a while, she got nasty. Said she'd make him pay if he didn't leave his wife. That woman was the devil!"

"Okay, this is very important." I sat forward. "Did you ever hear her name? Does the name *Eliza* ring a bell?"

"No. He called all of them *macushla*, or something like that." *Macushla* was an Irish term of endearment.

"You said *all* of them? More than one woman called him at home?"

"Yes. Whenever Mr. Quinn went into his office and closed the door, I knew he was up to something sneaky. That's when I'd pick up the extension if I could. A couple of months before he disappeared, he spoke to a woman with a sweet voice. She told him he was a grandfather to a redheaded baby girl named after him." She looked at me over the rim of her teacup. "Was she talking about you?"

"My daughter, Quincy. Please go on . . ."

"They laughed together and he asked for a picture. Said he couldn't wait until June when he could finally meet his girls."

I blinked back tears of anger. Just two weeks! I missed Quinn by two weeks. Now, more than ever, I was determined to find the person who deprived me of ever knowing my father.

"Did you ever hear him talk about gambling debts or money?"

"Once, when Miss Giselle was three, Mr. Jerome stormed over here and shouted at Mr. Quinn for losing so much money. Mr. Jerome was angry because it wasn't the first time. He told Mr. Quinn to take better care of his family if he knew what was good for him."

"That sounds like a pretty serious threat. What did Quinn do?"

"He just said, 'I know what my responsibilities are.'"

Did Quinn lie to his father-in-law about the extent of his gambling losses in order to hide where his money was really going—to Eliza Shiffer and to my secret account?

"How much did Giselle's mother, Louise, know about the gambling and the other women?"

"Enough to break her heart. Your father caused this family a lot of pain."

"I know. It seems he caused everyone pain. I've asked this once already, Figgy, but I need to ask you again. Do you think Giselle's grandfather could've been angry enough with Quinn to kill him?"

The housekeeper clasped her hands until her knuckles turned white. "Like I told you a week ago, anything's possible. But even if he did, what good would it do to drag that up now? The only thing Miss Giselle has left of her family is memories. Don't ruin that."

"Okay. Let's set that aside for now. Tell me about Edith Eagan, Giselle's grandmother."

Figgy frowned. "I didn't work in the big house back then. My job was to take care of Mrs. Louise and her family in the small house." *Small* was a matter of interpretation. I estimated that the house Jerome Eagan built for his daughter next door was a five-thousand-square-foot replica of the twenty-thousand-square-foot main house where we now sat.

"Sometimes, when Mr. Quinn and Mrs. Louise were gone, Mrs. Edith would sneak over and shut herself in Mr. Quinn's office. I'd bring her tea— even when she didn't ask for it—just to see what she was up to. I saw her go through his filing cabinet and the papers on his desk. Once, I opened the door a crack and peeked in. She rattled a drawer in the antique rolltop desk and cursed because it was locked. Later on, though, I'm sure she opened it."

"How?"

"When the police found Mr. Quinn's Cadillac abandoned at the airport, his key ring was still in the ignition. The man detective . . . what was his name?"

"Rohrbacher?" I poured myself another cup of tea with milk.

"That's right. One day, Detective Rohrbacher showed up to see Mrs. Louise, but she wasn't here. Mrs. Edith must've seen him park in front of the little house because she hurried right over. He held up the key ring and asked, 'Can you identify any of these?'

"Mrs. Edith said, 'Of course. I recognize all of them. We don't want these floating around. I'm sure our friend Chief Nelson would want you to return them.' Then she held out her hand, cool as a cucumber."

"Did Rohrbacher hand them over?"

"Right away. I was standing close enough to see an old-fashioned key with a long, round stem. I'm pretty sure it was for that desk drawer because, right after the detective left, Mrs. Edith ran to Mr. Quinn's office and shut the door."

And I knew what had been locked inside that drawer. All those papers that ended up as hexagons. I explained to Figgy how Edith Eagan had cut up Quinn's private papers and sewed them into the back of the Grandmother's Flower Garden quilt. "Do you have any idea why she went to all that trouble to hide the contents of that drawer instead of just destroying them?"

Figgy shrugged. "Mrs. Edith wasn't a bad person. She must've had her reasons."

Indeed. I could just picture the furtive little woman, sitting like Madame Defarge, stitching secrets with busy fingers. The question was, what drove Giselle's grandmother to such sneaky and bizarre behavior?

I thanked the housekeeper and drove back to the Valley on Coldwater Canyon then west to Encino on the 101. Bumper greeted me with a yowl just inside the front door. With his tail swishing sharply through the air, he marched into the kitchen, sat next to his empty water bowl, and complained again.

"Sorry! Sorry. I should've checked before I left." I promptly replenished his bowl and set it back on the floor.

The cat licked the water once and sauntered away in a clear reprimand.

I called Quincy to see if she had taken my advice about saltine crackers for morning sickness.

"Hi, Mom. I've been trying to reach you all afternoon. Did you forget to turn on your cell phone again?"

"No. I left it at home in the charger. Is everything okay? Did the crackers work?"

"A little, but morning sickness is the least of my worries right now. It's Noah."

"What has he done? Is he backing out? If he hurts you in any way, I'll kill him."

"Relax! He's not the problem. It's his father. Eli went ahead and booked the Hillcrest for the wedding. He doesn't care what we want. He and Noah had a huge argument. Noah was furious and disinvited his parents altogether. Now nobody is speaking to anybody else. I thought managing my dad was going to be a problem, but Eli is much worse. I don't know what to do."

"Didn't Noah tell him that it's the bride's family who's responsible for planning the wedding and paying for it?"

"You're living in the last century, Mom. Those rules don't apply these days. What Noah did tell Eli was that he trusted your judgment completely."

"He said that?"

Kaplan had resisted me on every murder investigation I'd been involved in. When did he go from nemesis to ally?

"Noah really respects you, Mom. He said you're one of the smartest people he knows."

Wow. I thought my recent discovery of the bank account in my name had turned my world upside down. But this declaration from Kaplan sent my head spinning into a parallel universe.

"Look, honey, I'm sure we can work out some sort of compromise. This should be a joyous event. It's time for me to meet Noah's parents anyway. Why don't we all have dinner and talk this out? You and Noah, his parents, your father, Yossi—if he's in town—and me? And if you still want Giselle to host the wedding at her estate, I'll ask her to be there, too."

"I'm sure Eli will insist we meet on his turf at Hillcrest."

"Then I'll ask Giselle to host a dinner. It'll be a good opportunity for everyone to see where the wedding will take place, and it's sort of neutral ground."

"Not exactly neutral, Mom. She's on our side of the family, and she owns an oil company. Better we do it here, at Noah's house."

"Don't you worry about your Aunt Giselle, honey. If she's capable of bringing Saudis to the bargaining table, she can handle someone like Eli Kaplan. By the way, what does Eli do?"

"He owns Kaplan Manufacturing. They make batteries for electric cars."

CHAPTER 25

No sooner had Quincy ended the call then my phone rang again. "I hope you haven't eaten yet, Sissy. I'm on my way over the hill to take you and Yossi to dinner. Don't expect me anytime this century, though. Traffic is crawling."

"Yossi's working late tonight." I checked the clock. "Why did you choose to drive over the hill at this time? Five-thirty is smack-dab in the middle of rush hour, G."

A half hour later, Giselle stomped through the front door and tossed her purse on a chair. "You should've asked for more money in your divorce settlement. You could've bought a house in the city and saved us both from having to make that heinous drive over the Sepulveda Pass!"

"Are you blaming me for the traffic, or my ex-husband?"

She glared at me. "Your divorce attorney. I need some wine."

I opened a bottle of my favorite Ruffino Classico Chianti and poured us each drink in the red Moroccan tea glasses with the gold curlicues. "How did your meetings go today with the Saudis?"

Giselle removed the jacket of her black power suit and slumped back on the sofa. She tossed her straight red hair out of her face and took a long drink. "It went well. We managed to break the stalemate and broker a good deal. As soon as the Saudis left, I rushed right over here because I'm dying to find out what you and Lucy discovered today. Then we're going out to celebrate. Harold will be joining us. He wants to meet you."

I led her to the murder board in my sewing room, where I'd pinned up the reconstructed baby photo of Quincy and the two notes—one from Eliza Shiffer demanding more money and one from my mother asking him to stay out of my life.

Giselle tapped her finger on the note from my mother. "According to this, he opened a savings account in your name. Apparently, he handed it over when you turned twenty-five. How come you never mentioned that?"

"Because he disappeared two weeks before my birthday. We never had a chance to meet, so I never learned about the money."

"Your mother never mentioned it to you?"

"I don't know if she even remembered. She was never a friend of reality."

"Do you know what happened to it?"

"That part was surprisingly easy to look up.

Quinn had been actively depositing money for fifteen years. After his disappearance, the account became dormant. Three years later, B of A handed the account over to the state. One-point-eight million dollars has been sitting in trust for me all these years."

Giselle gasped. "That's a lot of money! But I'm not surprised. The Daddy I remember was always giving me presents. One year he had a real pony delivered to our front door. A little pinto with a white mane. It wasn't even my birthday or Christmas. He bought it for me because he said he loved my green Irish eyes."

"The more we learn about Quinn, the more complex he seems. On the one hand, he was a compulsive womanizer and a liar. But he had another side, which Jayda Constable pointed out. He cared about his children. At least he had a sense of responsibility toward us."

I took a moment to sip the room-temperature Chianti, enjoying the full-bodied fruity flavor. "And that got me thinking about his so-called gambling problem. He may have liked to take the occasional trip to Atlantic City, but I don't believe he was a compulsive gambler." I paused for effect. "I believe he used his so-called gambling debts as an excuse to hide what he was really doing with the money—providing for his illegitimate offspring."

"That does sound like something Daddy would do. What about Figgy? Did she open up to you today?"

"Big-time. She admitted to spying on everyone." When I saw the shocked look on my sister's face, I added, "She was only being protective of you and your mother."

I told Giselle what the housekeeper overheard in Quinn's phone conversations with my mother. A wave of sadness washed over me. "Apparently, he was looking forward to meeting me and Quincy."

"Oh, Sissy. I'm so sorry."

"Figgy also witnessed your grandmother snooping through Quinn's office more than once. When Detective Rohrbacher returned the key ring from the abandoned Caddy, Figgy said your grandmother was finally able to open a locked drawer in Quinn's desk. That's where she must've gotten her hands on his private papers and photos."

"Okay, now we know how those papers got on the back of the quilt, but so what?"

"At the very least, we now have a clearer picture of how complex a person our father was. Unfortunately"—I chose my next words carefully—"Quinn's behavior could've provided anyone in your family with a motive for murder. Including your housekeeper."

She waved away my comment. "Just because it's possible doesn't mean it happened that way. You don't seriously think any of them could've killed Daddy, do you?"

"According to Figgy, after Quinn left the house on the day he disappeared, your mother locked herself in her bedroom and your grandmother hung around to look after her. But your grandfather could've easily arranged a hit. That would explain why Chief Nelson shut down the investigation."

"I'm beginning to think we'll never find out since both of them are long dead. Face it, Sissy. We're down to one lead. We'll find out this week if Wolf is our half brother. Jayda said Daddy liked to spend time with his son. We know Wolf remembers Daddy because he said so. I think he knows more than he told us."

"He was only nine when Quinn disappeared, G. How much could a young boy possibly know?"

"Maybe he overheard Eliza's threats. Maybe he saw something."

"What if he refuses to cooperate?" I raised my eyebrows.

Giselle sighed. "Eliza's dead, after all. Nothing bad can happen to her now. Money is a strong motivator. I might have to allow him to sell one of Daddy's paintings in exchange for the truth."

We finished our wine and Giselle pulled out her cell phone. "We're late. I'll text Harold we're on our way."

I remembered my sister telling me Harold was the CFO of Eagan Oil and her study partner from their student days in business school. When Jerome Eagan died, Giselle hired Harold to help rescue the failing oil company. Together they guided it back from the brink of bankruptcy.

Fifteen minutes later we walked into Noro, an upscale sushi restaurant on Ventura Boulevard in Studio City. A bald man in a black suit and black-rimmed glasses stood just inside the door. As soon as he saw Giselle, his eyes lit up and he covered the distance between us in two strides.

Giselle put her hand on his shoulder. "Martha, this is Harold Zimmerman, my right-hand guy."

Zimmerman? Jewish?

"Pleasure to meet you, Martha." His hands were smooth, but his handshake was firm. "I've noticed a change in Gigi since she met you."

"You call her Gigi?"

He turned his head toward Giselle, revealing a strong jaw and pleasant profile. When he spoke, his face softened along with the tone of his voice. "It's an old nickname from Philly." He referred to their time at the Wharton School in Pennsylvania. "She only lets me call her that when we're among friends." He signaled the maître d'. "Our table awaits."

Harold guided Giselle through the dining room, gently cradling her elbow in his hand and leaning slightly toward her. His body language broadcast volumes, but my sister seemed oblivious. When we sat down, I quickly inspected his ring finger. Empty. I'd grill him first, of course. But unless he was gay or committed, I knew what I had to do.

Harold gave me a knowing look. "I know you're somewhat concerned with *kashrut,* so I figured you wouldn't have a problem here."

I knew it! Harold was a member of the tribe. The term *kashrut* referred to Jewish dietary laws and wasn't generally known by non-Jews. And he was right. Fish with both fins and scales were on the permitted list and on the menu of every sushi restaurant.

He immediately assumed the role of host and ordered warm sake for the table to start off the evening. My usually bossy sister seemed satisfied to sit back and let him take over the dinner order, too. Maybe the Chianti had calmed her down. Or maybe it was Harold; clearly a good sign.

We spent the rest of the evening sampling rice balls covered in raw yellowtail and tuna. Harold expertly picked up a piece of salmon roll with his chopsticks, dipped it in a slurry of soy sauce and wasabi, and popped the whole thing in his mouth. I liked the fact he wasn't a dainty eater.

At one point Giselle asked, "What kind of food does Quincy want at the wedding? Does it have to be kosher?"

I cleared my throat. "Um, we're not exactly sure about anything at this point. It seems that Noah's father, Eli, booked the Hillcrest Country Club."

Giselle tossed her chopsticks on the table. "And just what is wrong with my place?"

"I gather the only thing wrong with it is that Eli isn't in control. Plus, he wants a huge production with at least three hundred of his closest friends."

"But didn't the kids say they wanted a small, intimate affair?"

"As far as I know, they still do."

"Well, if they change their minds, I can expand

the guest list. We can easily accommodate five hundred people."

"I'm afraid that's not the only problem, G. Noah and his father are no longer speaking."

"Problem solved." She brushed her hands together. "I'll just go ahead with my plans and the heck with Eli."

"We can't just write him off! We need to make things right between Noah and his family."

"What's the father's name again?" Harold asked.

"Eli. Eli Kaplan."

"I'm also a member of Hillcrest. Maybe I know him. What does he do?"

"Manufactures batteries for electric cars."

Harold's eyes widened. "*That* putz? He's brought more lawsuits against the oil industry than any other alternative-energy wonk. He even filed a suit against Eagan Oil over alleged pollution."

Giselle frowned. "Really? How come I never heard about this?"

Harold covered her hand with his. "Because it was a minor annoyance that legal took care of. I'm the one who sweats the small stuff, remember? You have enough on your plate."

Great. Now I had to deal with bad blood between the elder Kaplan and my sister. Could this wedding get any more complicated? "What happened?"

"It was thrown out of court, like most of his other lawsuits."

"So, if he loses all the time, why does he do it?"

"Because he can. The irony is, his battery yard has been cited multiple times for polluting the environment with heavy metals."

"So, his objections to having the wedding at the Eagan estate have more to do with his failed lawsuit?"

He dipped his head in the affirmative. "That and the fact we're competing energy providers."

When the waiter brought the bill to Harold, Giselle headed for the ladies' room.

As soon as she was out of earshot I said, "I notice you don't wear a ring. Are you married?"

He briefly shook his head. "Never found the right one."

"So, what do you think of my sister?"

"Huh?"

"You and Giselle."

He reddened and briefly looked away. "Gigi and I've been friends forever. That's all."

"Are you kidding me?" I rested my hand on his arm. "I can see right through you."

"Wow. You may not look like sisters, but you have a lot in common. You don't hold back, do you?"

"I'm a little more subtle when I have to be. Have you ever told her how you feel?"

"Don't say anything to her. When Ryan died, Gigi said she could never love anyone again."

"I'm pretty sure she's over that by now. If I were you, I wouldn't take the chance that another Ryan might come along and sweep her away."

Harold stared at me. "Do you really think . . ."

Just then Giselle came back to the table. "What did I miss?"

I winked at Harold. "Nothing,"

She gathered her purse and turned to go. This time he placed his hand ever so lightly on the small of her back.

CHAPTER 26

The following morning was Quilty Tuesday, and Giselle arrived early, gliding through the front door in a white, pin-tucked linen shift. "I know just what you can do with the money Daddy left you, Sissy. Move into a better neighborhood. Did you know this area is crawling with homeless people? I just saw one panhandling on the Balboa Boulevard off-ramp."

I bowed deeply at the waist and swept my arm toward the living room. "Was the drive over the hill any better this morning, your highness?"

She ignored the jab. "I came early because I need to talk to you about something." She yawned. "And I need more coffee."

I poured her a cup of Italian roast and we moved to matching easy chairs in the living room. "I'm listening."

"Something happened last night. When I arrived back home, Harold was parked in the driveway, waiting for me."

So he took my advice!

She stopped and looked for my response, but I kept my expression neutral. "Go on."

"As soon as I parked my car, he got out of his and said we needed to have a serious talk. He looked really worried. Naturally, I thought something was wrong with the business, so I went over to where he was standing and asked, 'Is everything okay?'"

"And?"

"And he kissed me." She took a gulp of coffee and stared at me over the rim of her cup.

"And?" I smiled at the thought of Harold finally releasing all those years of unrequited love.

"And he spent the night." She grinned and raised an eyebrow. "I guess it's true what I've heard about Jewish men. We hardly slept."

I wagged my head and sighed. I guessed if Jews had to suffer being stereotyped, that wasn't such a bad one. "I'm happy for you both."

"You know, Sissy, I always wondered why Harold never got married. I mean, he had girlfriends, but none of them ever stuck. I began to suspect he might be a closet gay. But when I asked him about it last night, he said he could never get serious with anyone because he'd been in love with me ever since our days at Wharton."

"I'm surprised you never picked up on that, because it was glaringly obvious to me last night how he felt."

"Looking back, I think I did and I didn't. He's been my best friend since college, and more a partner than employee. But if I'm honest, I have to admit I've always felt a sexy vibe with him. He's such a hunk, don't you think?"

"But you never acted on those 'sexy vibes'?"

She shook her head. "Nope. Dumb, huh?"

"I'm sure last night changed everything."

"That's what I wanted to talk to you about. Being with Harold feels right. You know? And, boy, is he great in the sack." She took another slug of caffeine. "Here's the thing, though. He wants to get married, and right away! He even talked about starting a family. I'm only forty-four. He says, with the help of modern medicine, there's still a chance we could have a baby, but we'd need to get started soon."

"Marriage? A baby? Is that what *you* want?"

She shrugged. "I know it's sudden, but I like the idea of being married to Harold. I just don't know if I want to start over again with another child. I already have a son who will graduate from Harvard Law in another year."

Boom! goes the H-bomb again.

"Listen, G, I don't know if you're asking for my advice, but I'm going to give it to you anyway. Harold has had a lot of years to think about how he feels and what he wants. But you need to take some time to figure out what *you* want. If you want to get married, fine. But that doesn't mean you have to start a family if you don't want to."

"I'm not a kid, Sissy. I know all that. But what if I do want to have a baby with him?"

"Then I'll be right there holding your head as you puke in the toilet with morning sickness."

We heard the front door closing and a moment later Lucy sat in her usual place on the cream-colored sofa. "Giselle has morning sickness?"

"We were talking about Quincy," I lied. "You've had five boys. You know what the first trimester is like."

A minute later, Jazz led an excited Zsa Zsa into the house. "*Bonjour.* We had a little tinkle on the lawn just now." He bent over, unhooked the pink leash from her pink collar, and straightened the rhinestone barrette in her topknot. "Daddy loves his little girl," he sang.

The Maltese immediately trotted off in her pink pinafore in search of Bumper.

"You know she's just a dog, right?" Giselle said.

Jazz adjusted the rolled-up cuffs on his pink shirt and sniffed. "Maybe she's just a dog to you, but she's my child. You should find yourself something to love. It might improve your attitude."

Giselle and I exchanged a quick glance and she held up her hand. "Don't be offended, Jazz. I think Zsa Zsa is darling. I just tend to blurt things out sometimes. You'll get used to me."

He raised an eyebrow. "Still waiting for that to happen."

He thrust a white paper bag smelling of onions and garlic in my hands. "My turn to bring the snack. I'm not doing sugar this week."

The bag was still warm to the touch from the

freshly baked bagels inside. He also gave me a smaller sack with a pint of whipped cream cheese.

We settled in the living room with our plates of food. Lucy sat in her usual spot on one end of the sofa and Jazz on the other end. She handed me a small sheaf of papers. "I printed these out from the computer. They're directions for how to file a claim with the state controller's office, along with an official form."

Jazz looked confused. "What's that for?"

I brought him up to date on the notes and photo we reconstructed on Sunday. He fanned his face with his hand. "One-point-eight million? *Quelle surprise!* Just think. With that kind of cash, we could open a quilt store."

Giselle frowned. "She'd be better off investing in real estate over the hill, a beach condo in Santa Monica, for instance." She opened her tote bag and dumped the limp quilt top and fabric hexagons on the coffee table. "I brought these back like you asked."

"And I stopped by the quilt store for these." Lucy reached in her tote bag and pulled out ten packages of precut two-inch white paper hexagons. "I bought a thousand. I figured that would be enough to replace the ones we removed from the quilt. If not, we can always get more."

"I don't think that'll be enough." Giselle lifted a fabric flower. "Aren't there more than eighty of these in the quilt?"

"We don't have to replace all of them, hon." Lucy

held up the unfinished top. "We only need to put paper in the outside edges to stabilize them for stitching. The hexes in the middle don't need to be reinforced. They're already sewn together. The same goes for the flower you're holding. Only the outside edges need paper hexes."

I tore open one of the small plastic packages and spilled the contents on the table—one hundred pieces of die-cut paper templates. "You're about to get your first lesson in quilting, G." I took a silver thimble from my sewing kit and placed it on the middle finger of my sister's right hand. Then I cut an eighteen-inch length of white thread, licked the end, and showed her how to thread a needle and make a knot on the other end.

"We're going to be using basting stitches, which means they can be bigger and don't have to be neat because they're only temporary. Just like the stitches we removed when we took out the original hexagons." I taught her how to push the needle through both the fabric and the paper underneath then bring it all the way up again.

"This thimble feels awkward. Do I really have to use it?" Giselle twisted the metal cap on top of her finger.

"Absolutely. Otherwise, the pointed top of the needle will poke right into your bare finger when you push it through the fabric. I know it feels funny at first, but I promise you'll get used to it. Using a thimble is an essential skill for every person who sews."

I coaxed and encouraged my sister for the next

ten minutes. After sewing her first hexagon, she was able to load the needle with two or three stitches before pulling the thread through the fabric.

"You're doing great, G."

Satisfied she had the basics down, I grabbed the top half of a garlic bagel and smeared it with cream cheese.

Lucy worked on reinforcing the edges of the quilt top, and Jazz stitched hexagons into a pink flower. "Something about this color speaks to me today."

I closed my eyes and enjoyed the dense, rubbery texture of my bagel. "Something about this food speaks to me."

Around noon Giselle's cell phone chirped. "It's a text to call the lab! Wolf's DNA results are in."

"That was fast."

"I paid them a hefty bonus to make this their top priority."

By the time I hurried over to Giselle's chair, her phone was already on speaker and ringing the lab. "This is Giselle Cole returning Dr. Chowdhury's text."

A moment later a man with a Hindi accent spoke. "Mrs. Cole?"

"Yes. You have the DNA results?"

"Quite so. I myself stayed over the weekend to perform the test. As a matter of fact, I ran it twice just to be absolutely certain. We take pride in being one hundred percent accurate at all times."

I looked at Giselle and made a rolling gesture

with my hand, trying to hurry them along. This was the breakthrough we'd been waiting for.

"And what did you find, Doctor?"

"The sample of the male DNA you gave me is not a relation of yours."

No! How can that be?

Giselle's face fell. "Are you sure?"

"Most definitely."

She looked at me and shook her head once. "Thank you for expediting the test, Dr. Chowdhury. I appreciate your thoroughness. Please FedEx a hard copy of the results to my office."

"The pleasure was all mine, Mrs. Cole. Cheers."

She flopped back in the chair. "I was positive Wolf was our brother."

"Tell me again." Jazz placed a blue flower with stiff edges in the "finished" pile and picked up a limp yellow flower. "Why were you so sure?"

I explained about the pencil drawings Quinn gave to all his mistresses. "We discovered one of Eliza Shiffer in the gallery office. And since Wolf seemed to be the right age, we assumed he was the brother Jayda Constable told us about."

Giselle tucked her cell phone back in her purse. "We were counting on it, because if Wolf was our brother, then Eliza could've been the killer. Plus, it would've been nice to connect with yet another sibling. Even if he does have dark purple hair. God knows how many more of us are out there."

"So, now what?" Lucy ended off a basting thread and picked up the next paper hex.

"For one," I said, "there's still Gabe Farkas. He said he'd search for Quinn Junior's birth records if Wolf's DNA test didn't pan out."

"That's right," said Giselle. "I'd forgotten all about that. We should call him and tell him to go ahead and contact Jayda Constable in New York. Maybe she can pinpoint the day in 1971 when she and Daddy first slept together."

"Why is that important?" asked Jazz.

"She said it was the same night that Quinn Junior was born in LA. Having that information would certainly make his search a lot easier."

"We also need to talk once more to Gabe's father, Captain Bela Farkas. I'm bothered by something Figgy told me yesterday. Don't get upset, G, but she didn't deny your grandfather could've arranged Quinn's death."

Giselle's shoulders slumped and she seemed to deflate. "I don't know . . . It's true Granddad was powerful. And he was used to getting his own way. You might even say he was a tyrant. But ordering a hit on Daddy? There was too much at stake. He'd lose everything if he were caught."

"Not if his friend Chief Nelson helped him cover up the crime. We know Nelson stopped the investigation into Quinn's disappearance. And he was in the perfect position to sanitize the missing-persons file. Plus, the sixty thousand Quinn carried when he disappeared in 1980 was an advance from Chief Nelson for a portrait Quinn was supposed to paint of Nelson's wife. I ask you, where does a cop get that kind of cash if he's not dirty?"

Jazz leaned forward. "What if the sixty thou came from Giselle's grandfather as a bribe to Nelson for looking the other way and shutting down the investigation?"

Lucy pushed her well-drawn eyebrows together. "That doesn't make sense. Nelson commissioned a painting of his wife *before* Quinn disappeared. If the money was a bribe for looking the other way, that means Nelson must've known ahead of time Quinn was going to die. And if that's the case, why would he hand Quinn all that money?"

Why, indeed? "Maybe Nelson was setting up an alibi in case the hit man was caught. Maybe the chief wanted it to look like he didn't know about Quinn's impending murder by paying the victim ahead of time for a job he knew he'd never live to fulfill."

"That theory seems pretty convoluted," said Giselle. "Nelson may have simply shut down the investigation to save Granddad the embarrassment of a scandal. Daddy's behavior was pretty awful."

"Maybe. Unfortunately, all the players in that little scenario are long gone. Now we may never know for sure."

CHAPTER 27

Crusher and I sat at a small table in Rafi's Middle Eastern restaurant, working our way through the Tuesday night special.

My giant fiancé tried to get comfortable on the small wooden chair as he speared a deep-fried falafel with the plastic fork. "Occam's razor, babe. The simplest explanation is usually the best. What you're describing is an elaborate conspiracy between an oil baron and a corrupt chief of police to commit a premeditated murder."

"I know, but that's our only solid lead right now."

"You still can't rule out jealousy as a motive. From the notes you pieced together, you know at least one of his women was pissed off enough to threaten him."

I pushed around my cucumber and tomato salad with my fork. "I know. And I thought we'd found her. But we were wrong. Eliza Shiffer may have been one of Quinn's women, but she wasn't the mother of his son or the author of those notes." I sighed. "The other thing is, Giselle and I were really hoping to find our brother."

"Maybe I can still help with that. But I'll need more to go on than just the birth year."

"Yeah. Gabe Farkas said the same thing. I called him this afternoon and told him about the DNA results. I reminded him there's a chance he could still find Quinn Junior, depending on Jayda Constable's memory. Gabe said I should contact her myself."

"Go for it."

"I tried this afternoon, but nobody answered the phone." I glanced at my watch. "It's too late to call New York tonight. But I'll call again first thing in the morning."

We finished our combo plates and started on our honey-drenched baklava and tea with *nana*, fresh mint.

"I spoke to Quincy this afternoon. She's trying to make peace between Noah and his parents. She's invited everyone to their place for Shabbat dinner Friday night."

"That's cool," he muttered through a mouthful of dessert.

"Maybe not." I told him about Eli Kaplan suing Eagan Oil. "The man is a jerk."

Crusher's blue eyes twinkled. "Don't worry. I spent time around the guy in the rabbi's office, remember? If he acts up, he won't be a problem for long. I've never met a bully I couldn't . . . you know."

"Crush?"

Jayda Constable picked up my call Wednesday morning at eleven New York time. I brought her up to date on what we'd learned, including the notes from Quinn Junior's mother. "We're trying to track down the woman who had Quinn's son. If we can find our half brother, we'll find her, too. And we need your help."

"How could I possibly—"

"You said the night the baby was born was the first time you slept with Quinn. Please try to remember when that was."

"It was ages ago, Martha, I can't remember the exact day."

"Would it help if we started with the time of year and work backward?"

"I can try." She paused for a moment. "Okay. I recall it was snowing outside. We rushed inside my apartment to get out of the cold. I poured us each a shot of whiskey to warm up. One thing led to another, and . . . well, you know."

"Okay, that's a good start. You said it was snowing. Was it around Christmas? New Year? How about holiday decorations? Do you remember window displays? Colored lights? Did you have a tree?"

"Oh God, I don't know.

"Do you remember where the two of you were before you went to your apartment?"

"Yes. We were at a gallery opening. I'd heard Quinn was in town. I knew all about him, of course. I'd seen his work and thought he was brilliant. So, I asked a friend to introduce us. It was instant attraction. For both of us."

Now we were getting somewhere. A gallery opening would appear in the arts section of the *New York Times*. "Do you remember which gallery or who the artist was?"

"Some funky little place in Soho that's no longer there. I have no idea who the artist was."

"Do you at least remember if he was a painter, sculptor, photographer?"

"Sorry. I only remember Quinn's green eyes, red hair, and sexy smile."

Darn! This was New York City, with countless art galleries and where winter could last for six months. I needed more details before sending Crusher to the archives of the *Times*.

"You took him back to your apartment that same night?"

"Almost right away. We both knew what we wanted."

"How far did you have to go? Did you walk, take a cab?"

"Since the show was only a couple of blocks from my apartment on Watts Street, we walked."

"You told Giselle and me this happened in 1971. Why are you so certain?"

"Because that's the year I left home and moved to New York. January. I'd only been there around a month before I met Quinn."

My pulse began to quicken with each new detail. "You're doing great, Jayda. That narrows it down to, what? February? March?"

"Well, I know it was before April because my birthday's in April. He was back in LA by then, but he sent me flowers."

"So, can we say for sure that you first slept with Quinn in February or March of 1971 on the opening night of an art show in Soho a couple of blocks from your place on Watts Street?"

"Yes. That sounds about right."

Bingo! "Okay, this helps a lot. If you remember anything else more specific—even if it's a tiny thing— will you call me?"

"Of course. I want to know as much as you do what happened to Quinn. I was the one who bugged that policewoman and insisted something bad had happened. Remember?"

"I remember. To be fair, Detective Gomez couldn't tell you more because the chief of police shut down her investigation."

"Bastard! I suspected something like that was going on. Only I couldn't prove it. Do you know why?"

"Chief Nelson and Giselle's grandfather Jerome Eagan were friends. Giselle believes her grandfather merely wanted to avoid public scandal over Quinn's behavior. The housekeeper, however, believes Eagan himself could have been responsible for Quinn's death. In either case, Nelson quashed the investigation."

"So, you're telling me you have two suspects? Either the mother of Quinn's son or Quinn's father-in-law?"

I sighed. "Yeah. The first suspect we still have to find, the second one is dead."

Just as the call ended, Crusher emerged from the bedroom and clomped across the hardwood floor in his leathers and biker boots. I told him what I'd learned from Jayda.

"Great work, babe." He grabbed his ATF badge from the hall table and hung it around his neck. "I'm on my way downtown. I'll see what I can find online in the *New York Times* archives and run it through the birth records."

He strapped on his helmet over the blue bandana covering his head and disappeared through the front doorway. A minute later the engine of his Harley fired up and roared out of the driveway.

Time for another conversation with Captain Bela Farkas in Green Valley, Arizona. He answered on the third ring.

"I know you want to avoid talking over the phone about certain sensitive subjects," I said, "but I'd like to bring you up to date on what Giselle and I have discovered and ask you a couple more questions without having to travel to Tucson."

There was a short silence. "I'm driving to LA as we speak to visit Gabe and my grandchildren. How about we talk when I get there?"

"Captain, you seriously think someone's listening in? I mean, who else would be interested after all this time?"

"Call me Bela. Let's just say I'm happy to drive five hundred miles to buy a gorgeous woman a drink."

I laughed. "Should I bring my fiancé along for protection?"

"Maybe you'd better." I could hear the smile in his voice. "See you this evening."

I spent the rest of the morning basting the new paper hexagons back onto Giselle's quilt. I kept wondering why Giselle's grandmother went to all the trouble of cutting up and incorporating Quinn's private papers and photos into a quilt. Why did she want to preserve proof of his indiscretions in this way? Was it to hide the information from her husband in a place she knew he'd never look? And what currency did she gain by doing that? The power to expose her husband as a killer? The power to make Quinn behave if he ever showed up again?

Crusher arrived home at six and gave me a long kiss. "I have good news and bad news."

"Okay. Give me the good news first."

"New York had hundreds of art galleries active in 1971. But I was able to narrow it down to fifteen in the general area of Watts Street in Soho."

"Wow! That's great. What's the bad news?"

"They all had openings during the months of February and March of that year. Some of them had two openings, one each month. Based on Jayda's comment that the show was at a 'funky little place,' I eliminated six well-established galleries. That still left nine, with fourteen possible dates."

"Well, fourteen is a lot better than three hundred sixty-five. Did you look up those dates on the birth register?"

"Yeah." He reached inside his jacket and pulled out a thick sheaf of papers. "Here's a printout of all the baby boys born in LA on those dates in 1971 and also on the days after. We know the mother of Quinn's son was in labor that night, but we don't know whether the boy was born before or after midnight."

"Good thinking!" I took the stack of papers and my mouth fell open. There were hundreds of names. "How in the world are we ever going to find him in this crowd? Wait." I remembered a detail Jayda told Giselle and me on our first visit. "Do you remember I once told you Jayda said Quinn didn't want the boy to have his name? He probably isn't even mentioned on the birth certificate as the father. Maybe we could eliminate all the records with the father's name listed."

"Already thought of that. What you have in your hands is a list of all the boys born in LA County on twenty-eight specific dates without a father's name. If you want to narrow the field even more, you need to come up with some other search parameter. For instance, do you have an idea of where the woman might've lived? I could go back and look at hospitals with maternity wards in that area."

"That's an interesting thought. Quinn's other LA girlfriends seemed to live in or near Beverly Hills. Maybe she did, too."

"Okay. Tomorrow I'll sort for boys born in hospitals in the West LA area."

After dinner, we'd just settled down for *Jeopardy!* when the phone rang. "Are you ready for that drink?"

"Captain Farkas! I see you arrived safe and sound."

"It's Bela, remember? I rolled into LA this afternoon. Had a nice dinner with the kids and wouldn't mind a beer right about now. Where can I meet you?"

"Depends on where you're calling from. You've driven all day. I wouldn't want to make you drive more than necessary this evening."

"Gabe lives in Culver City. He tells me you live in the Valley. How about someplace in between, like Westwood?"

After reassuring Crusher I'd be perfectly safe by myself, I left him throwing answers at Alex Trebek, and headed for the 405 south. Thirty minutes later I walked into the dimly lit Czardas Hungarian Restaurant near UCLA. Classical music spread a blanket of calm over the diners, some of whom spoke in foreign languages. This definitely wasn't a student hangout, judging by the linen tablecloths and leather-bound menus.

I spotted the white-haired Bela Farkas in the bar

and walked over to the small round table where a half-full glass of beer sat on a paper coaster. He stood as soon as he saw me and grinned. When Giselle and I had visited him in Arizona, he'd been wearing shorts. Now he sported freshly ironed gray Dockers and a white short-sleeved shirt. He gestured toward his glass and spoke in his gravelly voice. "Thought I'd get a head start while I waited for you. What'll you have?" He turned and signaled the barmaid.

"Just some Perrier. With lemon, please."

For the next ten minutes he listened quietly while I told him everything Giselle and I had pieced together. "My first question concerns the sixty-thousand-dollar advance Chief Nelson paid Quinn to paint a portrait of his wife. We have to assume that once the commission was filled, Nelson would've had to pay Quinn another sixty thousand dollars. In 1980 that was a lot of cash. How does a cop get hold of that kind of money?"

CHAPTER 28

Captain Bela Farkas pulled on his glass of beer then dragged the paper napkin across the foam on his upper lip. "You're right on one account. Even the Beverly Hills chief of police didn't make that kind of money in 1980. But his wife was a Garfield. Old LA money. She had plenty of dough to hire a famous artist."

"So you're saying the money Nelson gave Quinn for his wife's portrait wasn't dirty?"

Farkas nodded. "The money may have been clean, but shutting down the investigation and sanitizing the file wasn't."

"How did Nelson and Eagan know each other?"

"The wife's great-grandfather Garfield was one of the founding members of the Jonathan Club. Jerome Eagan was also a member, which explains their connection."

There it was, the 1980s version of the billionaire boys club, where being a member apparently put you above the law.

"We're talking about covering up a murder, here. Not fixing a parking ticket. Why didn't you report him?"

Farkas smiled at me and looked deep into my eyes until I looked away. "Nelson was as well connected as they came. There was no hope in hell of getting anyone to take him on. That's why I hung onto my notes for thirty-two years. I hoped someone would come along and expose the truth someday. It looks like that someone is you and that someday is now." He lifted his glass in a salute and drained it. Then he signaled the barmaid and ordered another beer. He looked at me and wiggled his eyebrows. "How about joining me this round?"

I shook my head. "I'm good. What can you tell me about the missing notes from the file?"

"About a week after we got the forensics back from the Cadillac, I reviewed what we had in the file. At the end of the day, I went straight to the chief and told him your father wasn't just missing. I was convinced we were now investigating a high-profile homicide, and, based on the evidence gathered, we needed to look more closely at the family."

"What was that evidence?"

"Detective Gomez had a hard-on for this case. She was adamant Quinn's wife was involved and wanted a chance to prove it."

I shifted in my seat. What if Gomez was right? How could I tell Giselle her mother might have been a killer? If only we could question Gomez and find out why she'd come to that conclusion.

Farkas took a healthy slug from the frosty glass of beer. "Nelson told me to leave the file on his desk. The next morning, he shut down the investigation. When I looked for the file, it was gone. Days later it turned up with several pages missing."

"Why do you think he removed certain information, but not all of it?" I lifted my glass of Perrier and took a sip.

"Nelson couldn't get away with cleaning out the whole file, so he left just the stuff about Quinn's sexual infidelities that suggested he'd either run off with another woman or was killed by a jealous lover. Since the Eagan family all had alibis for the day he disappeared—including the wife—none of them could be considered suspects in that scenario."

"How convenient."

"Here's the interesting part. The notes Nelson removed from the file suggested an alternative motive for murder. Rohrbacher was looking into large amounts of unexplained missing cash and rumors of gambling debts. That line of questioning might have led us back to the family. Eagan was a notorious control freak. Maybe he just got tired of an uncontrollable son-in-law."

"Do you think Eagan hired someone to murder Quinn?"

"I always thought it was possible, but, without a body, a murder weapon, or a witness, there was no way to know."

I thanked Captain Farkas for the drink and the information. He paid the bill and walked me out to my car. He opened the driver's door and leaned on the frame while I slid behind the wheel. His voice sounded like a coffee grinder at low speed. "You'd like it in Green Valley. I could teach you how to fish."

I smiled at the handsome older man. "As tempting as that sounds, Captain, I'm going to have to say no. I'm really quite happy with my present situation."

"My loss. Drive safe." He closed the car door and, with the flat of his hand, slapped the roof twice in a snappy farewell.

Thursday morning at eight, I phoned Giselle. Her sleepy voice told me she was still in bed. "Did I wake you?"

"We had another late night." She yawned. "Harold says he's making up for lost time."

A man's voice murmured in the background, and Giselle giggled.

I told her about my conversation with Jayda Constable and Crusher's search in the archives of the *New York Times* and the LA County birth records.

"That's great work, Sissy. Really clever of you."

"That's not all." I brought her up to date on my conversation with Captain Bela Farkas last night. "The thing is, G, Detective Meredith Gomez was going after your mother. Apparently, Gomez found something incriminating.

"No! I don't buy it. Mother was way too passive."

"Then why was Detective Gomez certain she was a viable suspect?"

"Ask her!"

I sighed. "You know we can't. Unless . . ."

"Unless what?"

"Unless we can find a way to question her in the morning when she might be more lucid."

"How do you propose to do that? Detective Gabe Farkas saw her and said she's too far gone. Her son, Carlos, refused to give us access. And we can't talk our way in, because Miss Leathy already knows who we are."

"We'll just have to get creative. Jazz and Lucy will help."

At ten-thirty, the four of us sat in my living room with fresh coffee and chocolate éclairs from Benesh Bakery, thanks to Giselle.

Lucy rubbed her hands together. "I've got an idea. One of Ray's customers is Acme Housekeeping. Ray maintains their fleet of vans. Maybe we could 'borrow' one of their vehicles and pose as cleaners." She tickled the air with finger quotes. "I brought his lunch to the shop yesterday, and I know he's working on two of them as we speak."

"We can't just show up out of the blue." Jazz offered Zsa Zsa a tiny drop of vanilla custard on the tip of his finger. "What makes you think they'd even let us inside the place?"

I typed on my laptop and immediately found what I was looking for. "Here it is. Thanks for the Memories Assisted Living is owned by the Hamilton

Group. Just a minute while I follow the link." Google took me straight to the corporate URL. "Okay. Hamilton operates memory care facilities all over the country." I went deeper into their web page. "The Western regional director is a Matthew Auerbach. We could say we're negotiating a contract with Auerbach and he sent us to do a trial cleaning."

Giselle made a face. "Won't work. Miss Leathy will recognize us right away."

"But she doesn't know Lucy and Jazz. Maybe we can figure out a way of disguising ourselves."

"Sounds like a plan," said Lucy. "Ray should be finished with the vans by tomorrow morning."

"I hate to bring this up, but we need to dress for the part." Jazz pointed to Giselle. "Especially you and your Alexander McQueen outfits. Nobody would believe you were a cleaner! We can't go waltzing in looking like ourselves. Well, maybe Martha could."

I could be so insulted, especially when nobody else contradicted him. "There's a uniform store not too far from here in a strip mall on Ventura Boulevard and Newcastle. We could go there now and buy matching outfits."

An hour later we left the store, each holding a sack with a blue jumpsuit. We had fake names embroidered in white thread on the left side of the chest of each. Jazz's said *Rock* and Lucy's read *Mildred.* Giselle spied a wig shop two doors away and insisted on buying us all fake hair to deepen our disguises. "Just in case we run into Miss Leathy."

I adjusted the "Dolly Parton," a blond bouffant teased into a frothy helmet. "How do I look?"

Jazz studied me for a nanosecond. "You look desperate. It's perfect."

Lucy selected a shoulder-length brown bob, Giselle chose a jet-black pixie, and Jazz opted for a bushy brown white-boy Afro. We agreed to meet the next morning at Lucy's house at six-thirty. We needed to allow extra time to join the rush-hour commute if we wanted to arrive in Burbank by eight a.m.

Crusher's Harley pulled into the driveway that evening. As soon as he came in the house, he handed me a printout of names many times smaller than the one the day before. "I think you're going to like what I found. There are only forty-eight names on this list."

"Thanks, Yossi. I'll look at this later." I set the printout on the apricot-colored marble countertop in the kitchen and told him about our plans to disguise ourselves and pay Detective Gomez a visit in the morning. I put on the blond wig and did a little pirouette. "What do you think?"

He smiled and shook his head. "Babe. Lay a little 'Jolene' on me."

CHAPTER 29

Crap! I rolled over and hit the snooze button on the alarm clock at five-thirty Friday morning. Ten minutes later the alarm pierced the air again. Crusher nudged me gently in the back.

"All right," I mumbled, "I'm going." I shut off the insistent ringing and rolled out of bed.

I zipped up the front of the blue jumpsuit I'd bought at the uniform store the day before. The pant legs were much too long, so I rolled up the hems several times. Finally, I pinned my gray curls on top of my head, put on a stretchy stocking cap, and pulled the Dolly Parton wig into place.

Staring back at me from the mirror was a zaftig, slightly bewildered-looking cleaner with the name *LaWanda* embroidered in white on the left side of her ample chest. If we ran into Miss Leathy, I doubted she would recognize me, at least not at first.

As I walked toward the kitchen to make some coffee, the cuffs on my pants slowly began to unfold.

So, I detoured into my sewing room, found a stapler, and tacked the cuffs together to keep them from falling back down.

Fifteen minutes later, hot travel mug in hand, I drove to Lucy's house on the south side of Ventura Boulevard. Even at six-twenty in the morning, traffic had started to accumulate on the streets feeding the 101 Freeway.

Lucy greeted me at the door wearing her "Mildred" overalls, long brown wig, and dark-rimmed reading glasses. She carried a clipboard holding a tablet of yellow lined paper. "Well?" She grinned. "Do I look official?"

"Not only official, but elegant. Too elegant for a cleaner." Jazz appeared behind me. "Kick off those kitten heels and put on some sneakers."

I turned to look at "Rock" and burst into laughter. Not only did he wear his curly brown wig, he'd pasted on a fake mustache that resembled a caterpillar in a long fur coat.

"What's wrong?" He frowned.

"Nothing. It's just that you look like a time traveler from the nineteen seventies."

"I am, in a manner of speaking." He examined his fingernails. "Those were my glory days."

Zsa Zsa tugged on the end of a blue leash that matched her tiny blue jumpsuit. A triangular piece of the same fabric was tied in a knot on top of her head like Rosie the Riveter.

"You can't bring her inside the facility," I said. "Who brings a dog to work?"

He picked up the little Maltese and showed me the *ZZ* he'd embroidered on the chest of her jumpsuit. "But she was counting on joining us. Look how excited she is."

Zsa Zsa's tail wagged furiously.

"She's really good with old people. Couldn't we say she's a therapy dog our company provides at no extra charge?"

"I'm sorry, Jazz. But we want to get in and out as fast as we can. She'll have to stay in the car."

"Fine." He pouted as he untied the miniature do-rag on her head.

Last to arrive was Giselle in overalls that said *Jane*.

"Well, I must say, the drive to the Valley at this time in the morning wasn't as awful as it usually is." She turned to Lucy. "Your house was easy to find. By the way, this is a much nicer neighborhood than Martha's. What does your husband do?"

Lucy opened and closed her mouth like a goldfish. Finally she said, "He fixes cars."

"That explains everything. Mechanics charge a fortune." She smiled brightly. "I guess you could say we're both in the oil business. Are we ready?"

Her black pixie wig made her look perky, but Jazz didn't seem satisfied. "You look like you're wearing a wig. Your red eyebrows are a dead giveaway." He turned to Lucy. "Do you have a dark eyebrow pencil?"

"No, but maybe I have something else that will work." She disappeared into the house and returned wearing sneakers and carrying a roller of black eyelash mascara. Jazz brushed the dark liquid into Giselle's eyebrows and stepped back to look at his handiwork. "Okay," he said. "Better."

A white van with ACME HOUSEKEEPING painted in red letters sat in Lucy's driveway. Below the words, a picture of a roadrunner winked at us with the motto SPEEDY SERVICE.

Lucy held up the key and said, "Shall we?"

We backed out of the driveway and headed toward the 101.

I asked, "How did you manage to get Ray to agree to letting you borrow the van?"

"I think he had a come-to-Jesus moment with his recent health scare, because he's been much more laid back about everything. I explained that we had a vitally important mission and needed the van just for the morning. When I promised that we wouldn't be in physical danger, he brought the van back to the house last night and handed over the keys."

At five to eight, we parked the vehicle on Bob Hope Drive and opened the rear doors. Jazz, Giselle, and I grabbed mops, buckets, cleaning rags, and a jug of purple soap heavily scented with lavender.

Giselle looked at me sideways. "You can't seriously expect me to mop and clean. I've always had staff to do the menial work. Besides"—she held up her soft hands—"it'll ruin my manicure. I think I should pretend to be the boss. I am, after all, a real CEO."

"Too risky, G. What if Miss Leathy recognizes your voice?" I rummaged through the supplies in the back of the van until I found a stash of stiff blue rubber gloves and handed two to Giselle. "Leave your good jewelry in the car and put these on." I passed another set of gloves to Jazz and, after removing my own diamond ring, shoved my hands into a pair. "If we all use these, we won't leave fingerprints. Just in case."

"What about me?" Lucy indicated her bare hands.

"Three pair was all I could find. Just don't touch anything. Let Jazz open the doors for you."

Lucy hugged the clipboard to her chest, tilted her chin toward the entrance, and took a deep breath. "Let's go." We all followed her to the front door of Thanks for The Memories Assisted Living, loaded with the tools of the trade.

The same blowsy blonde receptionist we'd encountered on our first visit buzzed us through the front door. Lucy stepped closer to the desk. "We're from Acme Housekeeping."

"Acme? Never heard of you."

Lucy stood taller. "Your corporate office hired us to do a trial cleaning today."

The blonde looked at her computer screen and frowned. "I don't see you on the schedule. Miss Leathy never said anything to me about any trial cleaning. I can't let you inside without her say-so, and she won't be here for another hour. You'll have to come back then."

Lucy frowned. "I understand you have a job to do, but so do we. And Corporate would not be pleased if you kept us waiting."

"No way! Miss Leathy would fire me on the spot."

Jazz stepped in front of Lucy and leaned toward the blonde. He spread a flirty smile across his face. "Believe me, I know how it can be. I used to work for someone like that."

The receptionist relaxed her posture, gave him the once-over and a coy smile.

If she only knew.

Jazz leaned even closer. "If you let us in, we'll make sure they know about your helpfulness."

"That's right, hon." Lucy clicked the top of her pen. "It's not your fault Miss Leathy failed to inform you we were coming. What is your name?" She prepared to write something on the yellow pad.

"Stella Price." The receptionist smiled again at Jazz and tucked a stray piece of yellow straw behind her ear. "And you can tell them I've never missed a day of work in ten years, not that anyone's noticed."

Lucy wrote on the clipboard again. "I'll do that. Now, if you don't mind?" She inclined her head toward the inner door.

Stella led us through, jangling a ring of keys in her hand. She stepped in front of Jazz, swung her hips straight to a closet marked MAINTENANCE, and unlocked the door. As she turned to go, she stopped and peered at my face. "You look familiar." She read the name on my chest. "LaWanda? Don't I know you from somewhere?"

Afraid she'd recognize my voice, I responded with what I hoped was a backwoods drawl. "Bless your heart. I have that kinda face. Folks is always askin' me that. But I ain't never met y'all."

Jazz stood behind the woman and rolled his eyes at me.

Stella raised her eyebrows. "Really? I'm almost never wrong." She shrugged. "Oh well, I might think of it later."

I smiled an apology and walked toward the maintenance closet, turning my face away.

Her voice gathered an air of authority. "Our patients already ate breakfast and some went back to their rooms. Try not to disturb them." She walked back to her desk.

An old woman with a vague expression on her face shuffled by.

Jazz lowered his voice and whispered in my ear, "That was slick, *LaWanda*."

I looked at my watch. "It's ten after eight. We have fifty minutes to find Gomez and talk to her before Leathy arrives."

He pointed down the hallway. "If we don't want to arouse suspicion, we should at least pretend we're cleaning." He filled our buckets halfway with water and added the lavender-scented cleaner he'd carried in from the van."

Giselle held her bucket and mop as if they were radioactive. "What do you expect me to do with this?"

I showed her how to wet the mop and squeeze out the excess water with the wringer on the side of the bucket. "If you see anyone looking at you, just start swishing it around the floor."

"Ewww." She made a face.

I rolled my eyes. "Think of mopping as a weird form of cardio."

Doors with nameplates lined the hallway on both sides. "These are the patients' rooms. Lucy and Jazz, you keep a lookout. Giselle and I will find Gomez. Come on."

Jazz removed yellow CAUTION WET FLOOR cones from the maintenance closet and blocked off the hallway. He began to mop while Lucy pulled out a metal tape measure and stretched it across the width of the corridor, recording measurements on a "report" we'd never submit.

Giselle and I carried our cleaning supplies down the hallway. She read the names on the right, I read the ones on the left. Meredith Gomez's room sat at the end on the left, immediately next to an emergency exit. I called to Lucy at the other end of the hallway and pointed to Gomez's door. She nodded in understanding and gave me a thumbs-up.

"This is it, G. Let's hope all this was worth it and her mind is sharper in the morning." I held my breath and knocked softly. Without waiting for an answer, I turned the knob and pushed the door open. "Cleaning service!"

Retired Detective Meredith Gomez looked up. "Do I know you?" She sat in a blue upholstered chair next to a window facing Bob Hope Drive. Her pink polyester pants matched a short-sleeved

T-shirt. A single braid of gray-streaked black hair hung over her shoulder and her hands rested quietly in her lap. Was it my imagination, or were her eyes a little brighter than the first time we saw her?

My sister quickly closed the door and approached. "My name is Giselle. We met thirty-two years ago. You investigated the disappearance of Jacob Quinn Maguire." She pointed to me. "This is my sister, Martha. We were hoping you could help us figure out what happened to our father."

Gomez frowned and narrowed her eyes, as if trying to retrieve a memory. "Quinn?"

"You remember him?" Giselle asked.

Gomez began to fidget with her fingers. "Where's Quinn?"

Yes! Gomez could remember something. Wasn't that exactly what a detective would ask about a missing person?

Then a chill ran up my spine. Those were also the exact words my mother spoke before she died. My poor mother had spent her whole life waiting for her lover to show up.

I squatted in front of the chair and gazed into the woman's eyes. I thought I detected a flicker of curiosity there. "That's what we'd like to find out, Detective Gomez. Do you remember your boss, Captain Bela Farkas? He said you were certain someone in Quinn's family was responsible for his death. Can you can tell us why?"

Gomez screwed up her face and blinked rapidly. I grabbed the woman's nervous hands and spoke softly. "I know it's hard, but please try to recall why you insisted Quinn's wife was his killer."

"Obstruction!" she spat out the word like a bad-tasting piece of meat.

Now we were getting somewhere. The anger of Gomez's response was proof she could still mentally connect with the long-ago investigation. Was she re-living what it felt like to be hot on the trail of a killer only to be thwarted by her superior officer?

"Martha!" Giselle's voice sliced through the air.

Why was she disturbing me? Didn't she hear how close Gomez was to telling us something? "Now's not the time to interrupt, G." I turned back to the woman in the chair. "What do you know about the Eagan family that Chief Nelson wanted to cover up? What do you think happened to Quinn? Who do you think killed him?"

"Look, dammit!" Giselle again.

I turned around. "What, for heaven's sake?" The color had drained from my sister's face and her left hand, still enclosed in a blue rubber glove, flew to her neck. She raised her right hand and pointed to the wall.

A small pencil drawing of a young and beautiful Meredith Gomez hung in a simple frame. I lifted it from the wall to get a closer look and my stomach plunged to my ankles. The signature in the lower right-hand corner read *J. Q. Maguire.* I turned the picture to the back and read out loud: "'For the love of my life. Your Quinn.'"

"I don't believe it!" Giselle gasped and stated the obvious. "Another one."

Thoughts tumbled around my head like colorful pieces in a kaleidoscope, rearranging all the facts we'd uncovered into new patterns. "Not only another one, G. I think we've just found *the* other one."

I took photos of the picture with my cell phone and shoved it toward Gomez. "You not only knew Quinn, you were one of his women, weren't you?"

Her mouth snapped shut and she crossed her arms. I touched her shoulder, but she jerked away and refused eye contact.

Suddenly the door to her room burst open. Stella stood with her hands on her hips. "I know where I've seen you before!"

CHAPTER 30

My heart pounded as Giselle and I moved closer to each other. Stella must've seen through our disguises.

The receptionist closed one eye and pointed at me. "Corbin Bowl. Tarzana. We're in the same league. I'm on the Rowdy Rollers team. Aren't you one of the Ball Crushers?" She crossed her arms in triumph.

I blew out a sigh of relief, because even though this woman had an eagle eye, she hadn't yet discovered our true identities. I deepened my drawl. "Bless your little heart. Not a day goes by that someone don't swear they know me. Like I said, I just have one of them common faces." My voice sounded hollow in my ears as the needle on my BS meter edged to the right.

Stella snapped her finger. "Fudge! I'm usually accurate at this. I never forget a face." She turned the doorknob and looked back at Giselle over her shoulder and frowned. "You know, you look familiar, too."

Giselle raised her eyebrows in mock surprise. "*Moi*? Zat would be, 'ow you say, impossible, *non*? Maybe you see me in France. 'Ave you ever been to Paree?"

I closed my eyes and shook my head once. Only Giselle would think a beautiful French woman from Paree would immigrate to America and become a maid.

Stella stuck a finger through her brittle yellow hair and scratched her scalp. "I'll keep working on where I know you from. I never forget a face."

As soon as she left, I grabbed my sister's hand. "We'd better hurry before she figures it out. Let's see what else we can find."

"Like what?"

"We'll know it when we see it."

Giselle began searching through the dresser. "There's nothing here but enough polyester to sabotage the fashion industry."

On the upper shelf of the closet I spotted a clear plastic container labeled PHOTOS stacked atop a piece of expensive-looking luggage. I couldn't reach the pictures, so I grabbed the handle of the brown leather suitcase and slid it toward me, being careful to balance the plastic box on top. I set both pieces on Gomez's bed.

Giselle rushed over. "Open it."

The loose photos inside chronicled the lifetime of Meredith Gomez, including images of her son, Carlos, from the time he was an infant. Then my heart stopped.

In one photo, holding the little boy's hand, was my father.

"Holy mother of God," said my Catholic sister. "Carlos Gomez, TV weatherman, is Quinn Junior?"

"Our long-lost brother." I snapped a picture of the photo with my cell phone.

"If Carlos is our brother"—Giselle snarled and pointed to the confused woman sitting in the blue chair—"that means *she* was the one who threatened Daddy with blackmail and demanded more money."

I replaced the photos in the shoe box and my gaze fell to the leather suitcase underneath. Embossed in gold were the initials *JQM*. Sometimes, only a Yiddish word could adequately express someone's shock and dismay. "*Gottenyu!*" I blurted out. Dear God.

Giselle peeked over my shoulder and quickly sipped in a breath. "This is Daddy's suitcase."

I attempted to snap open the heavy metal clasp, but it was locked.

"Let me try." Giselle removed one of the hairpins holding her wig, stuck it inside the keyhole, and wiggled it around. But the lock stayed shut.

I knelt in front of Gomez's chair again and softly held her hands. "Meredith, where is the key to your suitcase? We need to open it."

She pulled her hands out of mine and covered her face. "Go away."

I looked at my sister and sighed. "We'll just have to find it ourselves."

For the next five minutes, Giselle and I examined every little box and container in the room. We even opened the bottles and jars in the bathroom cabinet. But if Meredith Gomez still had the key to the suitcase, she wasn't about to give up its location—assuming she could even remember where it was.

Giselle threw her hands in the air. "Why don't we just take the darn thing and open it at home?"

"First of all, that's theft. Second, this suitcase is evidence. If we remove it, how can we prove it came from this room? I'm afraid we've gone as far as we can on our own. Time to call Detective Gabe Farkas and tell him we may have found the luggage Quinn carried on the last day of his life."

Her face froze with a new understanding. "That means . . ."

"Yeah," I said. "We most likely found our father's killer."

After I photographed the suitcase, my taller sister helped me replace it and the box of Gomez's photos on the top shelf of the closet. Then we gathered the cleaning supplies and left the woman sitting alone in her blue chair, humming to herself and gazing out the window at the cars passing by on Bob Hope Drive. We hurried down the hall and met Jazz and Lucy still standing guard near the maintenance closet. Jazz emptied our buckets in the sink, replaced the CAUTION WET FLOOR cones, and closed the closet door.

Lucy pressed the button next to the reception room door and waited for Stella to buzz open the lock so we could leave. When nothing happened for thirty seconds, she pressed the button again. "What's keeping her?" She looked through the little glass window on the door. "I can't believe this! Ray's going to be *sooo* mad."

I stretched on my tiptoes and saw Stella talking to two uniformed police and two men in suits. She pointed them toward the door and buzzed it open. I looked at Giselle. "We're busted."

I had just enough time to pull my cell phone out of my pocket and send a quick text before staring into the stern faces of a Burbank detective, two police officers, and *Could it be?* Noah Kaplan. At first, he didn't recognize me with the wig. Then his eyes widened in slow recognition and shock. He must've realized he was about to arrest his future mother-in-law. Again.

Kaplan grabbed my arm in a gentle but firm grip, pulled me aside, and whispered, "What are *you* doing here?" He read the name on my uniform. "LaWanda?"

"Please, Noah. I can explain everything."

"Do it fast!" he hissed, barely moving his lips.

"It's complicated."

He glanced nervously at the other detective. "Simplify."

"The quick answer is, Giselle and I just found our father's killer."

He regarded me for a split second. Then he said, "I hope you know you're in deep trouble. The receptionist finally reached her boss. The boss told her she'd been conned and ordered her to call the police."

I pulled my head back. "By the way, what are you doing here? This isn't even LAPD's jurisdiction."

He jerked his head toward the other detective. "I happened to be having coffee with my friend Mike when he got this call."

"What are the odds?" I said.

The Burbank detective, Mike, announced in a loud voice, "You're all under arrest for trespassing and attempted robbery. You have the right to remain silent . . ."

Giselle snapped off her blue gloves. "Why would I want to steal anything from a bunch of senile old people? Go ahead and search me."

"That's right." Jazz stepped toward one of the officers and raised his arms. "Go ahead and search me, too. The only thing I've done is mop their floor for free. Besides, you can't arrest me. Who will take care of my little girl? She's been waiting all alone in the van this whole time."

The detective gaped. "You left your kid in the car? I'm adding felony child endangerment to those charges." He spun Jazz around and cuffed his hands behind his back. Then he barked at one of the uniforms, "Go get that poor kid. NOW!"

"But . . ." Jazz sputtered.

The detective growled. "I'd exercise my right to keep silent if I were you."

Kaplan walked me back to join the others and squeezed my arm in a secret signal. "This may not be what it looks like, Mike. LaWanda here thinks they made a mistake and got the wrong address."

Bubbles of warmth tingled in my chest, and I regarded my future son-in-law with a new respect. Not only had he just lied for me, he'd manufactured a brilliant way out of our predicament. From now on, even if he reverted to acting like a weasel, he would be *my* weasel. I quickly queried my cell phone for nursing homes in the area. Almost instantly five of them popped up on my screen. I chose the nearest one. "Isn't this Providence Nursing Home on Buena Vista Street?"

"You must've taken the wrong off-ramp," the remaining cop declared. "The Buena Vista exit is a mile east of here."

"Dang!" Lucy threw up her hands. "That's the last time I use GPS."

A short time later the first cop walked back into the room. "There's no kid in the car. Just a little white dog in a blue costume." He made tiny circles with his finger in the air next to his temple.

Kaplan let go of my arm and walked over to the other detective. "Listen, dude, I don't know if it's worth bringing them in. I think this was just a stupid mistake on their part. I mean, look at them. Their combined IQ can't be over one hundred."

Mike, the detective, scanned our faces and narrowed his eyes and muttered out of the corner of his mouth. "You can say that again."

Giselle bristled. "Now, just a minute!"

I put a restraining hand on her arm and gave a quick shake of my head. "Keep quiet," I whispered. "Noah's got this."

"It's your call, of course," Kaplan continued," but I'd cut them loose. Save you some paperwork."

The detective barked. "Search 'em."

He scowled the whole time the uniforms patted us down. Thank God we'd left our jewelry in the van. When the officers were satisfied we weren't hiding stolen property, they stepped back. "Nothing here, Mike."

The detective was silent for a moment then signaled Stella to buzz open the reception room door. He removed the cuffs from Jazz and gave him a little shove. "Get out of here."

CHAPTER 31

Lucy raced the white Acme Housekeeping van back to Encino as fast as she dared, knuckles white on the steering wheel. She believed doing sixty miles per hour in a sixty-five zone was speeding. Jazz sat next to her in the passenger seat. I brought them up to date on everything we'd discovered.

"Holy moly!" he said. "Why did she kill your father?"

"Because," said Giselle, "he wouldn't leave my mother and marry her. When Meredith Gomez said the word 'obstruction,' she wasn't accusing Chief Nelson of shutting down her investigation. I think she meant Mother refused to give Daddy a divorce."

Jazz made a big deal out of rubbing his wrists. Lucy glanced over at him. "Did the cuffs hurt you, hon?"

"A little."

"What does it feel like to wear handcuffs?" asked Giselle.

Jazz sniffed. "This wasn't my first time."

She strained forward in her seat belt to get a better look. "You've been arrested before?"

"Not exactly." He cleared his throat. "To change the subject, we were darn lucky Noah showed up, Martha."

Giselle twisted her ring back onto her finger. "I'm going to make sure their wedding is spectacular."

My cell phone chirped and I read the message. "It's from Detective Gabe Farkas. He's meeting us at my house in an hour."

"Did you call him?" asked Lucy.

"I texted him right as the Burbank police came through the door. When they released us, I sent him an all-clear message."

My best friend glanced at the watch on her left wrist. "I wish I could be there. But my grandson's got a soccer game in about an hour."

"And Zsa Zsa and I have a business to run." Through the gap between the front seats, I watched Jazz remove the miniature blue jumpsuit from the sleepy Maltese and dress her in her work clothes: a ruffled red pinafore with white polka dots. As soon as he finished, she rotated once in his lap and lay down again to finish her nap.

"You've both been great," I said. "Giselle and I can handle this."

Lucy pulled the van into her driveway and turned

off the engine. "Swear you'll never tell Ray how close we came to being tossed in jail this morning!"

Jazz raised his hand. "I solemnly swear. And so does Zsa Zsa."

"Ditto," Giselle and I said together.

She followed me back to my house on the other side of Ventura Boulevard. We hurried inside, where I grabbed the birth records Yossi had printed out. I found the information I'd been hoping for, hidden on the fourth page. Teresa M. Gomez had given birth to baby boy Carlos Gomez on February 25, 1971, at Brotman Memorial in Culver City. Father unknown. I showed it to my sister. "No wonder I didn't notice it before. Meredith must be her middle name."

"Whatever her name is, she got away with murder all these years." She parked her fists on her hips. "What do you think they'll do to her?"

"She's too far gone to stand trial. But I'd sure like to ask her son, Carlos, a few questions. He was nine at the time Quinn disappeared."

We changed out of our wigs and costumes and put on normal clothes. Jeans for me, an Eileen Fisher linen dress for her. At twelve noon, the doorbell rang.

Gabe Farkas wheezed an asthmatic hello and lumbered into the house. "Do I want to know what you were doing this morning?"

"We found Quinn's killer!" I brought him up to speed on my interviews with Jayda Constable and Anna Figueroa—"Figgy." Then I led him into my sewing room and showed him the murder board with the threatening notes from Quinn's lover and the birth record from Brotman Memorial. "Meredith Gomez was another of Quinn's lovers, and the mother of Quinn Junior."

I gestured toward the few remaining reports from Quinn's missing-persons file. "She was in a perfect position to pull out anything that incriminated her from this folder."

"Was Chief Nelson in on it?" he asked.

"Here's what I think. Nobody in the police department knew she did it. The investigation was dropped because the Eagan family didn't want a scandal and Chief Nelson did them a favor. When Gomez heard the case was closed, I think she was the one who cleaned out the file."

The younger Farkas shook his head. "And my dad never suspected a thing. Wow." He studied my notes pinned to the white sheet. "This is all very impressive, Martha, but it doesn't prove that Detective Gomez killed your father."

"What about this?" I showed him the photos on my cell phone I'd taken that morning of the pencil drawing, the photo of Quinn and his son, Carlos, standing together, and the leather suitcase with Quinn's initials embossed in gold. "I think this is the piece of luggage taken from his Cadillac the day he disappeared."

Farkas narrowed his eyes. "Where'd you get these?"

When I told him, he gnawed on the corner of his

mouth. "How'd you manage . . . never mind. Sorry I asked. Did you open the suitcase?"

I shook my head. "Locked tight. I don't think it was empty, though. It felt a little heavy."

Farkas paused for a moment. "We're lucky. If you'd been law enforcement, only the drawing would be admissible as evidence since it was out in plain sight. Without a search warrant, anything else would be considered fruit of the poisonous tree—including the suitcase and photos, because they were hidden in the closet. But since you're not the law, I can get a warrant and seize the evidence based on a tip from a private citizen. Send those photos to my phone."

He pulled out his cell phone and called West LA. "I'm already in the Valley. Show Judge Crown the photos I'm about to send you. She'll grant the warrant. Fax it to Burbank PD and ask one of them to meet me there."

"When are you going to talk to Carlos Gomez?" Giselle asked when he ended the call.

"I'll wait till Monday. First, I want to know what's in the suitcase."

I glanced at my sister. "Can we sit in on the interview? He is our brother, after all."

"Dream on," Farkas grunted. "That's one meeting you'll have to arrange on your own. But I will let you know what the search turns up. Do you have any large Ziploc bags?" He began to unpin all the notes and evidence from the murder board. "I'll need something to put these in."

"Wait!" Giselle raised her hand. "You can't just take all our hard work."

Farkas continued to gather the evidence. "Do you want to close the case or not?"

After he left, I slumped against the door. "Now we just wait."

Giselle still simmered. "How come we did all the work and he gets all the credit?"

"Sometimes it's not about credit, G. We set out to uncover the truth, and we found it."

"Not quite. I want to know what she did with Daddy's body. And there's still the matter of our brother. How much did he know?"

I sighed. "I want to know those things, too. But trust me when I say Gabe will take us to the finish line. Right now, we have bigger things to worry about. Remember, the kids have invited both families to Shabbat dinner tonight. If Eli Kaplan is still demanding to hijack the wedding, it'll be up to us to make him back off. Are you ready for the fight?"

"Can I bring Harold? I have the feeling Eli will more readily accept defeat if the rejection comes from a man. It's a little trick we resort to when dealing with the Saudis and, well, most male-dominated cultures."

"By all means, G. Harold's a part of the family now, too."

At five o'clock West LAPD Chief of Detectives

Gabe Farkas called. "It had a man's shirt, two toy cars, a seashell collection, kid's birthday cards, and a drawing of a young boy signed by J. Q. Maguire."

"Was anything written on the back?"

"Yeah. 'With love to my son.'"

Bingo!

CHAPTER 32

At six o'clock, Crusher, Uncle Isaac, and I parked in front of a spacious two-story cottage-style home in the foothills of Sherman Oaks.

I peered at the brass numbers near the front door. "Are you sure you have the right address, Yossi? How does a young detective afford a place like this?"

"His old man's loaded. Remember?" Crusher wore a blue tie with his suit. Clutching a bouquet of white roses from the supermarket, he rounded the car to open the front passenger door for Uncle Isaac. I grabbed the pink box from Bea's Bakery off the backseat and got out, glad to be wearing my good pearls.

Noah Kaplan opened the front door even before we had a chance to knock. He smiled, shook Uncle Isaac's hand and then Crusher's. "Shabbat shalom."

Noah hugged me and whispered in my ear, "Glad to see you, *LaWanda*."

I hugged him tight and whispered back. "You

were brilliant this morning. I owe you. But don't tell Uncle Isaac."

We pulled apart and he grinned. "Only if you promise to stay out of trouble."

Uncle Isaac's eyes widened and he gave me a *Where did that come from?* look. I'd explained to Crusher earlier about the evidence we'd found in Gomez's room, including the suitcase with the man's shirt and children's items, but I wasn't about to scare my uncle with the knowledge that I almost got arrested.

We followed Noah into the house, and Quincy rushed out from the kitchen, wearing an apron. Her face was flushed under her coppery curls, and her green eyes shone with happiness. After greeting us, she said, "Dad had an emergency and won't be coming tonight. Noah's parents will be here in about ten minutes. Giselle and Harold are already inside the living room."

Crusher thrust the flowers toward her, and I handed her the pink box. "It's a chocolate babka from Bea's. Do you need any help?"

"No thanks. Go and sit with your sister." She turned around and disappeared into the kitchen again.

Noah's living room looked like he'd hired a decorator. A heavily textured brown sisal area rug anchored two navy blue sofas and gray leather chairs. Giselle and Harold sat holding hands at one end of a sofa. They both wore black power suits; red blouse for her and red tie for him. I guessed this was part of their strategy to stop Eli Kaplan from taking over the wedding. Everyone knew red was the color to wear if you were planning to confront someone in a power struggle.

I left my men standing together and sat next to Giselle and Harold. I'd barely had time to tell her what odd things Gabe Farkas found in Quinn's suitcase when the older Kaplans appeared.

"Stand up," she whispered. "We have to be eye level or he'll think he's the dominant one."

Wearing an expensive silk suit and flashy gold Rolex, the short Eli Kaplan reeked of new money and expensive cologne. When we were introduced, a smile creased his olive complexion. But his dark brown eyes glittered with the smug authority of a man used to getting his own way.

Bernice Kaplan, dressed in a conservative St. John knit, hung back and gripped the life out of her green Birkin handbag. Either she was undergoing chemotherapy or suffered from alopecia because I glimpsed a tiny patch of smooth scalp underneath the edge of a short brown wig.

Giselle must have noticed it, too, because she said, "Are you one of those Orthodox women who shave their heads under their wigs? Does it itch?"

Bernice's face blanched and her hand went straight to her synthetic hair.

Oy vey!

I elbowed my sister. "What Giselle means is how

religious are you? She grew up in a Gentile home, so she's very curious about Jewish customs and practices."

Eli's head snapped in my direction. "You're not Jewish? My son is marrying a shikse?"

Crusher placed himself directly in front of Eli, bent slightly toward the much smaller man, and spoke in a controlled voice. "Be careful how you speak in front of our family." Eli took a step backward and Crusher leaned in even closer. "Martha's mother was Jewish, which makes Martha and Quincy Jewish. Giselle's mother was Catholic, which makes her a Gentile. I trust you'll never need to bring that up again."

Eli Kaplan swallowed but said nothing. I glanced at Noah, who had covered his eyes with his hand.

In the dining room, the nine of us sat in uncomfortable silence around a square-legged mahogany table, like one I'd seen in a Pottery Barn catalogue. My heart ached with a combination of pride and melancholy as I listened to my daughter recite the blessing over *her* Sabbath candles at *her* table in *her* home. Noah handed the honor of reciting the Sabbath prayers to Uncle Isaac, the oldest man at the table.

As the plates of food were passed around, Eli addressed his son in a loud voice meant to be jocular. "So, all that money we spent on your bar mitzvah and you can't recite a few prayers? At least we know when we throw you a big wedding, you'll have a kid to show for it."

Noah clenched his jaw. "I told you before, Dad. Quincy's family is doing the wedding. Period. And it will be just the way *we* want it."

Eli looked at me through half-closed eyes. "If it's a matter of money, you don't have to worry. I'm more than capable of footing the bill for my only son. Frankly, a backyard wedding is not our style. My son . . . the kids deserve better than that." Giselle stiffened next to me as he continued. "Besides, we have dozens of close friends and their families who expect an invitation."

Now Giselle fumed.

Harold put a warning hand on her arm and spoke. "Apparently, Eli, you've never been invited to the Eagan estate in Beverly Hills. If you'd been a guest, you'd know that it's on the same National Register as the Vanderbilt estate and Monticello."

Harold ignored the surprise on Eli's face and breezed on. "I'm also a member of Hillcrest Country Club, and I can tell you that every wedding I've attended there, however flashy or elaborate, felt like a hotel event. The Eagan estate and its priceless art is far more gracious and impressive. And believe me when I say our caterers will surpass anything you've ever experienced."

Giselle lifted her chin. "Money is not a problem for this family. But tone and style are. Your son and my niece have made it quite clear what they want. So, we will give them a small but spectacular wedding. And if they do change their minds, we can easily seat five hundred people without sacrificing an ounce of quality. When we entertained Prince William and Kate, we accommodated at least that many."

Eli perked up at the casual mention of English royalty.

Quincy said with a sweet smile, "Eli . . . Dad, Noah and I really appreciate your offer. You and Bernice are so kind. I know you'll be the best grandparents."

Eli's face softened. I sat in awe of my daughter's ability to defuse the tension between father and son. I feared, however, that would be her role for years to come. I just hoped it wouldn't put a strain on their marriage.

"So, what would you think about hosting a big party at the country club when we return from our honeymoon? We'd love to meet and greet all of your friends then."

Bernice Kaplan, who had remained silent throughout the evening, reached over and grasped her husband's hand.

He pursed his lips. "I only want the best for my stubborn son." Then his voice softened. "I think for once he found it in you."

And that was it. Crisis over with hardly a shot fired. And Eli had managed to take *no* from a woman.

Uncle Isaac, who sat at the end of the table in the place of honor, had keenly observed the sparring without joining in. In the relaxed silence that followed, he looked at me and Giselle and asked, "So *nu?* I love weddings. Who's next?"

What's next, is more like it. With Quincy's problem resolved, I could once again focus on the unanswered questions about Quinn's murder. Where was his body? Why hadn't Meredith Gomez gotten rid of the suitcase, such an incriminating piece of evidence? What were the meanings of the items Farkas found inside, and how much did our long-lost brother, Carlos Gomez, know? We'd have to wait until Farkas interviewed Carlos on Monday to find out.

CHAPTER 33

The call from Detective Gabe Farkas came on Monday afternoon. "The DA's refusing to press charges for obvious reasons. Meredith Gomez will never be fit to stand trial."

"That doesn't surprise me. But I feel cheated. She got away with murder. What did her son, Carlos, have to say?"

"Nothing. He was only nine at the time and doesn't remember anything." I heard the whoosh of Farkas taking a hit from his puffer. "He did ask to talk to the two of you, though. Gave me his private number to pass along. Got a pencil?"

My doorbell rang at eight that evening. Crusher moved to get up, but I stopped him. "No, Yossi. Let me." I glanced at Giselle, who sat on the sofa gripping Harold's hand. "Are you ready to meet our brother?"

She nodded once. "This has been a long time coming."

I inhaled deeply to calm the fluttering in my chest and walked to the front door. Carlos Gomez stood taller than he looked on TV. *Great. Am I the only one who inherited short genes?* He wore jeans and a black Lynyrd Skynyrd T-shirt. *Well, at least we got the same comfortable clothes gene.*

He stood stiffly with his hands shoved in the pockets of his Levi's. Except for the green eyes, he bore only a vague resemblance to the photograph of Quinn in the silver frame, the one Giselle had given me the first day we met. His gaze darted from my face to the ground and back again. The muscles in his face were tight and guarded, but he managed a small smile. "Martha?"

I offered my hand and drew him over the threshold. "Thank you for coming."

After introductions, Giselle blurted out, "You could've saved us a lot of trouble if you'd just let us speak to your mother. Instead, Sissy and I went through a lot of trouble and almost landed in jail."

Carlos sat on the other end of the sofa and accepted the frosty bottle of Heineken Crusher offered. "I was protecting her."

Giselle leaned forward and pointed her finger at him. "Protecting her from what? You told the police you were too young to remember anything. But I don't buy it. I think you know a whole lot more than you've admitted." She flopped back against the sofa cushions and crossed her arms, never taking her eyes off his face.

Carlos ran his fingers through his hair. "You don't know what you're asking. I've never talked about my dad to anyone. Not even my ex-wife."

Afraid that Giselle's confrontational attitude might stop him from talking, I stepped in. "Maybe if you tell us what you do remember, it would help the three of us. After all, he was our father, too."

He gazed downward, as if he were attempting to dig up secrets buried beneath the floor. "For many years, the last thing I remembered about him was when I saw his face on the news one night. They said he was missing. Mom told me not to worry. She said her department had put her in charge of the investigation and they were doing everything they could to find him. Then she made me promise to never tell anyone he was my dad. She said she'd get in trouble and they would take me away from her. That really scared me into keeping my mouth shut."

How despicable. To frighten a little boy like that.

"A couple weeks later, she told me he'd gone to Australia and was never coming back. I believed her. And that's all I remembered for years."

My ears pricked up. "But your memory changed?"

He took a deep breath and nodded. "When I went away to college, I walked into the men's shower room at my dorm, right after the cleaning crew left. A strong odor of bleach hung in the air. Suddenly, I was walking into our living room at home. Mom had spent the whole morning scrubbing it with bleach. Then the vision vanished, and I was back in the showers again. The sensation was so strong, I felt like puking." He paused to take another pull at the bottle.

Repressed memories could bubble up in bizarre ways, sometimes distorting the facts. I wondered how much of his account was real. "Did you remember more?"

"God, this is hard." He closed his eyes and blew out his breath. "The next time something happened was when I came home for Christmas break that first semester. I was in my bedroom when Mom called to me from across the house. I don't know what she wanted, because hearing my name shouted out triggered another memory."

He gazed into the distance, as if he was watching something the rest of us couldn't see. "I heard my mom and dad yell at each other in the living room. I heard my name a couple of times. The image passed, and the next thing I know, Mom's standing in the doorway asking me about dorm food."

"Did you tell your mother what you were beginning to remember?"

Carlos shook his head. "No! I knew better than to discuss my dad. He was a closed subject as far as she was concerned. Anyway, that night I had a dream where I heard them arguing. Then I heard a slap and something crashed on the floor. A broken lamp. Shards of green pottery." His eyes brimmed with sadness. "Dad shouted, 'Wait!' Then I heard a loud bang. Then silence. After that I heard Mom crying." He swiped the tears from his cheeks with the back of his hand.

Had Carlos just described Quinn's murder? "Did you think the dream was real?"

"I hoped it was just a false memory, that my mind was playing tricks on me. I didn't want to believe she could've shot Dad. But as time went on that first year away from home, I remembered more and more about that day. Me being told not to leave my room. The bustle of Mom cleaning and always the smell of bleach. The sound of her dragging something heavy across the floor.

"I was sick with anger. At him for being a lousy creep who took advantage of Mom and failed me as a father. But I was most angry with her. She put a nine-year-old kid in the position of either sending his mother to jail or keeping their drama a secret. Who does that?"

Giselle had remained quiet, letting me take the lead on questioning our brother. Now she reached over and lightly touched his arm. "What a terrible thing for you to go through, Carlos. I think it takes a lot of guts to face the truth."

He finished his beer, and Crusher got up to bring us each another. I shoved a plate of salty crackers and an assortment of cheeses in my brother's direction and channeled my bubbie. She would've said, *Ess, faigela.* ("Eat, darling.") *You need to keep up your strength.* I said, "Did you have a chance to eat before you came? I have some roasted chicken and rosemary potatoes left over from dinner tonight. It'll just take seconds to warm it up in the microwave."

He managed a brief smile. "Thanks. I'm good."

I cleared my throat. "I don't know how else to do this, so I'll just come right out and ask the hard question. Do you know what she did with his body?"

"I have a good idea. That evening she drove me in her Triumph to spend the night in my grandmother's house. She usually stored the tarp that covered her car in the trunk. But when she opened it to put my backpack inside, I noticed the tarp was missing. I remembered that as we pulled away from the curb to go, Dad's Cadillac was still parked in the driveway."

"It's obvious what happened," Giselle said. "The Triumph was too small to hold a body. She wrapped Daddy in the tarp and put him in the trunk of the Cadillac."

Carlos grabbed a dry white cracker and broke it in half. "I think she took his body to Big Bear. She grew up in the area and knew all the neat places to go camping. He's probably up there somewhere. I think that's why she left me at my grandmother's the whole night. It's almost a three-hour drive each way."

Crusher spoke for the first time. "You know about Locard's exchange principle? Whenever two things come in contact with each other, like a body wrapped in a canvas tarp for one and a car trunk for the other, there's always something left behind and something taken away. A tiny bit of something. What did the missing-persons file say about trace evidence in the Cadillac?"

I rushed into my sewing room and returned with

the forensic report Farkas had left behind. "It says here, 'The trunk of the vehicle contained the following: Standard repair kit including jack and spare tire. Unidentified coarse fibers, possibly from canvas cloth.'"

"So there it is." Giselle waved her arm in a grand gesture. "She dropped Carlos at his grandmother's, dumped poor Daddy's body, and abandoned the car at the airport. She probably took a taxi home from there." My sister stopped and blinked back tears. "We'll never find Daddy in those mountains."

Harold circled my sister's shoulders with his arm. "Maybe we could bring some flowers up there anyway and leave them on the side of the road."

Crusher said, "I can do some research on unidentified DBs that've been found in the San Bernardino National Forest. There should be a database somewhere."

One more thing puzzled me. "Carlos, if your mother was so meticulous about getting rid of any evidence connecting her to Quinn's murder, why did she keep his suitcase? The one with his initials, no less?"

"She didn't. I found it in the garbage can the next day where she'd stuffed it next to the broken green lamp. I emptied out all his clothes except for one shirt—the one I'd given him for Father's Day the year before. Then I hid it in my room with all my memories of him inside; birthday cards, a picture he drew for me one Christmas, the seashells we'd collected on a trip to the beach, and two

Hot Wheels he had given me that day as a present."
His voice caught in his throat. "Those cars are why
he's dead."

"Why do you say that?"

"When he handed me the box with the Hot Wheels
inside, I begged him to stay and play cars with me.
He said he had to go on a trip, but he promised to
take me for ice cream when he came back." Carlos
grinned sadly. "He always did that! Promise to take
me places and then never show up. Anyway, I
hurled the cars across the living room and began
to cry. I said I hated him and ran to my bedroom
and slammed the door. The next thing I knew,
Mom and Dad were shouting at each other. You
know the rest."

"How did the suitcase end up in her room at
Thanks for the Memories Assisted Living?"

"I put it there. Those things were all I had left of
Dad. I meant for everything to be found *after* she
died. I was hoping that someone would discover it,
put two and two together, and figure out the truth.
So, when I moved Mom into the facility, I figured
her closet was the perfect place to hide the suitcase.
She never even realized it was there."

"What about the pencil drawing Quinn did of
her? Why did she risk keeping that?"

"She treasured that drawing more than anything.
I believe she never stopped loving him. But after
that day, she took it off the wall and hid it. One night
when I was in high school, I woke up and heard her
crying and talking to someone. I wondered who

was in the house late at night. I crept toward the living room. She sat all alone in a chair, hugging the drawing. She said over and over again, 'I'm sorry, Quinn. I'm so sorry.' Then she kissed the picture and cried some more. Since I had blocked out the memories of that day, I didn't understand why she was apologizing. I just figured she missed him. She never saw me."

My heart broke at the word picture he painted. "And you never told anyone what happened to Quinn?"

"How could I? Despite what she did, I loved my mom. I never planned on someone showing up while she was still alive and figuring out the truth."

Giselle had been leaning against Harold. Now she shifted toward Carlos and squeezed his hand. "But Martha and I did come along, which is pretty amazing when you think about it."

"Absolutely." I moved to the other side of Carlos and sat on the arm of the sofa. "Look at the three of us. A few short weeks ago, each of us was an only child. Yet, despite the odds, we managed to find one other. Like it or not, you're stuck with us now, baby brother. Welcome to the family."

Carlos threw some internal switch that lit his face with a charming TV smile, completely obscuring the man with the vulnerable secrets. "I gotta admit, learning I had two sisters really threw me. I've got questions of my own."

"Ask away," I said.

"Martha, why do you call him Quinn and not Dad?"

"Because unlike you and Giselle, I never met him. I grew up believing my father had died in a train wreck before I was born."

"So you don't have an emotional stake in this?"

What did I feel about the father I never met who casually mistreated those who loved him? He was a hedonist and a liar, yet he provided for his children and their mothers. It wasn't his fault I only recently discovered the seven-figure bank account he left for me. He was preparing to give it to me on my twenty-fifth birthday but was killed two weeks before that could happen.

I could hear Uncle Isaac's voice in my head cautioning me that Torah commands not once, but two separate times to honor your parents. So, what could I honestly say about the man who fathered me? "In the past few weeks I've learned that Quinn was gifted and complex. Men like that are often deeply flawed as well. He and my mother gave me life, and for that I'll always be grateful. But while I care about him in the abstract, my true emotional attachment is to my uncle Isaac. He's my real father."

Seemingly satisfied with my answer, Carlos turned to Giselle. "You knew him best of all, because you lived together as a family. What kind of father was he to *you*?"

"Daddy may have been a lot of bad things, but

he never gave me reason to doubt he loved me. And when he disappeared, my whole world collapsed. I vowed to never stop looking until I found out what happened to him. Then I met Sissy, and that's when things really started coming together. Now, thanks to you, we have an answer."

I had the feeling Carlos measured every word that came out of our mouths, searching for something. Was it kinship? Absolution?

Finally, he put his beer on the coffee table. "I have one more question. The two of you managed to bully and trick your way into solving a thirty-two-year-old missing-persons case. I'd like to know what to expect from you if we're all going to be family. I mean, are you guys always this pushy and nosy?"

Giselle and I looked at each other and burst out laughing.

CHAPTER 34

We gathered in my living room the following morning on Quilty Tuesday, stitching hexagons into the Grandmother's Flower Garden quilt. Jazz and Lucy sat openmouthed as Giselle told them about our meeting with our newfound brother, Carlos Gomez, the night before.

Jazz picked up Zsa Zsa and hugged her to his chest. Today she wore a pink jumpsuit with a hole cut out for her rear end. "Oh, that poor boy! Having to keep a secret like that his whole life. Did you persuade him to go back and tell the police everything he knows?"

I looked up from the blue floral hexagons I whipstitched together. "What's the point? Meredith Gomez can't be prosecuted, and they might take away her police pension. Assisted living doesn't come cheap."

"I don't mean to be indelicate, hon"—Lucy shifted in her seat—"but what about your father's body?"

"Yossi's looking into that for us. Over the years,

the police have recovered various human remains from those mountains. Most of them go unidentified and are eventually cremated. *If* Quinn's remains were recovered, and *if* it was after the nineties, when they started keeping DNA samples, we might find a match. It's a long shot."

I didn't want to dash my sister's hopes, but privately, I had no illusions. Without testimony from Meredith Gomez, the chances of finding Quinn's bones in that vast wilderness were almost zero.

"I've been dying to ask you this." Jazz cupped the side of his mouth with his hand and lowered his voice to a stage whisper. "What about all that money your father left you?"

"I haven't had a chance to do the paperwork yet. They say it might take a couple of months to transfer the funds to my account."

"I've got a bit of disappointing news," sighed Lucy. "I talked to Birdie this morning. She and Denver won't be able to make Quincy's wedding."

Birdie Watson, the other member of our Tuesday morning quilting group, had been absent for the last month because she'd been traveling with her new husband, Denver, in their Winnebago.

Jazz looked stricken. "Why not?"

"You remember how she refuses to fly?" Lucy asked. "Well, she and Denver will be on a transatlantic cruise ship at that time, headed for Rome. Denver is being awarded some kind of medal from the Italian government for his invention of an improved tractor rototiller thingy. Apparently, it revolutionized Italian farming."

Zsa Zsa jumped down and ran toward my orange cat, Bumper, who must have been sending mental signals to her from the kitchen.

"On a happier note," Jazz said, "Quincy's coming to my shop tomorrow for a fitting. I found the most divine ivory silk charmeuse for her wedding dress. It'll drape beautifully over her baby bump. I'm constructing the princess bodice with underwires. When I'm done, she won't have to worry about a bra."

"Is it the strapless design you showed me?" Giselle asked.

A resigned expression dulled his face. "If only. Quincy insisted on a more modest dress for a traditional Jewish wedding. So, the neckline will cover her collarbone and the sleeves will be long."

"What?" Giselle snorted. "I'm only beginning to learn about Judaism, but in every religion, getting pregnant before marriage isn't exactly modest or traditional."

She was right. My daughter was living proof of the conflict between modern lifestyles and cherished traditions with their old mores. "No argument here. I'm just happy they want to make it official. Some couples have multiple children yet never get married."

Lucy reached for a piece of *mandel broit*, the almond biscotti I'd picked up from Bea's Bakery earlier that morning. I made sure to get the ones with chocolate chips she loved.

She asked, "Do the kids know the sex of the baby yet?"

"It's a little girl." I beamed with the anticipation of holding my first grandchild in my arms.

"Have they picked out a name?"

"Quincy likes Sarah. But Noah says he's suddenly fallen hard for the name LaWanda."

My friends joined me in a laugh.

Four weeks later, the late-August heat wasn't noticeable inside the air-conditioned Eagan mansion. Upstairs in a blue and gold rococo bedroom, I helped Quincy dress for her wedding. Her copper-colored curls had been skillfully tamed by Giselle's Beverly Hills stylist into an updo, with tendrils cascading down the back of her neck. Subtle makeup accentuated her green eyes.

I helped her slide the soft silk gown over her head so she wouldn't wreck her hairdo. The ivory fabric cascaded over her growing belly and lay in folds in all the right places. As a concession to Jazz, she'd allowed him to make the long sleeves and the top of the bodice out of unlined lace, her bare skin slightly visible underneath.

I pulled a cloth bag from my purse, removed my bubbie's pearls, and fastened them around her neck. "Something old," I said, referring to the tradition of dressing the bride in *Something old, something new, something borrowed, something blue, and a sixpence in your shoe.* It wasn't a Jewish custom, but I loved it.

Quincy reached up and caressed the pearls. "Oh, Mom, I know how much these mean to you. Wearing my great-grandmother's pearls makes the baby and me feel connected to you and all the women who came before us."

"You should also consider this to be your something borrowed," I joked. "I'm not ready to part with them quite yet."

Giselle and Lucy had been watching us quietly from a velvet settee in the corner of the room.

Giselle stepped forward with a black fuzzy box of her own and handed it to the bride. "Something new."

Quincy gasped when she opened the small square box. Inside was a pair of diamond stud earrings, each two carats. She gaped at my sister. "Don't you mean something borrowed?"

Giselle chuckled. "These are yours, sweetie. I hope you like them." She led Quincy to a huge, gilded mirror hanging opposite the canopied bed and helped her secure them into her earlobes.

Quincy beamed. "I love them! You've already done too much, Auntie G. I don't know how to thank you."

"Just be happy, sweetie."

"And here's something blue, hon. It's from me and your aunt Birdie. She wishes she could be here." Lucy came forward and handed Quincy a heavy gold bracelet with a white cloisonné amulet in the shape of an eye. A deep blue sapphire winked from the middle. "Your mom tells me this charm will protect you against the evil eye."

Quincy held out her left wrist. Lucy fastened the bracelet and my daughter cooed. "I love it, Aunt Lucy."

"That just leaves this to put in your shoe." I handed her a copper penny I'd cleaned and polished the night before. "I didn't know where to find a sixpence, so this will have to do."

Jazz knocked softly on the door. "Incoming!" He strode inside the room, carrying a long garment bag and stopped when he saw Quincy all dressed up. "God, I'm good! That dress is fabulous. You look like redheaded angel."

He seemed a little startled when he saw me in my black Rachel Zoe dress from New York and my hair and makeup professionally done. "I swear to God, I didn't recognize you. Are you wearing Spanx? You could be beautiful if you'd only let me throw out everything you own. Except that dress, of course. You look gorgeous."

He hooked the bag over the top of a door and unzipped it. Inside hung a long, diaphanous veil of delicate netting embellished with pearls and sequins around the crown. He carried the gossamer confection over to Quincy. "If you'll allow me?"

She dipped her head slightly forward while he fastened it to her curls with tiny white translucent combs. He finished, stood back, and fanned the air in front of his face. "Tears to the eyes."

Another knock on the door. Aaron Rose, my ex-husband, stood in a perfectly tailored black wool tuxedo with narrow, black satin trim and not a speck of lint. His face was clean-shaven and his gray hair closely cropped. He strutted over to me and gave me a tight little smile and a peck on the cheek. "Do you think I could have a moment with my daughter before we take her downstairs?"

What is it about his attitude I always want to slap off his face? "Sure." I gestured for the others to leave with me. "I'll wait for you outside in the hallway."

Ten minutes later, Quincy walked between Aaron and me, tightly clutching a bouquet of white roses. A live string quartet played Mozart in the distance. We headed toward the music and the grand ballroom of the Eagan mansion. With all the plus-ones and a few small concessions to Eli Kaplan and Aaron Rose, the guest list had expanded to over one hundred souls.

Giselle's "people" had transformed the ballroom into a dazzling fantasy. The air was filled with a sweet fragrance from thousands of white roses massed with white ginger flown in from Hawaii and countless gardenias floating in crystal bowls alongside flickering tea lights. Silver ribbons and more flowers festooned the walls, reflecting light from a dozen crystal chandeliers. Off to one side, round tables and chairs covered in white linen and dressed with white floral centerpieces waited for the party to follow.

The wedding ceremony would take place at one

end of the spacious hall. Guests chatted noisily in their seats, which had been arranged in a more intimate semicircle around a bima, or raised platform. After the ceremony, the chairs would be relocated, the platform removed, and the area transformed into a dance floor.

As soon as we entered the room, the quartet switched to Pachelbel's Canon. Everyone stood and focused on us as Aaron and I escorted our daughter to the chuppa, the wedding canopy. Eli Kaplan had wanted a traditional man's prayer shawl to form the top, but Quincy insisted on using the one sewn of white satin, velvet, and lace I'd carefully appliquéd and quilted years ago in anticipation of this day. Over the past few weeks I'd used white thread to embroider their initials, *NKQ* in a space I'd left blank for that purpose.

Uncle Isaac stood next to the rabbi and watched our approach. Noah wore a *kittel*, a snow-white robe, over his clothes and a large prayer shawl draped like a blanket over his shoulders. A white Bukharin yarmulke embellished with embroidery and sequins sat like a square pillbox on top of his dark curls.

Once Quincy took her place next to Noah, I joined Crusher already standing on her side of the bima. Aaron's third wife also waited for him there. Eli and Bernice Kaplan stood on the other side of the bima near their son.

Standing beside Noah was his best man and partner, LAPD Detective Arlo Beavers. My ex-boyfriend.

Who now stared at me. With those incredible dark eyes. And an unhappy look on his face. Crusher must've seen it, too, because he reached over and grabbed my hand.

Oy vey. Who else in the history of Jewish weddings ever had to stand with their fiancé next to her arrogant ex-husband and sexy ex-boyfriend on the happiest day of her daughter's life?

But I soon forgot about my own personal discomfort when Quincy began to walk in a circle around Noah seven times. According to tradition, just as Joshua circled the walls of Jericho seven times until they fell, so would the bride conquer the groom's heart.

When she returned to his side, Noah opened his prayer shawl and drew her to his side. From that point forward, they would become each other's shelter and home.

The rabbi blessed a cup of wine and gave a sip to the bride and groom. At a signal, Beavers reached into his pocket and pulled out two gold rings. Noah recited in Aramaic the declaration, "Behold you are consecrated to me, with this ring, according to the laws of Moses and Israel."

As he placed the ring on her finger a great sobbing broke out nearby. I turned to see Jazz melting into his handkerchief. Lucy patted his back and whispered something in his ear. Quincy looked over her shoulder, smiled at him, and blew him a little kiss.

I love you, he mouthed.

Lucy rolled her eyes.

Quincy turned back around and recited her part of the ring exchange. Then the rabbi stepped aside and invited Uncle Isaac to sing the traditional *sheva brachot*, the seven blessings. The old man's reedy voice sweetly rendered the Hebrew words as he closed his eyes and swayed. The last blessing was lifted straight from the Bible:

"'Once again will be heard in the cities of Judah and the streets of Jerusalem, the sound of joy and the sound of happiness; the voice of the groom and the voice of the bride.'"

When he finished, warm tears coursed down my cheeks. My heart filled with the moment and, for the next ten minutes, my uncle spoke with love and wisdom to the bride, his "Quincy girl," and her groom.

At last Noah stomped on a goblet, and the sound of glass breaking beneath his heel marked the completion of the ceremony. A loud shout of *Mazel tov!* filled the room as my new son-in-law lifted Quincy's veil and gave my little girl the most tender kiss the universe had ever witnessed.

Crusher raised my hand to his lips and whispered, "That could be us."

"Yes," I sighed. "That thought also crossed my mind."

The string quartet had been replaced by a klezmer band playing "Siman Tov," and the guests were invited to find their tables for the *seudat*, the celebratory meal. Quincy and Noah shared an intimate table by themselves in the center of the room for all to see. My expanded family filled our table for eight: Uncle Isaac, Crusher, Giselle and Harold, my nephew, Nicholas Cole, and Carlos Gomez with his current plus-one.

As the celebration started, the three waiters assigned to us kept our champagne glasses filled with cold Cristal.

Uncle Isaac looked around our table at each of our faces and raised his glass. Everyone stopped their conversations and listened. "Family is a funny thing," he said. "Two months ago, you three were strangers who found each other under the most difficult circumstances." He looked at Carlos. "Your *tsuris* was the worst, I think."

Carlos seemed to hang on every word the old man spoke. He leaned toward me. "What's that word?"

"It means 'trouble.'"

"But instead of letting jealousy and hatred get in your way," Isaac said, "you treated each other with love and generosity, *keinehore.*"

Again, a blank look from Carlos.

"He means the evil eye shouldn't steal the good in us."

Giselle grinned and gave me a thumbs-up. "I knew that."

Uncle Isaac's kind face seemed to take on an almost saintly aura. "The three of you may have been Quinn's children, but you are all my children now."

Through a blur of tears, I watched him bring his glass to his lips.

"L'chaim."

To life.

Please turn the page for a quilting tip
from MARY MARKS!

QUILTING THROUGH THE GENERATIONS

For tens of thousands of years, all sewing was done by hand. The oldest needles (28,000 BCE) were made of bone. They didn't have an eye, just a slit to insert strips of gut or sinew to sew fur and skins. After the dawn of the metal age (7,000 BCE) needles with eyes were made of copper, bronze, or iron. This style of needle, refined over thousands of years, was used to construct everything from clothing to tapestries, to bedding.

In many cultures, sewing by hand was an essential skill taught to every girl in preparation for her life as wife and mother. Beginning as young as the age of four, little girls practiced their stitches. (Even girls from upper-class families, who were not expected to sew their own clothes or household items, were taught the fine art of embroidery.) In Colonial times until the late twentieth century, sewing was a mandatory part of the school curriculum for girls.

Our American foremothers raised sewing to an art form with their beautiful quilts. They managed to create striking designs using up scraps of material saved from dressmaking, often trading scraps with other women to collect a variety of colors and patterns. Traditional quilting persisted as an art form—one of the few ways women could express their creativity. With the introduction of precision steel needles, women were able to refine their quilting stitches. A skillful quilter could produce at least ten stitches per inch.

The popularity of quilting reached a zenith in America during the Depression era. With the prosperity following World War II, quilts were considered "old-fashioned" and a symbol of poverty. Quilt making experienced a slow decline until the latter part of the twentieth century when a revival took place. The 1976 bicentennial of our country's independence spurred a renewed interest in American history and folk arts.

A whole new generation of women became fascinated with quilting. This renewed interest created a demand for fabric and tools which gave birth to a multibillion-dollar industry. A 2010 survey by *Quilters Newsletter* magazine estimated that there were more than twenty million quilters in America.

My granddaughters love to sew. So does my grandson. I fervently hope that all the quilters out there are teaching their children and grandchildren not only how to use a sewing machine, but how to lay down even stitches by hand using just a thimble and a needle and thread. Those girls and boys are the future of the art of quilting.